Dear Reader:

Jessica Holter has mesmerized audiences for over a decade with her live performances exploring sensuality and sexuality—two totally different things—through poetic word and physical expression. She is undoubtedly a prolific poet. In *The Punany Experience*, she shows the world how prolific she is as an author.

Korea and Stormy had traumatic childhoods, like so many women, and end up becoming involved later on in life. But their relationship—their love—is not an easy journey. Both have different needs and desires, and both have a lot of emotional baggage and scars inflicted on them by men. They want the American dream; a nice home, financial freedom, and true love. They have it, for a period of time but soon realize that it is not enough. That is the amazing thing about life. Once we achieve everything that we have ever wanted, we begin to yearn for something different. Why? Because all of the challenges and hurdles have been overcome. That is human nature.

The Punany Experience is engaging, sensual, suspenseful, and a real eye-opener. This book is for anyone who wants to learn more about how people think, how they love, and how they cope. It is possible to beat the odds, to repair damage, and find what it is that you truly seek. Once Hartford enters the lives of Korea and Stormy, everything changes. Hartford is a complicated man, with unusual desires that his wife cannot fulfill. That is when "the war between tops and bottoms" begins.

Thank you for giving this book a chance. I am sure that you will enjoy it. Thank you for reading the books published by all of my Strebor authors. I try my best to bring you out-of-the-box titles that you will not find at other publishers. I have always been a risk-taker and believe that every good story has an audience. You can visit me online at Eroticanoir.com or join my online social network at PlanetZane.org.

Blessings,

Zane

Publisher
Strebor Books
www.simonandschuster.com/streborbooks

ALSO BY JESSICA HOLTER
Verbal Penetration

ZANE PRESENTS

THE PUNANY EXPERIENCE

THE WAR BETWEEN TOPS AND BOTTOMS. NOT YOUR AVERAGE DOWN LOW STORY

A NOVEL BY

JESSICA HOLTER

STREBOR BOOKS

NEW YORK LONDON TORONTO SYDNEY

Strebor Books
P.O. Box 6505
Largo, MD 20792
http://www.streborbooks.com

ISBN 978-1-59309-161-3
ISBN 978-1-4165-5330-4 (e-book)
LCCN 2010925103

First Strebor Books trade paperback edition July 2010

Cover design: www.mariondesigns.com
Cover photograph: © Keith Saunders/Marion Designs

10 9 8 7 6 5 4 3 2 1

Manufactured in the United States of America

For information regarding special discounts for bulk purchases,
please contact Simon & Schuster Special Sales at 1-866-506-1949
or business@simonandschuster.com

The Simon & Schuster Speakers Bureau can bring authors to your
live event. For more information or to book an event, contact the
Simon & Schuster Speakers Bureau at 1-866-248-3049 or visit our
website at www.simonspeakers.com.

To Patience

ACKNOWLEDGMENTS

I would like to thank God for keeping me alive through it all.

To my patient and loving son, KLH, for being my motivation to improve myself.

To Zane and Charmaine, for accepting, editing and publishing this book; to Shay, for being a confidante and a friend throughout this writing process; even though you *don't even know me*. To Artisha "Mack" McCullough, for waking the sleeping lover in me, so I could write and be about sex again. To Olaywa and Porsha, for listening. To Lisa Blackwell, Jeannie Arnold, Terenda and Jack, Julie and Todd, for giving me a home when I had none, and for taking care of me when I was sick, hurting, or traveling; to Britteni (Honey T) Taylor and all of The Punany Poets; to Denyse Ford and all of her ladies who give love to Ghetto Girl Blue—thank you for feeding me; to Dwayne, Yulonda, and Sven, for the game. Special thanks to Ms. Sonni Collins and Terenda Goodwin for taking the time to read and edit this book. But, especially, to all of THE FANS who have truly given me a Punany Experience.

INTRODUCTION

When I was asked to present a second book to Zane, I pondered over how to deliver a novel the fans of the Strebor authors would appreciate. I decided to base this book, *The Punany Experience*, on a poem from my first book, *Zane Presents The Punany Poets' Verbal Penetration*. Far from the average down low discussion, *The War Between Tops and Bottoms*, a story-poem about two lesbians in a sexual battle with one another and a married man, shocked audiences when it was first presented in live form by the talented actress and AIDS activist, LOVE the poet. This poem initiated discussions during my Punany-branded cabaret shows about the power of the prostate, and began conversations about what is "gay" and what is "straight." *The Punany Experience* is a provocative excursion into a world where the lines of sexual identification are seductively rubbed away to reveal the unobstructed truth; that orientation is simply the process of becoming accustomed to something that is new to you.

So, with no further ado, I present to some, and introduce to others…

THE WAR BETWEEN TOPS & BOTTOMS

Late.
her hips pressed
against my ass

Hot.
because he was watching

It's like that?

It could be.
but what she
really wants to do
is fuck a man in the ass

Like that?
Yep.
She's never done it before. I lied, not knowing it yet.
Forty-five minutes and a bridge ride later
my phone rang...

"Booty Call,
  Booty Call,
    Booty Call!"

I wondered if I could download that ring
and set it for the men

who phone disrespectfully
after 10 o'clock pm

It was 2:15 in the morning
"Is it cool?
I'm on my way to your pad."
I looked at my woman
as if to ask permission
She returned a sly glance as if to say,
"Bring it on!"
Five minutes inside
he was just parking
but she was already
showered and strapped

I had seen her that way many times
her plump ass squeezed between three black leather
   straps
holding in place a 9-inch dick
I had handpicked from Good Vibrations
to match the John Henry hunk of the man
I used to call my husband
It was large, slightly flexible, jet black
and bulged with human vein-like texture
I had a special relationship to this dick
It was mine
and I was particular about it.
to me, it was as real as any dick,
as in relationships

it would only stray if I got careless and lost it
or as in tonight, chose to give it away.

It was huge next to her small body
but trust,
she wore it and used it like she had grown it
She was soft butch, bisexual by admission
and beautiful by even Hollywood standards
If she were an ice cream she'd be a Creole Mocha
  Blend
A tiny package, she was full of surprises
Hairs on her chin
Egotistical and a Taurus
even her cum smelled like a man's
Yet her breasts were nearly as large as mine
and I was busting provocatively out of a double D

I'd lie if I said living this life
didn't bring thoughts of
Jerry Springer to my mind from time to time
I giggled like the child I felt like,
Anticipating…
Nowhere to hide

She made a cup of coffee
sipped it wearing nothing
but the dick and strap
I blushed
abandoned her to the shower

doorbell rings
I scrubbed and tried to wash off the vodka
so I could know that this was really happening
Now let me get this straight...
rinsing my cigarette breath again
spitting water
My former lover
Is coming over
to let my lesbian lover
fuck him in the ass
I shook my head a couple times
but the thought was still there
My heart would not stop racing
it wasn't sexual excitement
I was pretty sure of that

It felt more like the nerves that flutter about your
    stomach
when you know you have done wrong and your
    momma has found out
but you haven't made it home yet
and your sister is running toward you
shouting
ooooh, you gonna get it!
Accepting the inevitable
you can only hope she falls.

I had known him for as long as I had known my own
    sexual being

I was a virgin when we met
He introduced me to the freak in me
and has kept her skills on point for nearly twenty years
but never this way
Damn!

My momma told me he was gay!
I was thinking this when he stepped into the shower
He washed my body
kissed me everywhere
just like he used to
and did that thing he does with his thumbs
massaging my inner thighs down to the bone
gently stretching my pussy with circular motions
until I had the urge to press down
and give birth to another level of
our homie-lover-friendship
I was melting in the heat
I cooled the water down
Kissed the softest lips I have ever known
and said goodbye to love making as I had known it
    with him
My momma
and the women of her generation
would have stopped us dead in our tracks
because there are some things you just don't hang out
    to dry
What was going down tonight
was definitely going to leave some dirty laundry

She made it easy to get started
She didn't believe in awkward moments
He stepped out of the shower
She pushed me into him
He held me tight
lit a joint, passed it around
The kissing commenced quickly
I couldn't suck her pussy with the strap on
and her legs so tight, like they always are for me
so I sucked her dick
then his
He ate my pussy
then tongue kissed her ass
She ate my pussy then tongue kissed him
then put her tongue to his rim
for a very long time

he wanted to enter her
she wasn't having it
I stepped out of the room to grab two rubbers
while they decided who's on top
and what's on second
I don't know,
third base came so quickly
I didn't have time to think

I sat back and took a lesson in testosterone
waiting just a few moments to see if
he would give the ass up right away

A few more of her famous tongue lashings
inside and outside of his asshole
she was going to be in there
I couldn't bear to watch him go out like that
I wanted to know, but I couldn't watch

So I did what any woman
in denial about the sexual preference
of a man she's loved since childhood would do...
I slipped my body under his
shoving hips into his
I spread my legs
Spread them wide
opened my pussy up in the candlelight
Wet my finger
slapped my clit
pushed two fingers in and out of myself
testing the waters with my own tongue
and
attempted to flood the room
with the intoxicating pheromones
of my good pussy
but all I could smell was ass
as she dug into him
with such aggression,
her force urged him deeper inside of me.

Part of me hoped for a fast win in this
war between tops and bottoms

for the sake of my health
Cuz this was 2004
and I had been fucking a man who
desired a dick in his ass
for nearly half of my life

The other parts of me were
extremely turned on
extremely jealous
and angry
over how I had been a sexual fool
seeing all the signs, heeding no warning
What was more, I hadn't even been giving him,
what he was really looking for

My body grew hotter
as he kissed me and briefly remembered me
calling my name
I drew my pussy like an M16
and fired into the dark
He spread my thighs wider
Fucked me with his tongue
Sucking my fat pussy lips
on the up stroke
a couple feet away I could hear her tongue
lathering up his ass
His hips began to roll
Pow! She slapped it with a magical sting

and raised the ass high into the air
with the power possessed in her fingertips

My man was now my woman's bitch
And the 9-inch dick I had picked
from a little Berkeley sex boutique,
that reminded me of my husband,
and gave to my lesbian lover
to fuck me with,
was in my soul mate's ass
deeply, in his ass
"Stop."
he pronounced
candy in my ears

She withdrew

He caught his breath
Then whispered
"Tell her to put it back in."

My pussy got numb.

He continued to fuck me, I think.
Mostly, she fucked him
She fucked him, and busted so many times
before they finally came together
Their unified moans and grunts

were like a song, a dirty rap song
I added some curse words and moans
of my own but my pussy was only wet
with her juices
as they shot on his ass and thighs
and dripped down to tease me.

But he still wanted to enter her
in four years, I hadn't even put a finger inside of her
she almost didn't lay down for that
gave it the political lesbian try
before her legs were spread so far apart
I didn't recognize her or her porn star vocabulary

The pair weren't fighting anymore
"Thank you, thank you, thank you"
he repeated emphatically
over and over as he dressed

He really meant that shit.
I had two G's in my bed
giving me the kind of truth
you don't even get in church
I had no reason to be mad
I set the whole thing up
I had asked for a pass to a game that was not for suckers
He wanted something that I wasn't willing to give
and now that I know this
I can choose not to put myself at risk

I wasn't mad anymore.
because I was no longer a fool,
just maybe a little grossed out.
I mean, except for the fact that
the entire room smelled like ass
It might have even been cool.

But the thought of where his ass goes
on nights he can't find a woman
so willing to engage in anal play
was a little bit scary

It was 4:15 when he went home to his wife
I drank my girl's cold coffee
Sat down at my computer and ordered
a new dick online

—T. CALLOWAY

CHAPTER 1: THE VIRGIN FILES:
STORMY IN THE HOUSE OF THE LORD

He wasn't like any of the other men in the church. He did not dress like a deacon. He did not speak like a saint, but Brother Marcel Samuels could sing like a Temptation. He was nineteen years old, suave, and confident. He was a regular guy from the neighborhood, like the ones with Jheri curls, and puff coats that hung in front of the Dolomite Liquor store where Stormy Talbert shopped for candy after Sunday school; the store with the spinning rack of pantyhose and stockings that got her in all that trouble one day. Brother Samuels had all of the traits that made people stand out in the Oakland, California neighborhood—light skin, good hair, green eyes, and savoir-faire. He could have been a pimp, a player, or a gigolo but instead, he was newly saved, baptized, and filled with the Holy Ghost, making every Sunday feel like Motown as his long, neatly manicured fingers danced across the ivory keys with the Midas touch.

"This young man can spin gospel into gold," Pastor told the church on the day he appointed him Minister of

Music at Faithful Baptist Church. Pastor and the entire church body hoped young Marcel would lead them to gospel stardom in a land that had been dominated by the Hawkins family for years. The truth was, most folks knew little to nothing about him. He was a pied piper from the projects, who had increased church membership by nearly thirty percent in a few months, with his silky voice and golden touch. Pastor never even asked him if he wanted to be baptized. He offered him a salary and dipped him for political posture in the pool beneath the movable floor of the choir stand. He fought a bit as Pastor and a deacon pushed him under, a washcloth over his mouth, a hand on his hands, which were folded over his chest, as he went down into the water.

Brother Marcel Samuels brought the mothers' board to weeping and wailing as he arose from the pool in a heartrending rendition of "Soon-a Will be Done."

On the first Sunday following Brother Samuels' baptism, Stormy sipped the unfinished portions of grape juice from the tiny communion glasses she had been assigned to wash in the church kitchen, and tried to be invisible as she eavesdropped on her mother's conversation in the hallway right outside the kitchen door.

"I don't like it; I can't help the way I feel," her mother said. "That young man is too worldly to be in this church."

"Now, Sister Talbert, that's not fair; we were all worldly before we came to Faithful Baptist. Lord, have mercy on my soul, for the woman I used to be, and the things

I used to do!" Sister Thompson exclaimed with a hand in the air.

"Amen to that!" Sister Sarah chimed.

"Bless you!" Sister Thomas retorted.

"You know, Sister Thomas, I understand where you're coming from, but you're hardly influencing these young people from where you sit on the second pew. That little heathen is in a very important position, leading the choir. He's got all these girls showing out."

"It's not only the girls," Sister Thomas said, cutting her eyes at Sister Sarah. "It's the women, too."

"Hmm," Sister Sarah said. "Well, I, for one, don't see any harm in having him."

"You wouldn't."

"No, I wouldn't. And you two shouldn't either. He's representing the neighborhood. We haven't had so many people from this neighborhood join the church since Brother Samuels came," Sister Sarah told the women.

"That's what I am afraid of." Sister Talbert felt herself becoming angry. "We don't want too much of the neighborhood inside the church."

"My, you're judgmental lately," Sister Thomas said.

"If recognizing trouble means I'm being judgmental, Sister, then I'm guilty as charged. You can judge me all you want, but one thing I know for sure is that being Christian doesn't make you Devil-proof."

"This is true," Sister Sarah said. "But being Christian doesn't mean you aren't human either. Listen, I love

Jesus as much as the next Christian; you see what I'm saying? But I'm also a woman. Haven't you noticed how many women are coming to church, now that we have Brother Samuels?"

"They're coming for the wrong reason," Sister Talbert complained.

"No, no, Sister Talbert, she's right," Sister Thomas said. "No matter why they're coming, they still get the same word of God that we do. Pastor sees to that. You have to keep your faith. Besides, with women come children and, in their lives, Christ Jesus can make a real difference."

"I agree. So what if they're coming for the music or simply to look at him? It's not a sin to look," Sister Sarah replied.

Sister Thompson laughed. "That depends on how many times you look."

"No, it doesn't," Sister Talbert said. "It depends on what you're thinking about when you're looking."

"You can say that again," Sister Sarah said, giggling.

"But really, ladies, I think Pastor should be ashamed of himself for letting a sinner lead the choir simply because he can sing and play like a professional," Sister Talbert said.

"Sister Talbert, you're much too bitter for your own good these days. I don't mean any disrespect to you at all, so please don't take this the wrong way, but I think bitterness and anger can make you sick."

"Oh yeah? Well, I'll have to ask my doctor if he has some happy pills for my Cynical Cancer."

"Stop it, you two." Sister Sarah glanced over Sister Talbert's shoulder at the young, green-eyed beauty gliding down the church hallway, removing his choir robe. "Shhh, here comes the little pretty boy now."

Underneath his robe he wore a white shirt, unbuttoned at the neck, revealing the silver cross all newly baptized members received, and a pair of pleated baggie slacks that kind of danced in the breeze of his trail. There was a hint of a player's drag in his right foot as he walked toward them in midnight blue, snakeskin Stacy Adams.

"Ladies…" Brother Samuels nodded at the women as he passed, leaving them in a fog of Calvin Klein cologne. He walked into the meeting hall, opened the closet where the choir robes were stored, and hung his inside.

"Stop staring at that boy's ass," Sister Sarah said under her breath. She cleared her throat. "That was quite a performance you gave today, Marcel."

Brother Marcel looked up at the women, then up and down at Sister Sarah to find out if the flirtation in her eyes was also in her hips. He smirked and nodded slowly as he walked toward the church hens. From this direction, with the kitchen light shining through, he could see that Sister Sarah wasn't wearing a slip under her pink silk dress. Just behind her, he could see Stormy washing communion glasses.

"Thanks, Sister," he said. "But it's these beautiful angels

ya'll have given me to work with; they make the heavenly sounds you heard." He stepped behind Sister Sarah, letting his shoulder brush against the woman's back. He leaned into the kitchen door. "There's one of them now. Hey there, Stormy." Stormy could feel those familiar butterflies flutter about her insides when he said her name. "I'll see you at choir rehearsal next week, right?"

"Yes, of course, Marcel. I'll be there."

"That's a grown man you're speaking to. You'll address him as Mister or Brother Samuels. That is your name, right?" Sister Talbert checked with him.

"Oh, yes, ma'am. Brother Samuels will do fine."

He smiled softly at Stormy and brushed against Sister Sarah once more, before retreating back down the hall.

"Please don't get any bright ideas about calling me by my last name, Stormy," Sister Sarah said. "If I hear anyone say Sister Dippman, I'll be looking around for my mother!"

"Never mind all that," Sister Talbert said. "Stormy, you mind your manners around that young man. You understand? He's not a boy. He's a man."

"Yes, Momma," Stormy said.

Sister Talbert could feel Sister Thomas and Sister Sarah looking at her suspiciously. "Bless you, sisters. Bless the both of you!"

She tossed her nose in the air and walked down the hall. She hoped to speak to Brother Samuels, but she was stopped in her tracks by Pastor, who prayed over her

Cancer in front of the church. When she opened her eyes, Brother Samuels and nearly everyone else was gone.

STORMY WOKE UP EXTRA EARLY ON SATURDAY MORNING so she could leave the house before her mother woke up. Stormy was only fourteen. Too smart, her mother said, for her own good, and too young to be wearing black stockings with a seam up the back. Her mother had told her to throw them away when she bought them at the liquor store on Sunday. But she liked the way her legs looked in them. They made her legs look exactly like the ones on the package. So instead of tossing them, she had stuffed them into her purse and had been posing in them in the mirror all week long; sitting on her dresser, legs crossed, toes pointed, stomach sucked in, budding breasts forward, silently laughing, and touching fingertips to her chest, she had practiced being grown up in them.

Her dress was short enough to show them off as she walked to the bus stop. The bus driver noticed them with a bright golden grin. The old ladies, with huffs and snubs, noticed the grown-up legs on the teenage girl. Stormy silently hoped for a more favorable reaction from Marcel Samuels as she crossed her ankles and turned her face away from the women.

Stormy and Melissa, the soprano that stood next to her in the choir stand, had been jabbing each other in the thigh during rehearsal, in girlish competition for the young director's attention. Melissa, he said, had a voice like Tramaine Hawkins, so he offered her the lead on "When You Pray." Stormy was sulking in defeat as Melissa melted in the sultry attention of the director, whose hands manipulated their way from her shoulders to her diaphragm, compelling the young vocalist to push the song out. Melissa giggled when Brother Samuels told Stormy that her voice was shaky and compromised his entire choir, but she swallowed her laughter whole when Brother Samuels offered Stormy some personal assistance after rehearsal.

Saturday afternoon, when choir rehearsal was over and all of the good Christians were gone, Stormy lay cradling herself on the floor, where young Brother Samuels had abandoned her wilted body, with her virginity bleeding slowly down her thighs in the Pastor's study.

Stormy didn't know how he had removed her pretty black stockings. She had only wanted to kiss him. She had only wanted to see what kissing his special mouth would be like. That first kiss was the sweetest thing she had ever felt. Everything else happened so quickly that she couldn't think straight. Her face was stinging, there was something around her neck, his salty hand was over her mouth and nose, and she couldn't breathe. Then she was on the floor with her hair being pulled back so far she thought her neck would snap. Her fists pounded the flesh and muscles of his big, strong back, and someone was screaming "no" and "stop" and "it hurts" and "please, Jesus, stop him." Things in her stomach were being pushed around as her bones seemed to split and give way to a digging inside of her and everything between her legs was throbbing, aching, and bruising. Then time was still and she left the room and floated into space and looked for Jesus. She was calling His name and looking and calling and looking, but she couldn't find Him anywhere. She found a quiet place, lay down and waited, unsure of what she was waiting for.

Suddenly, there was a loud grunt in her ear, and then panting, squeezing, shaking, and breathing and then… he was soft again, kissing her with his special mouth.

"Now that's some pussy that can make a brother sing," he said, kissing her again. Stormy didn't say anything. She stared at the cross on the wall behind him, where Jesus hung. "Hey, are you in there?" Brother Samuels knocked on her head with his knuckles. She turned her empty eyes toward him. "Don't worry. It won't hurt the next time."

He stood up over her. She saw his dick; the first one she had ever seen. It had blood and white stuff on it. She felt her stomach retching and thought she would throw up, until she swallowed hard and looked away, at the cross again.

Brother Samuels picked her dress up off the floor and wiped his dick with it. "You ain't never even seen one before today, huh?"

Stormy lay there. She did not answer. She did not cry. She kind of lay numb and wondering. What had she done wrong? Why was God punishing her? Was this what she had to look forward to with men? *If God is everywhere*, she thought, *why couldn't He hear my prayers from inside a Pastor's study?* Her eyes were fixated on that cross, where a hippy-looking white man hung with nails in his hands and feet. Her Sunday school teacher said Jesus was a carpenter. *Maybe he built his own cross, too*, she thought. *Jesus, where were you when I was looking for you?*

She shivered.

"Are you cold?" Brother Samuels asked. "Here, put your dress back on." He tossed the dress onto her body, but she didn't move a muscle.

For a moment, there was tenderness in his voice that Stormy appreciated. Even when he wasn't singing, praising God with his tenor tone, his voice sounded like a song. *Are you cold?* Even in the aftermath of him stealing her virginity, Stormy was drawn to his voice and waited for him to say something that would make her feel better.

"Is something wrong?" he asked her. "Why are you laying there, staring up at that cross?

"Oh, so now you're not talking. What happened to '*Oh Brother Samuels, you sing so pretty?*' And '*how old are you? Hee hee hee*'; I saw ya'll up there in the choir stand giggling. I be seeing ya'll all the time, talking about me. Now that you have my attention, you can't talk. You all hurt. Shit." He curled his lip in disgust at her. "You know, you females make me sick, prancing around in front of dudes, dressing like little sluts, switching your little asses around, batting your eyelashes, flirting and shit. Then you have the nerve to cop an attitude when men want to fuck you; especially you young chicks. Sometimes I think God be playing games. I mean, He be giving ass and titties, like the ones He gave to you, to kids, and expects a man not to want them. It don't make sense. It's just wrong. That's why I'm in this church, playing the piano, singing and getting paid. My pretty hands make seventy-five dollars every time they touch the keys on Sunday. All this shit is fake. You are hell of fake." He kicked Stormy's leg. "I'm going to give you some advice, young lady. You would be smart to take it. Don't take this situation and try to use it to play victim. You'll only be fucking yourself up for later. Pussy wasn't created for anything but fucking and having babies. So if you think I've done you wrong, think again. I simply got you ready."

He knelt at her side, watching her lay still. Young Brother Samuels spoke slow and deliberately to her. "I know you're feeling kind of bad about it right now, going out like a hoe and all; especially at church, and being only fourteen. But I can see it in you. You're going to be one of those bitches who love to fuck. Trust me; don't worry about it right now. Hey…" He waved his hand in front of her eyes. "What are you doing? What are you looking at?" He followed her eyes to the cross on the wall behind him. "What? Do you think He's going to climb down off that cross and whip my ass? Hey, my cousin said that Mary, you know, from the Bible, Jesus' mother, was around fourteen years old. So you're in real good company."

Stormy just lay there, not responding. He looked at the catatonic girl on the floor, laughed, and stood on his feet.

"Naw, for real though; that's some real good pussy you got. You were fighting me for a minute. That's something you can hold on to, for sure, for your honor. But I could feel you wanting to fuck me back. I could feel you holding yourself back. You even got a couple of good pumps in there, didn't you?"

Stormy turned her face away. He reached for her chin and turned her face back over to him. She closed her eyes.

"Open your eyes. I want you to look at me and remember me. I want you to remember what I smelled like, what I tasted like, what I felt like, before all those other men come rushing up inside you. You should do yourself a favor next time; don't hold back. You ain't being raped if you're fucking back. Remember that."

Stormy watched Brother Samuels as he walked away from her, shaking his head. He checked his hair in the mirror by the coat rack, where the Pastor's robe, hat and coat hung, and continued to talk.

"Pussy ain't all special like you females try to make it out to be. That's all I'm saying. Men know what pussy is for. We have to have it. We would kill to get it. We pay for it! I mean, I don't pay for it but some fools do. Men are the ones that give it value; not women. Pussy ain't worth anything; not really. It's just that men have a need for it. So in the future, if any of these fine, upstanding church men want to run up in you, you need to get a little something for your college fund. You know what I'm saying?

"Besides, fucking is in our nature. It's something people do. We're all animals with urges to procreate and shit. That means have babies," he said, looking back at her on the floor. Stormy was starting to look like she was going to cry. "You need to get up off the floor, and stop feeling sorry for yourself. You don't even know. I did you a big-ass favor." Brother Samuels pulled his arms through his choir robe and zipped it. "I swear," he said, "Females can be so unappreciative." He walked toward the door. "Every girl has got to become a woman some time. It's probably better that you became one in the house of the Lord, don't you think?"

In that moment, a single tear crawled through the corner of Stormy's eye. She could feel a well of them rushing in to pity her. He was almost out of the door. She willed her tears away; she would not give him the satisfaction of seeing her cry.

Brother Samuels opened the door to the Pastor's study and was stepping through it when he had an afterthought. "I know you don't want to embarrass your momma with any of this. With that cancer eating her up like it is already, you might kill her with foolishness. I heard, back in the day, your momma knew what pussy was for, too."

With that, he disappeared behind the door. Stormy could hear him, already humming his next musical gift to God as he shut the door and walked down the hall with her innocence still ripe on his dick, under his choir robe.

After a few minutes, when she could hear the organ flooding the sanctuary, Stormy stood up on her trembling legs. She pulled her pretty stockings from around her neck and tossed them in the trashcan by the Pastor's desk. She picked her pink cotton panties up off the floor and stepped into them. Then she put on the dress her mother had warned her was *"too short for the church house"* and folded her choir robe. She could hear Brother Samuels on the organ in the sanctuary, singing…

"I find no fault in God; He's wonderful. I find no fault in Him…"

CHAPTER 2: THE VIRGIN FILES:
THE GIFT THAT KEEPS ON GIVING

he night Korea gave her virginity to Keith, she didn't even bleed. Over the next couple of months, she let him hit a few more times, hoping it would get better, but she was starting to wonder what all the excitement over sex was about. She was about to stop fucking him altogether when he started getting more creative.

Keith was pretty sure that he wasn't getting Korea off with his usual moves, so he decided to try something different. *He wasn't usually a weak fuck, but he had to admit to himself that he could understand if Korea thought he was.* After all, she never made a sound when he fucked her, even when her pussy was dripping wetness. Her silence was so intimidating. It was all he could do to stay hard most of the time.

Korea found a package in her gym locker with a note attached. "Baby, I bought you something. Please put on only what is inside this package and meet me on the corner behind the gym after school. I love you. P.S., make sure you don't wear anything but what is in the package."

It was an old trick he hadn't used in years, but it was failure proof, Keith thought, as he waited with his Mustang idling behind the high school. For a fleeting moment, he thought he might be tricking himself when he saw her strutting toward his car in the red silk wrap-around dress and elegant Evan Picone pumps he had given her. Half an hour later, Korea lay on a hotel bed, spread-eagle, with her full pussy exposed to his razor's edge. *He had shaved her*, then sucked, kissed, and licked inside her bald pussy until she had moaned for him, for the very first time. But right when Korea was getting into it, rolling her hips and fucking his lips and tongue, Keith had grown excited. He had pulled his face from between her legs and climbed on top of her. Before long, he was spilling his hot milk on her clean-shaven skin.

Korea couldn't stop thinking about the sweet sensation of having a tongue on her pussy. Every night, she was touching herself and searching for the spots that got her the hottest. But after three days, when her hair began to grow back, her desire to touch herself became an intense need to scratch, as hair bumps began to form, leaving tiny pus-filled blisters. The skin of her pussy became inflamed and hot to the touch in the next days and she could not scratch enough to soothe the powerful itch.

"Aw, baby," Keith said into the phone. "That happens sometimes. Your skin has to get a little tougher. It'll heal in a few days."

"It better," Korea said, calming down a bit, as she pressed a warm wet towel against her punany.

"You've been thinking about me licking on you, huh?" Keith said, in a sexy voice.

"No."

"I'll bet you have. I'll bet you've been touching yourself, and thinking of my tongue inside you."

"Yeah. That was good. That was real good," the girl admitted finally. "But I'm not trying to have a tough pussy; I want a pretty pussy. So, you won't be shaving me again. I hope you understand that."

Keith ignored her command. "You want me to come over?"

"No, my mom will be back in a minute."

"I could come later, when she's sleeping. You know, hang around your window, like last time."

"Now see, that's what I get for giving you a bullshit answer. I'm over here with a disco inferno blazing between my legs and all you can say is that you want to get a blowjob at my bedroom window? Yeah, that's really going to happen. Keith, please hang up now, so I don't have to disrespect you and hang up in your face. I can't be getting angry at senior citizens like that."

"Aw, no you didn't call me a senior citizen!" Keith laughed into the phone. "All right then, young lady. Take it easy though. The bumps are going to go away. Maybe you could throw a perm on it when the hair comes back."

Korea searched for a quick comeback to stick him with, but all she came up with was a dial tone. Keith was right, though. After almost two weeks, Korea's hair was coming back nicely and there was only a cluster of small itchy bumps left, near her vaginal opening.

"It could be an STD, huh?" she asked the doctor, shyly. This was her first pelvic exam and pap smear. She lay on the examination table with her legs wide open and her feet lodged in stirrups.

"It could be," the milky-skinned blonde woman said as she slipped her long narrow hands into two rubber gloves. "Then again, it could be nothing. Why don't we wait and see what it is?" The woman smiled so warmly at her young patient, Korea felt it.

This doctor is pretty, she thought. *No, she is beautiful.* To Korea, she looked more like a model than someone who would be working at the local free clinic. Her eyes were such a pale blue, they were almost translucent. Her cheekbones were high and well-defined and her small, pouty lips looked like somebody had drawn them on her face with a calligraphy pen.

Korea was lost in these thoughts when the pretty doctor nudged her knee a bit to get her to open her legs wider.

"Relax," she said. "This won't hurt. I'm going to…"

As Doctor Model went on to describe the next steps she would take, Korea could feel a warming sensation running completely through her body as two well-lubricated gloved fingers reached inside of her. With her other hand, the doctor pressed around on her stomach, leaning forward just enough so that Korea caught the scent of her cotton candy breath, flooding her belly with butterflies. At first, Korea thought she had to pee. As the doctor reached her fingers deep down inside of her, tapping and searching around for "lumps, bumps or anything unusual," Korea felt something she had never felt before; a strong increasing urge to bear down and squeeze.

"Wait," she said, grabbing a fist full of the plastic pad underneath her. "I…" Korea tried to warn the woman of the impending flood, but suddenly her entire body seemed to sneeze.

"Whoa, young lady…," the doctor said. "That was a first," she said, taking her fingers out of the patient so quickly, Korea had an aftershock of tiny jolts and quivers.

"I'm sorry," Korea said. Her heart was pounding inside her chest; it's rhythm spreading through her veins, clear down to the little button she had been pushing on all those nights since Keith had licked her there. She lay on a soaked pad, hiding behind the hand over her face.

Korea decided, in that very moment, that she might never need a dick, or a man, again. Keith's dick had never made her feel this way; whatever *this way* was. She wanted to feel it over and over again. She wanted to feel it forever. And if it only existed in the fingertips of a beautiful woman with cotton candy breath, so be it. She was going to make a way to leave Keith immediately.

"Don't worry. You'll have it all under control before you know it," Doctor Model said, peeling the gloves off of her hands and dropping them into the trashcan. She handed a clean, dry, blue plastic and cotton pad to Korea.

"Was that what I think it was?" Korea asked her.

"I'm pretty sure," the doctor replied over her shoulder as she washed her hands and forearms in the sink. "Okay, let me start the exam over." She walked back over to the table and slipped her hands into a new pair of gloves.

"Thanks," Korea said. Then, realizing that it may have sounded like she was thanking the woman for making her climax on the table, she corrected herself. "I mean, thank you for not making me feel embarrassed."

"Of course," she said and exhaled.

There's that cotton candy again, Korea thought as she closed her eyes.

"Okay," the woman said, preparing her young patient. "This part might not be quite so pleasant," Korea could hear the magician say as she lay feeling the tingles slowly dissipate.

Suddenly, all sense of pleasure came to a quick freeze when the cold speculum slipped inside of her. She could feel the cool clinic air rush into her open body; the swipe of dry cotton, a pinch, a squeeze, and then another swipe and it was over. Korea exhaled and relaxed her pelvis, and then the rest of her body.

"Okay, Miss Smith," Doctor Model said. "We'll have to send these samples to a lab for tests. One of the nurses will be back in to talk to you."

"Tests," Korea repeated softly, having been reminded of exactly where she was and why she was there. "Doctor, can you tell me what you think it is?" she asked in a voice that sounded much more frightened and tiny than any voice that had ever emanated from her throat before.

She momentarily wondered if it was hers, and then she cleared her throat and tried again, repeating the question, this time with more assertiveness and adding, "Could they be hair bumps? See, I let Keith, that's the guy…I let him shave me down there. When I told him about the bumps, he said they were probably just hair bumps," Korea finished confidently.

The doctor dropped her gloves into the trash receptacle and turned to look at the sixteen-year-old girl who had probably gotten herpes before she had even had her first orgasm. "Well, I'd rather not say until the tests are back. There's no point in getting you all *excited*, until we know for sure." Then she winked one pale blue eye at Korea and disappeared behind a cold clinic door.

In the ten days that it took to receive her test results in the mail, Korea ignored Keith's calls, played basketball, and found it difficult to stop thinking about the doctor and that strange sensation she had had on her table.

Korea was still pretty sure the bumps were nothing. They had scabbed over and fallen off without even leaving scars.

CHAPTER 3: THE VIRGIN FILES:
DREAM CROW

Keith studied Dream Crow from across the room, examining her reaction to the screams and bumping sounds pounding against the wall. Titus, the pimp in the condo next door, was beating his unruly new hoe again, and every time her head hit the wall, Dream Crow flinched like her nerves were pinching her. She sat at her dressing table, nervously trying to apply lip liner to her full, heart-shaped lips, but she kept going out of the lines and had to keep starting over. On top of the screaming and pleading and slaps and booms crashing through the wall, Keith's phone was ringing but he wouldn't answer it. Her pager was buzzing with persistent reminders from her brother, Hartford, that she needed to get a new life. Her stomach was tied in knots and beginning to hurt.

"Baby..." she said finally, hoping the sound of her own voice would calm her. "Do you want me to answer the phone?"

Keith stood in front of his undraped panoramic windows with a sea of San Francisco skyline framing him. "No," he said, smiling wickedly.

He looked at the anxious phone, knowing Korea was on the other end of it, probably in a tailspin. It had been a while since she had told him about those bumps. She probably had her test results back from the clinic. He walked over to the stereo and turned the knob to raise the volume on Whitney Houston's latest release, "Didn't We Almost Have it All."

"Don't answer the phone yet." His voice was airy and loaded as he walked toward the back of Dream Crow's red velvet stool and laid his hands gently on her shoulders. "Why are you so nervous?" Keith asked into her ear as he bent down and looked into the mirror at her.

"I'm not nervous."

"Really? You seem nervous. I thought you might be because Titus is over there drunk and acting a fool again."

"I have a date that I can't be late for. He's pretty big time, I think. He won't wait. I *know* he won't wait if I'm late. That's what it is. That's all."

"Well, he's going to have to wait."

"Huh? Why?"

"I need you to fix those shaky little hands of yours and trim my mustache." Keith reached for her hand and grabbed the pager from it. He looked into the tiny screen to check the number. "Is that who I think it is?"

"Yeah, I called him back when I got out of the shower. It's my mom. She's sick."

"And?"

"And Hartford wants me to go to the hospital to see

her. That's all. But I'm not. I'm not going." Dream Crow gave Keith a nervous smile and changed the subject. "Daddy, why don't you go get me the scissors so I can trim you?"

"Yeah, alright," he said.

Keith disappeared into the master bathroom. Dream Crow cleared the numbers in her pager and tucked the gadget into her tote. Between the incredible voltages of Whitney Houston's crooning, she could hear Titus grunting through the wall. Their neighbor's fights always ended with sex; *always*. Exactly like Dream Crow's mother and father had.

"Whose pussy is this?" Titus was commanding his green little runaway to answer, when Keith game back with the mustache scissors.

"Sit down," Dream Crow told him.

"What did you say?"

"Not like that, honey. I'm just saying, please, baby, sit down. My time is short."

"Life is short." It was a warning she didn't miss. "I'm not sitting on that stupid little stool. Do me in the kitchen."

"Okay."

She followed Keith into the kitchen and tried to hold her hands steady but her nerves were fucking her up and now she had to shit.

"Your stomach's growling," Keith said. "Maybe you should eat before you head out."

"No. I'm not hungry."

"Maybe you need to shit then."

"No," she said, embarrassed. "I don't have to shit."

"Do you ever shit?"

"Please, stop talking; you're going to make me mess up your mustache."

"You better not mess up my Billy Dee Williams. We been together for some years and I've never even smelled your shit. What do you do? Wait for me to go to sleep, or leave the condo or something?"

"Eeew, Keith, I really don't want to talk about this."

"Why not? Are you too much of a lady or something?" Keith asked sarcastically.

Dream Crow worked on his mustache and sang along with Whitney Houston, who was getting all "Emotional."

"I've been waiting for the phone to ring all night
Why you wanna make me feel so good
I got a love of my own
Shouldn't get so hung up on you.."

Keith got irritated whenever he heard Dream Crow singing. It meant she wasn't over the stupid-ass fantasy she had about becoming a singer.

"Ain't you finished yet?"

"Almost, baby," she said, continuing to hum along with the diva on the stereo as she clipped and snipped.

The kitchen phone rang. "You can answer that now. And please don't be singing all up in my ear while I'm talking. This ain't a fucking concert hall."

Dream Crow put the scissors down, wrung her hands, and fetched the phone. The voice of the teenager on the other end of the line pissed her off and reminded her of the white girl Keith had found and spent all kinds of money on. Had he learned nothing? After working for only a few weeks, the little ingrate had traded up and left her holding the bag. Between Dream Crow's new car, Keith's endless car renovations, the rent on the condo, and the heavy recruiting efforts he was making on this new "child" he was trying to mack on, they had twice the bills and half the income. Keith was barely helping her with anything, complaining that powder cocaine wasn't moving because base rock was taking over.

"It's for you," she snapped, as she walked back over to him and handed him the phone.

Korea was in a rage on the other end of the phone. "You gave me herpes, you fucking bastard!" she screamed.

"I know," he said dryly, trying not to move his mouth too much while Dream Crow trimmed the last few hairs of his mustache.

Korea was nearly inaudible as she screamed and cried through slobber and tears on the phone. All Keith could manage to understand of what she said was, "You scarred me for life."

"Look at it this way," he said in a cool tone, waving Dream Crow and her scissors away from his face. "Now you don't have to worry about catching it."

"Keith…you…" Korea couldn't believe he was admitting to giving her herpes. She could not say another word.

"Don't say my name like a little bitch. As a matter of fact, don't call me again until you ain't actin' like a little punk."

Keith hung up the phone. He sat for a few moments, contemplating his next move. He hated to have to come off the way he had to Korea on the phone. It had already been three months since he had spotted her at her high school basketball game, whipping ass like a dude on the court. If she had been any other chick, he would've had her working his track by now, but there was something special about her. He could start her out in the best hotels and he could get more money for her because she was young and had a unique look. She was unlike any female he had ever met. She was calculated and mannish in a way that he respected. She was also poor and desperate to get rich, so he thought he could present the game as a business opportunity that she could appreciate. He had planned on doing this a week ago, but now that she had caught the virus, he was going to have to change up the game plan. He sat for a minute in the kitchen, thinking about what he was going to do.

"Man, I'm telling you, this girl is different. I can't seem to break her," Keith said, when he found Dream Crow sitting at her dressing table again.

"Mmmm," she mumbled, as she primped one last time in the mirror, thinking of her brother, Hartford, and her promise to him to meet a friend of his who was in town for a music convention at the Moscone Center. He had been blowing up her pager all night with reminder calls that the man would only be at The Bellevue Hotel until six o'clock the next morning. Hartford was desperate to get his sister out of the life. He was only nineteen and already on his way to the big time in the music industry. When they were children, he had made a promise to her to make her a star.

Hartford was always complimenting her. He would say, "Your voice is almost as beautiful as you are, big sister."

Part of Dream Crow thought that Hartford was simply being a good brother, or working on her self-esteem to get her off the track and back on track. The other part of her knew that it was his way of taking care of her, as she had taken care of him, all that time their mother was too broken to even take care of herself. Their natural father, the late Jay Crow, had been a well-respected musician whose talents were as well known as his sins. He was a good provider, but he was also a violent and suspicious husband, prone to jealous rages. On nights when their father would come home drunk, the nights when a beating could be anticipated for their mother, Dream Crow would feed Hartford and Blue early and keep them in their room, entertained by concerts featuring herself as Chaka Khan, Patti LaBelle, or Donna Summer.

When Jay Crow died at forty-four with an enlarged

liver and a surprised look on his face, staring at his wife from the pillow beside hers, he still had a fistful of her hair in his hand. Except for the house they lived in, he had gambled away most of his possessions by then. He didn't have life insurance or a savings of any kind, leaving his family impoverished and his uneducated, inexperienced wife severely depressed. She had always stayed in the house, day and night. Their father forbade her to leave. But when he died, their mother could not get out of bed. Dream Crow became the woman of the house, and raised Hartford and Blue on pure love and a diet of Oodles of Noodles. Asking for help from the government meant asking for trouble, so Dream Crow did whatever she needed to do to survive and keep her family together. Her younger sister, Blue, was assigned to nurse her mother back to health and Hartford made sure he did his part with his paper route.

"Girl, you got a body that could make a blind man blush," a voice said to her from a Lincoln Continental, driving five miles an hour beside her as she walked home from school one day. Dream Crow was budding into a promising young artist with vocal, dance, and acting skills. She was focused on her education, but desperate for a break from the poverty and responsibility she had faced by the time she was only fourteen years old. So when Seth came along, she was all ears.

Seth was thirty-two, and had been a player all of his life. He had a good car and some decent hustles that included an uncanny ability to find things for people. But he needed a place to stay. When he found some anti-depressants for her mother, Dream Crow named a price and cleared a space for him that he could call a room.

One Saturday morning, the children and Seth were sitting down for breakfast when Seth looked up and saw the children's mother standing in the doorway. "Who are you?" she asked him. "Who said you could bring my children pancakes?"

Seth looked to Dream Crow for an answer. "Momma, this is Seth. He's been waiting to meet you…"

Seth married her mother, but everyone in the house realized that he was there for Dream Crow. He was a supportive and present adult in Dream Crow's life, and had won her heart easily with attention. He attended her recitals and showed up for parent-teacher conferences when her mother was too medicated and numb to be a parent at all. Dream Crow might have stayed there with him, seen her brother and sister off to college, and taken care of her mother, but Seth got caught up and started using. When she was seventeen, he traded Dream Crow to Keith for a brick of cocaine.

Hartford hated his stepfather for what he had made his sister become. He wanted to save her. He wanted her to realize that she needed to save herself and that she had the talent to do it. Now that he had both feet in the door, and a hit song waiting to be recorded, he was inviting Dream Crow and their sister, Blue, to come inside.

Dream Crow noticed the roots of her hair sweating back and her curls going limp. She checked the clock. *Ten more minutes and I need to be walking out of the door,* she thought, firing up her curling iron again.

"I can't believe it, man. I think I love her." Keith had not meant to say the words out loud, especially not in front of the only girl on his team, but they had been said and he couldn't take them back.

"You think you love her? What kind of shit is that for a pimp to say?" Dream Crow hissed at him. She grabbed her curling iron and playfully lunged at his image behind her in the glass.

"Aw, baby, that's what pimps do. We love everybody." Keith kissed at her annoyed reflection in the mirror. "But, for real, the bitch ain't budging. Here she is, going to be able to leave home soon, and she's talking some bullshit about business school. And she had the nerve to be talking about 'ain't no basketball scholarships for this school,' like I'm supposed to pay for the shit. She's got me twisted."

"It sounded to me like she was mad about something else."

"Huh? Don't get beside yourself. Not now. I really don't feel like beating your ass tonight."

Yeah, I've heard, an outbreak can make you tired, Dream Crow thought as she avoided his eyes charging at her in the mirror. In the early 80's, Castlemont, the high school in her East Oakland neighborhood, had been nicknamed

"Herpes High" when the *Oakland Tribune* newspaper reported that a lot of the students had been infected. The high school clinic made a point of preparing all incoming high school students with information on the incurable virus, so Dream Crow knew exactly what to look for. The second she saw the scars on Keith, she laid down the law about sex with him. If he wanted her to work for him, she would, but there would be no fucking between them.

Sex was more than a pastime or a good time for Dream Crow. She was not an innocent girl when she met Keith. Sex was neither a sin nor a misdemeanor punishable by God, or by law, in her book. Sex was a business, like any other business, and it was not to be compromised or jeopardized by incompetence, ignorance, and especially not sexually transmitted diseases. She could spot a man who was not clean over the phone. When she met Keith, she had examined him thoroughly and knew the scars were the mark of the beast. So theirs was not a relationship based on sex. She was loyal to him like one was to a job or a boss, but she was beginning to see his weaknesses. She was beginning to see that he wasn't qualified to pimp her or anyone else.

"I can hear you thinking," he said. His words were code for, "Get the fuck out and make us some money before I get my belt."

He was threatening her a lot lately, but he had only used his belt on her once. But once was enough for her to know that she should never disrespect him. The whipping she had endured had been vicious and painful. The very thought of it had been enough to keep Dream Crow in line ever since.

She had been with him for a year; it was her eighteenth birthday and he had taken her out for dinner. They had a nice time, but back then she didn't know how to control her alcohol. So when one drink led to another, her mouth had started running. Over dinner she had let him pick her brain. She confessed that she had fucked an associate of his. She had laughed into her brandy glass when she told him that she didn't charge a dime. She wanted to fuck the guy, so she did, she told him.

"You can't imagine how liberating it was to fuck for pleasure," she blurted out in the car when he strapped her in her seat belt. Then, she passed out. When she woke up, naked in the bed, Keith was pouring water on her sheet. He had a belt in his hand.

"Are you sober now?" he asked. "I want you to be sober so you can feel this shit." *Whap!* His belt came down on her. "*Happy Birthday to you. Happy Birthday to you…*" He sang the birthday song while he dropped his belt across her ass, thighs, and back over and over again.

Dream Crow screamed and tried to get off the bed as he burst into the second chorus: "*How old are you?*" But Keith had tied the sheet down so Dream Crow was stuck between it and the mattress. After a minute or so, she was getting numb. "I might not be fucking you, but you *will* respect me."

Dream Crow wasn't surprised that he had beaten her. She lay in the aftermath with the feeling in her skin returning and burning. She was thinking, *"Maybe I wanted him to beat me."* She thought, *"It wasn't that bad."* And she thought, *"It could have been worse."* She never thought of leaving.

"At least I know you ain't a punk," she had said when he untied the sheet.

She deserved to get her ass whipped that time, she told herself, but it would not happen again. So she did what she was supposed to: brought in the money, kept her personal business to herself, and never got drunk again. Now, with money getting funny, she was afraid that it would not be long before his ego brought his pimp hand out again. She would not be able to live like that girl next door, getting beaten every night.

Ugh, Ugh, no way, she thought.

There was a moment of understanding silence between Dream Crow and Keith. Then he continued to talk about "Korea Smith, a high school basketball player, beautiful enough to model, smart enough to run a corporation someday…she loves her mother…she wants to move her mother out of the projects…she lives in the 69th Avenue Village Projects…"

"Bla, bla, bla…" Dream Crow said inside her mind as she curled her hair. She checked the clock every thirty seconds, and let him talk until her hair was finished.

"Keith, can I ask you something, and you promise not to get mad?"

"If I might get mad, maybe it's something you shouldn't ask."

"Why do you want to turn a girl like that out? This life isn't any kind of life for the girl you're describing. This life is for women who don't have so many choices; women who aren't so talented."

Keith ignored Dream Crow as if she hadn't spoken at all. She exhaled in defeat and started straightening up her dressing table.

"She needs to come to an understanding about this here," he said. "Maybe you can help me, baby. I think she may have a thing for girls. It's not that she plays hoop; she naturally has a lot of dude in her. I think she might even shave her chin."

Distracted from her own thoughts, Dream Crow looked at Keith and repeated what she thought she had heard. "Did you say she has a beard? Damn, at sixteen? Gross! Now you know I'm strictly dickly. If I wasn't, I'd be licking my way to riches all over Nob Hill, getting paid for real. I've heard lesbians and lonely widows can be real generous."

"So you'll consider it then?"

"Me, fuck a bearded kid, to pull her for you? No, absolutely not. Some things are simply out of the question. I wouldn't do that, not even for you, Daddy. Sorry."

"That's cold, Dream Crow. That's real cold. But for real, she's really pretty though. She's brown-skinned with a real tight body, big titties, a fat ass, the whole nine, you know? I thought…I mean, this is San Francisco, and with things being kind of rough around here, it wouldn't hurt you none to open your mind up a little bit. Who's going to know you're munching on fur burger?"

"Gross."

Keith laughed. "Yeah, I knew you wouldn't be down with that shit. I was fucking with you."

"Look, Daddy," Dream Crow said, "I don't have to keep staying around for this crazy talk. You sound kind of desperate, like you're losing your confidence. The Keith I know wouldn't be chasing after some kid and spending money like you've been doing. Besides, we don't need a child to do a woman's work. I heard there were some outlaws over in the Tenderloin. I could take off tomorrow night and go recruit there."

"I like top-notch bitches. You know how much I dropped on Seth for you? It took you a long-ass time to work off that debt. Shit, I'm just now seeing any real profit, since you've been taking calls instead of making corners. When I saw you, I realized we could do some real business. You think my stable cut out on me, don't you?" He looked at Dream Crow with seriousness in his eyes. "Don't you?"

"Didn't they?"

"Hell no; I traded them hoes."

"Traded them?"

"Yes, I did; Mickey, Trina, and Sasha. I traded them twenty-dollar bitches to Rico. He ain't pulled shit from me. I didn't need them anymore. I didn't need them once I had you. I didn't want to tell you; I didn't want you to get all beside yourself, thinking too high. I didn't know you like that. I didn't realize how loyal you are. When I was dealing with street hoes, I didn't know anything about business. I got you off the streets as soon as I could line up the kind of clientele you should have. In no time, you were pulling in what all three of them put together were making working those corners."

It was a rude awakening for Dream Crow. She hadn't realized how valuable she had been to Keith until that very moment.

"Now that we've learned that street money ain't money at all, you want to go pick up some trash in the Tenderloin and bring it here? Here? I don't think so," Keith said. "This ain't the Open Door Mission. I'm only dealing with the best, baby, so we can make that top money. If we start scraping the bottom of the pond, we'll have a stable full of bitches in and out of county jail and rehab. Instead of paying for Gucci bags, we'll be stacking up medical bills. Remember how Trina was always getting her ass beat because of her mouth?"

Dream Crow had to laugh at that. Trina could fuck up a dude's wet dream with her foul mouth. She had no business trying to sell fantasies.

"Korea is going to work, just like you did. She's fine, she respects money, and she's got a little class on her ass. Korea's young and I'm the only one who's had her so far. She's the one. She ain't got a daddy and I don't think her momma is about to be checking for her."

"Is that a fact? How can you be sure?" Dream Crow asked him, turning around on her stool to look at him.

He ignored the disbelief on her face. "I'll make sure."

"Oh, like you did with that blue-haired white lady from the trailer park in Vallejo? She basically gave you her daughter. Remember Pepper? You went all out for that little ingrate…buying shit. She still left us. We still haven't recovered from that yet. That little trailer park trash. She better hope I never run into her ass again. I mean, just as quick as I cleaned her up in designer knocks and shoes, she turned my best trick into her husband." Dream Crow could feel herself getting upset. She wanted to stop talking but she had to get her say in. "She got a fucking husband, baby!" She stood up and looked at him with pleading eyes. She wanted to say, *"Don't make me do this. Don't make me leave you, too,"* but instead, she painted a simple and vivid picture of his misfortune and their mutual sacrifice. "Keith, we invested thousands on her gear and her car, and now she's married to a banker in a gated community in Blackhawk. I don't want to sponsor another green bitch."

"I don't want to talk about that white girl," Keith said, cutting his eyes at her.

Dream Crow's voice softened and soothed his mood with the tenderness of a love ballad. "Darling, baby, baby…" she said, walking toward him. Pressing her breasts against his chest, she cooed, "I won't keep talking about Pepper. But I thought you said, after she left us, that it was going to be you and me. I thought you said we were going to slow our roll and pace ourselves, maybe invest and do some real business together. You know, we could have a Laundromat or a car wash by now. It's like this shit is never going to end. It's supposed to end. I'm getting ready to be twenty-five. I'm not trying to do this shit forever. Do you think these rich tricks are going to pay a forty-year-old a thousand dollars to meet them in their penthouse suites? I don't think so." She paused for effect. "This right here…" She opened her hands and spread them to present the beautiful and extravagant California Street condominium to him. "Look around, baby. I can take care of this right here. It's all this extra stuff that's making everything all bad."

"Well, damn. I thought you could handle this whole situation, now that I got you those thousand-dollar clients, but…" He sucked his teeth. "I guess I was wrong." His drag may have worked on Dream Crow years ago, but tonight she could see through him like a silk screen.

"I would have it handled and I would keep it handled, but you're spending faster than I can return a phone call," Dream Crow said, backing away from him. "We're just gambling. I could be working on my singing career if I'm going to be gambling. I'm still young and sexy, you know?"

"Yeah, and you could learn to parse Greek."

"I could learn to do what?"

"Exactly. That's why your job is on your back."

"That was hurtful, Keith. You don't have to be mean to me because you're mad at that kid." She pouted, quickly trying to divert him from any thoughts of violence.

Dream Crow's heart-shaped pout could have stopped the conflict in the Persian Gulf. If Keith could figure out how to profit off of it, he'd have contracted her pussy out to the United States government. Her beauty was undeniable in the soft light of the dressing room. Her caramel-colored skin was a smooth, milky promise. Keith had not really looked at her for a long time. She was perfect in every way. Her skin never had a blemish and all of her womanly parts were perfect and well-pronounced. She always smelled delicious and inviting, like hot apples and cinnamon.

"Is that what I'm doing?" he asked softly, giving in to her perfections. "I'm sorry, baby, you're right. I apologize." He kissed her cheek and inhaled her baked goods. "I love the fact that you're a dreamer. There's nothing wrong with having your head in the clouds as long as you have your feet on the ground."

"You mean on the track, don't you?"

"Excuse me? What track? I've brought you clients and opportunities that make it so you haven't had to walk the block in years. Shit, I even got you judges so you don't ever have to see a jail cell. I got you into hotels and high-rises. I'm not pimping you; we're pimping them. I'm your manager and your friend. You wouldn't have been able to buy your car without me; Seth had your credit all fucked up before you were even old enough to have a credit card. I cleaned your credit up. I even let you send money home to your brother and sister and I helped you put Blue through nursing school. Would a pimp do that?"

"No," she admitted.

Keith had been unlike any pimp she had ever met. He had really been a friend to her.

"So you think that it's just you out there, woman? That ain't you out there; that's us. That's us out there. I can think of a million other things I could be doing. My daddy wasn't a pimp; he was a preacher. I could do that, and a whole lot more, but this thing we got is what it is, you know what I'm saying? This is going to get us where we need to be. You, making the sacrifices you make, so we can get ahead, means a lot to me. I hope my commitment to you means a lot to you, too. I mean," he said, rubbing his mustache. "How many times have I had to get with one of your clients about breaking you off after you already put it down? You appreciate me having your back out there, don't you?"

"Yeah, I do."

"Well then, act like it. You keep talking about being a singer because your jive-ass brother says you have a voice and he could manage you. He's selling you and your sister wolf tickets. She needs to keep herself at General and you need to get your head out of the clouds. Do you know how many singers never get discovered and die broke? Baby, we're pulling in close to twelve G's a month, sometimes fifteen. And you only work part-time. The rest of the time you're shopping. You're complaining about that little money I spent on them bitches to get us ahead, while you're keeping Dolce & Gabbana and Chanel in business all by yourself."

"Keith, those are business expenses. I can't keep quality clientele if I look like a walking billboard for Montgomery Ward," Dream Crow said, self-consciously pulling her strapless silver Giorgio Armani dress up to secure it over her breasts.

"If I could get this tender on our team," Keith said confidently, "we could double that and move into a big house. We could get that Laundromat you want, with the daycare in it," he promised *again*.

"That's what you said before."

"Did you hear any fucking thing I said? You should be helping me and supporting me, like I support you. Not threatening to bail out like some punk bitch. You mess around, wasting time trying to be a singer, and you'll be fucking for free…laid up on some music exec's couch somewhere. Come on now, you're smarter than that. Don't lose the faith. You have to trust me on this."

Keith was talking fast until he saw the defiance in Dream Crow's eyes dwindle down to defeat. He liked to keep that look in her pretty brown eyes; it made her look sexy, sad and sexy like a blues singer. He lifted her chin with his pinky finger. "Baby, I'm just saying the truth to you. If I didn't have mad love for you, I wouldn't tell you the truth. If I didn't love you, we would be over there like Titus and that crazy bitch. He's messing up her face, bruising her up, probably shooting her up, and using her pussy all up for himself. He's turning her into a twenty-dollar hoe. I'm not like that. I'm good to you, right?"

"Yes, you are, Keith. You've been real good to me, for what this is."

"For what this is?" Keith repeated, unbelieving, "For what this is? Trina and them never lived with me; they didn't share my space. I moved you in. I share everything with you, like we're partners. And except for that one time when you got drunk, I've been real cool to you. I be letting shit slide, you know, letting you express your opinions and shit. I have more love and respect for you now than ever before. When Seth brought you to me, you were only seventeen. You had a little past with him; I figured that out when you were holding on to his legs like you were. He couldn't get out of here fast enough with that brick of cocaine under his coat. He was dragging you across the carpet, trying to get out of the door. Do you remember that?"

"Of course I remember," Dream Crow said sadly, thinking of Seth. She had heard that he was in West

Oakland somewhere, walking the night like a toothless zombie.

"I'm sorry. You probably don't want to think about that now." Keith had promised never to bring it up. "But I never held that against you. Never once did I think, *Oh, I can get this nasty bitch to do anything*. Now look at you, classy as all get out. You can hold a conversation with anyone. You can go anywhere and feel right at home. You're all woman," he told her, flashing the smile that used to melt her. "I'd like to think I had something to do with the beautiful woman you've become."

"I know," Dream Crow said, wanting to get him to shut up so she could get out of this loud place that had been sounding off like warning sirens in her head for hours. "I have your back, Papi, like you have mine."

Satisfied, Keith stepped away from her. "What am I going to do about Korea?"

Dream Crow replied, "Leave her alone. She'll come to you. Daddy, I would love to stay and talk, but I have a date. I have to go. I'll be back tomorrow with so much cash, you'll forget all about that little fucking teenager."

"Tomorrow?"

"He's new; I'm breaking him in."

"Make sure he's paying double, if you're staying over."

"Of course, Keith. If I have any problems, I'll call you."

"You can break him in all you want, as long as you break him."

"Will do," she said, pecking Keith on the cheek.

She grabbed a small Louis Vuitton tote, her Gucci handbag, and left the condo. Over her silver mini-dress she donned a luxurious vintage three-quarter-length, brown mink. Dream Crow stepped into the night with her strappy silver stilettos beating the pavement quickly to her car. The minute she walked out of the door, her stomach had stopped hurting. She wasn't nervous anymore. Her hands weren't sweaty or shaking. She didn't have to shit.

The clock on the dash reminded her that the time on her dressing table was set thirty minutes ahead. She wouldn't have to meet Hartford's friend for another forty-five minutes. She drove down California Street, thinking about the girls that she used to work with and had left behind. She didn't know that they had been traded. She wondered what Keith had traded them for. She was headed for the 101, but decided to take a left onto Leavenworth and drive by her old stomping block. It was Friday night and the 500 block of Jones was popping with rich white potential clientele. Besides the music convention at the Moscone Center, a big charity fashion show called Macy's Passport was going on. She had heard that Elizabeth Taylor would be helping to raise money for AIDS. The event was sure to bring a lot more Hollywood players to town.

Dream Crow drove around the turf, showing off her shiny black convertible Spider, waving at girls that she used to know. It had been a long time since she had seen or talked to any of them. Looking at the scene, she almost felt like a traitor. She stopped for a traffic light when a girl leaned against her car.

"I'll suck your pussy for fifteen dollars," the girl said. Dream Crow pulled her car over to the curb. The girl followed and stood outside the passenger door. "So we got a deal?"

Dream Crow could see that she was high on heroin and there were needle marks all over her arms and neck. "I don't know, yet. You got a man around here?"

"Yeah," the girl said. "He's over there in the car, watching."

"Okay." Dream Crow reached into her purse and pulled out a fifty. "Here." Dream Crow handed the money to the girl. "Go ahead, get in."

"Damn, how did you go from hoeing to tricking?" Someone on the sidewalk was talking to her. Dream Crow looked up and saw Trina standing there in a dingy white pleather dress and white boots. Her blonde wig was matted and her lip was healing from where it had been recently busted. There was a black patch over her left eye.

"I see you're still giving those tricks more than they bargain for," Dream Crow said. "Who blacked your eye?"

"Ain't nobody blacked it," Trina said. "It's gone."

Dream Crow wanted to stay and talk, but she didn't have time. "You take care of yourself, Trina."

"You, too," Trina said. "Hey, where are you going

with Pillow?" Trina called after the car as Dream Crow hit the corner.

"I can't go too far for too long. Pull over in the alley over there," the girl said. "I can do you in the car."

Dream Crow turned into the alley, but she did not stop. "How old are you?" she asked, guessing she wasn't more than fifteen under her makeup.

"Don't you know it's not polite to ask a lady her age?" the girl said, nodding off.

Dream Crow checked her rearview mirror to see if she was being followed as she pulled out of the other end of the alley onto O'Farrell Street.

"Hey, wake up!" Dream Crow smacked her face and pulled her eyelid open at the stoplight. "How old are you?"

"Twelve. But I can suck your pussy like a grown-ass woman. For this fifty bucks, you can even suck mine."

"YOU KNOW, HARTFORD, I'LL DO MOST ANYTHING FOR you, but your sister is late and I'm supposed to be taking a very large check to Macy's Passport tonight. If I don't show up with that money, Liz will hogtie me. How much of my time did you promise to your sister?"

"Mr. Bandarofski, I promise you that Dream Crow is well worth the wait. She's fantastic. You won't be disappointed. Please, hold on. Give her fifteen minutes; she'll be there."

"I'll give her ten," Bandarofski said, and then Hartford was talking to a dial tone.

IT WAS A TEN-MINUTE DRIVE TO POTRERO AVENUE. She parked in an emergency room stall and helped Pillow out of the car.

Dream Crow put the child in a waiting room chair and walked up to the reception desk.

"Hi," she said to the nurse behind the counter. "Is my sister on duty? Her name is Blue Crow."

"Yes, she's in the Children's Health Center."

"Will you call her please? I can't stay. Tell her that her sister was here. Tell her that I brought this little girl here," she said, pointing to the child. "She needs to be fixed up."

The nurse winced when she saw the little girl with a painted-on face and festering needle marks. "Oh my God, child! What has happened to you?" She looked curiously at Dream Crow. "How do you know this girl?"

"I don't know her. I found her like this. I don't even know her name."

"My name is Linda," Pillow said. "Lady, you're going to be in so much trouble. You took me." She was slowly shaking her head and waving her finger back and forth. "He's gonna be mad."

"Who's going to be mad?" the nurse asked.

"Titus. Titus is gon' be real mad."

"Is he the one who did this to her?" the nurse asked.

"I don't know. I don't know who did this. I have to go," Dream Crow said.

"We'll take care of her. She'll be okay. I'll tell Blue you were here."

"Hey, lady," Pillow called after Dream Crow in a weak voice. "Do you want your fifty dollars back? I didn't get a chance to eat your pussy."

THE OLD MAN TOOK OFF HIS SMOKING JACKET AND LAID it on the bed. He stood in the mirror and straightened his bowtie and took his green paisley tuxedo vest off of the hanger and put it on his body. He checked his profile in the full-length mirror. He checked his watch and decided to give the girl a few more minutes while he had a glass of wine.

In Friday night traffic, it took Dream Crow twenty minutes to drive five miles. She was hoping she hadn't messed up her opportunity when she pulled up in front of The Bellevue Hotel. She gave her keys to the valet, and got directions to the lobby bathroom from the concierge. Dream Crow stepped into the stall a hooker, and stepped out a star-in-the-making. Her simple black dress clung to her curvaceous body in all the right places, its neckline plunging nearly to her navel. She tossed her silver mini-dress into her tote, dressed her slender neck with a single strand of black onyx, and twisted her long hair into a French roll. She put her demo tape into a simple black clutch and strutted through the lobby to the elevator with a winner's stride.

He gasped when he saw her standing at the door of his hotel suite. His appreciation for her stunning beauty was obvious and honest. "Your brother told me you were talented but he didn't say you were so beautiful," the man said, handing her a glass of wine. "Name's Bandarofski; Jerome Bandarofski."

Dream Crow took the wine and sipped from the glass. "I'm Dream; Dream Crow. Here is my demo."

"Yes, of course," the old man said, smiling. He took the cassette tape from her hand but did not look at it. "We'll get to that. Have a seat. Why don't we start by you telling me what you want?"

"What I want?" Dream Crow was confident and certain when she answered him. "I want *everything*."

"What a coincidence," Jerome said. "So do I."

Between sweat suits, basketball shoes, nail maintenance, dining, hotels, and movies, Keith figured he had spent a few thousand dollars on Korea, but she was rationing her pussy like she only had a limited supply. *I'm going to have to fix this*, he thought to himself, as he dialed her number. She didn't answer. He had tried to take Dream Crow's advice and wait for the girl to call him, but he couldn't.

His golden skin was naturally tanned and glowed, no matter the season. His thick eyebrows arched down to the corners of his almond-shaped green eyes that were clear and sparkling between thick, long lashes that women envied. His jet black hair had been permed and finger-waved into a silky Lord Jesus-style that cascaded down his neck and lay coolly on his back. Bringing his full lips together in the mirror, he checked his mustache.

Something didn't look right. Something was off. He tried smiling again and cocking his head left, then right. His mustache was crooked.

"That hoe cut my shit crooked," he said out loud. He

tried the smile again, this time like Billy Dee; wide and sexy-like.

Yep, his shit was crooked.

"Bitches!"

AFTER GETTING HER TEST RESULTS, KOREA CRIED ALL night. She cried hard and soft. She cried tears of anger and tears of self-pity. She gasped and whimpered, and nearly lost her breath. She cried until her stomach hurt and her body convulsed and shook. She cried until her crying was merely a noise her mouth made and no more tears would come. She cried until she fell asleep.

In the morning light, she was already beginning to heal. She had showered and dressed and was standing in the bathroom mirror when she heard a knock at the door. Korea didn't open it but answered, "Yes?"

"It's Mom, honey," Gladys said through the closed door. "Are you all right?"

"I'm fine."

"Was that you that I heard crying last night?"

"No, Mom. I wasn't crying. That wasn't me. It must've been my television."

"I guess. That must've been *some* program," her mother said suspiciously.

"Yes, it was, Momma. It was something else."

"Well, alright then. I wanted to let you know that I'm here if you need to talk about anything…anything at all.

I work a lot, but I'm still here for you; even if all you want to do is watch TV together."

Korea appreciated the gesture and she didn't mean to lie to her mother; she didn't share trauma or drama with her mother. Gladys was fragile and given to mood swings that could last a few weeks or more.

"Okay, Mom," Korea answered. "Maybe we can go get some ice cream."

"Let's do that, baby. Ice cream always makes me feel better. I'm going to go ahead and get dressed. I'll meet you in the kitchen in ten minutes."

"Okay, Mom."

Korea didn't mean that she wanted to go get ice cream right then. She had a lot on her mind. Walking down East 14th was like taking a cool test. Anything could happen to test your cool. And whenever they went to the ice cream parlor, they walked. The last time Korea and Gladys took the walk, two women had fallen out of a car door, fighting, and had almost knocked Gladys down. Another time, a boy had threatened to sick his dog on them if he couldn't get Korea's phone number. To avoid injury or rabies, she had given him a fake number. Once, there was a bum peeing on people as they walked past him. If her mother hadn't been with her, she would've knocked him in the head with the gallon jug of wine he was pissing out. But Korea wasn't feeling cool and level-headed today. *If anyone does anything to piss me off today,* Korea thought, *Momma might see another side of me.*

Korea stood in the bathroom mirror, trying to see if she looked any different. The doctor said the virus would be manageable; that it may never even return if she kept her stress level down. She had no intention of dealing with Keith ever again. But she wasn't the type of girl who let offenses to any part of her, especially her pussy, go down without retribution.

"Stop it," she warned the young athlete looking back at her. "Stop your fucking whimpering. Shit happens. Deal with it. It could've been worse. He could've been some broke-ass street niggah who gave you his baby, or infected you with that new deadly disease, AIDS. What if I had his baby and it looked just like him, and reminded me of his stupid face every day for the rest of my life? I really need to be grateful," she told herself. "Just be grateful and walk away."

Then she thought, *What if I'm one of those people who break out all the time? What if I get it on my face, or on my mouth? Everyone will know! Hell no!*

Korea almost started to cry again. She could feel her throat knotting up, and her nose beginning to run. She hardened her face in the mirror and blew one final time into a tissue. She tossed it into the toilet and watched as it spun around in the bowl, flushing her tears and anxiety.

By the time the toilet stopped running, a light bulb had turned on in her mind and she felt suddenly better. The epiphany had come to her as quickly as a flash flood; the details of her retribution falling into her mind like raindrops, flooding her consciousness like storm clouds, images of Keith's pain flashing like lightning bolts. He would pay. He would pay with his blood. She could taste it already.

The trip to the ice cream shop was sweet and un-eventful. No dudes stopped in their cars to holler at her and disrespect this rare time Korea had talking and walking with her mother. None of the employees at the ice cream parlor did or said anything to set her off, and all the bums had taken the day off.

Her mother ordered black walnut ice cream and was carrying some home in a container for later. They talked while they walked home and Korea revealed enough of her teenage life and adult plans to make her mother feel hopeful. She painted visions of gated housing and secu-rity that her mother had only dreamed of. There was a garden in the plan, and a minivan and golden years of nothing to do but plan vacations to exotic places.

"See that building over there, baby?" Gladys asked.

"Yes, Momma, I see it, that little broken-down shack next to the liquor store across the street?"

"Liquor store? Now when did that get there?"

"It's been there for a little while, Mom."

"Nothing around here really looks like much now, but that little place used to be a clubhouse…a kind of meet-ing place. That's where I first saw your father."

"My father?" Korea repeated.

Korea was more surprised that her mother had conjured

up her father's memory than at the fact that they met directly across the street from where she and her mother now stood. When she was younger, she used to ask about him, but it always seemed to upset her mother. They hadn't discussed him in years. All that Korea thought she knew about him, she had heard in the streets. And what they said in the streets was that he was a drug dealer that had gotten himself killed. Korea hadn't been interested enough to know much more than that.

Suddenly Gladys stopped walking. She watched the little building as a man wheeled a dolly stacked with boxes of liquor to the door. When the door was open, she could see that the place had become a liquor warehouse. She shook her head and asked her daughter, "When did you say that liquor store got there?"

"Oh, he just opened a few weeks ago. He's pretty cool. His name is Hasaan."

"That's Mr. Hasaan to you."

"Mr. Hasaan," Korea repeated. "Anyway, he and his brother own it. They're Egyptian. I didn't know Egyptians had nappy hair, did you?"

"You've been inside that liquor store, Korea?"

"Yes, Momma; all the kids go there. They sell pickles and candy and chips and stuff," Korea answered defensively.

"Listen, I don't want you inside that store or any other liquor store. Do you hear me?"

"Yes," Korea answered.

"You don't know what that shit can do to you. Those men aren't selling candy and pickles. They're a couple of ghetto farmers, cultivating a crop of future clientele."

Gladys was getting that look in her eyes that always made Korea nervous. She was sensing her mother was getting ready to have one of her anger or sadness episodes. Korea changed the subject.

"Let me guess, Momma. My father had on one of those polyester shirts with a collar out to here?" Korea touched her mother's shoulder, snapping her out of the glazy gaze she had fixated on the building. "Momma, your ice cream is going to melt."

"Huh?" Gladys replied. "Oh yeah, I was just thinking." Gladys took her eyes off the building and put them in front of her and walked with her daughter.

"Oh, oh wait, I know," Korea said. "He had on some platform shoes and bellbottoms!" Korea made her mother laugh. It was nice to see her mother laugh. It didn't happen a lot. "I bet he had a big ol' Afro, too…with a fist in it."

"Well, even though it was 1966, your father never dressed like a clown," Gladys said. "The day I first saw him he was looking real fine, dressed in all black. Everything was black; beret, turtleneck, pants, belt, all the way down to his jump boots."

"What are jump boots?"

"A special kind of military boots. He said they were for jumping out of helicopters or planes."

"Was he in the Army?"

"Only in his mind," Gladys said. Korea laughed at that. "And for your information," her mother continued, "your father had a very small, very neat Afro."

"And?"

"And what?"

"And…What about the fist? You know the Afro pick with the fist on the end."

"Oh, that."

"Yes, that."

Gladys burst into laughter. "Korea, child, I'm telling you…if it wasn't stuck in his head, it was in his back pocket. I was passing by the place, and he was standing outside handing me some papers. He asked me if I was ready for the revolution. Well, I giggled a little, because he was so cute, but I wasn't about to join up with some Black Panthers or any other color panther. I told him that my daddy would kill us both. Then, he would march down there and burn the building down. My father was like a one-man army. He had strong principles that weren't available for compromise. You remind me of him, Korea."

"My father was a Black Panther?"

Gladys didn't answer; she kept talking and walking with that glazed look in her eyes. "I don't guess I cared anything at all about police brutality in Oakland, or the war in Vietnam. Except for the free lunch program, I didn't personally get involved in much of it. I was like a lot of the women. We were there for the men. I got involved because it was so nice to see Black men standing up for themselves. Actually, it was nice to see them standing up for anything. It was attractive. And they were dedicated. I got a few turtlenecks and a really nice black leather jacket. I even rocked an Afro for a couple of years, but I never did really join or anything. I went to enough meetings and read enough literature to understand what it was all about. The deeper I fell in love, the more I defended the organization to my father. I tried a few times to explain to my folks that the work they were doing was important.

"'A lot of them are real smart,' I told my daddy. Some were college students; some already had degrees from schools like UC Berkeley and UCLA. They were organizing the community to unite together to complain about the way the cops were beating on people and things. They were preaching all about a ten-point plan. They even started their own newspaper. But my parents, especially my father, didn't want me to have anything to do with those troublemakers. That's what he called them, *troublemakers*. My father said they were the reason the drugs came in to pacify the Blacks and that they chased all the White folks out of East Oakland. When the White folks packed up, property value went down, so he always blamed the Black Panthers for his house not being worth more. Daddy whipped me when he found out I was going to bed with your father. He put me out the house and cut me off entirely when he found out I was pregnant by him. But I've never regretted a thing. I miss your father. No other man could ever replace him. I'm still married to him."

"So, my father was a Black Panther. I never realized that."

"Oh, I thought you knew."

"How could I, if you never told me?"

"Didn't I?"

"I thought he was a drug dealer," Korea said. "That's what they say."

"I don't talk about him much; it makes me sad, I guess. But, he sure was, for a little while. But, being in that group is the least of what the man was. The fact is that messing with the Panthers is probably what got him killed. I mean, maybe dealing drugs was how he got his start. I really don't know. I never asked, though people do say that he was peddling. But when I met him, when I was married to him, he wasn't doing any such thing."

"Damn," Korea said in awe.

"Hey, young lady?"

"I mean, dang, Momma, dang. I'm sorry. I can't believe it; my father was a Black Panther!"

"Words like that come slipping out of your mouth and I can assume you use them often."

"No, I don't really. But you know how it is out here. You need to know how to cuss or you'll get punked."

"Well, there's no arguing with that. Do you want to

know what your father really was? He was a numbers man; very smart with his money and charming to talk to. He could buy a loaf of bread from a baker, slice it, and sell it back to the same man at a profit. He was a brilliant businessman. There isn't one thing in his pedigree that should shame you. He helped to establish that free breakfast program over at St. Augustine's Church.

"He was smart; too smart sometimes. But he underestimated the corruption in people. Right after you were born, he started working on business arrangements with food suppliers for the lunch program. I think that may be how he got himself killed; trusting the wrong folks."

"Maybe he wasn't so smart after all," Korea said.

"What do you mean?"

"There couldn't have been much room for capitalism in a socialist program."

"Listen to you! Did they teach you about them in school?"

"Only that they were radicals and communists and reformists... the usual brainwashing stuff. I read between the lines, Momma."

"You make sure you're smarter than he was. Use the system instead of working against it. You can't win, working against it."

"So somebody shot my father? Was it somebody from the Black Panthers?"

"No. One day I opened the front door and there he was, dead in the hallway with his throat cut. The police told me a cut throat probably meant he was killed by somebody he knew. But who can really say? I didn't have the time to think about it. I had you to care for by then. And your father was a prideful man so welfare wasn't an option for me. I buried the man with the savings we had and got me a second job. I disappeared from the scene altogether and focused on being a mother to you and keeping a low profile so I wouldn't get noticed by the pimps and players. I've learned that some questions are better left unanswered."

"Momma?"

"Yes, baby?"

"Why didn't you marry another man, instead of working so hard?"

"Baby, men are work. Besides, I never loved another man."

"Oh."

AFTER THEIR TALK, KOREA FELT LIKE A SOLDIER IN A war for human rights. It was her human right and female obligation to bring Keith to justice. When she heard a woman's voice on Keith's phone, she figured that he must be a pimp or something like a player. She wasn't a girl from the projects with nothing to look forward to but babies and government aide and she didn't like fucking enough to be anybody's whore. If that was what he was thinking, he had another thing coming, she thought.

Korea was a businesswoman in the making. She would use the system to attain the tools she needed to make magic happen in the hood. But first she was going to get her revenge on the last hood niggah she'd ever allow to enter her body.

Korea had been waiting all night for her mother to fall asleep. After their walk, Gladys had left the house on three separate occasions, to go to the store, before settling down in her room for the night. Korea could hear the life improvement tape playing through the walls.

"Envision what you want…a new car, a new house, Caribbean vacations. Imagine yourself, living debt-free or simply enjoying a well-deserved vacation on the beach in the Bahamas or on the French Riviera…"

Korea wondered if the woman on the tape had ever lived the life she was describing. If she was recording tapes about it, she was probably an actress who could never afford the things she was describing.

Gladys was finally asleep and probably dreaming of a better life when Korea walked into the kitchen. *Whatever she was getting at the store, it sure wasn't groceries*, Korea thought as she stood in the light of the open, empty refrigerator.

Korea put a small pot on the stove and poured a half-cup of water in it. From the pantry, she pulled a package of instant noodles. She opened the wrapper and pulled out the seasoning packet and ripped it open with her teeth.

"That bastard is mine," she said as she dumped the seasoning and the dry block of noodles into the boiling water. When the noodles were soft, she put them into a bowl and sat in front of the TV, with little but revenge on her mind.

Korea picked up the phone.

"It's about time you came to your senses," Keith said. "Don't you know it's disrespectful not to call a man back?"

"I'm sorry, Keith. I didn't mean to be rude or to disrespect you."

Keith was talking fast. "What's up with you? Do you think I meant for that shit to happen? What, you hate me now?"

"I know you didn't mean to give it to me. I don't hate you. I love you, baby. How could I not? You've been so good to me. You know, Keith, I never got a chance to thank you for the new Air Jordans you got me. Even the players on the boys team are jealous." Korea was as sweet as candy as she spun her sugary web. "You really need to come over to let me thank you."

Keith grinned like a Cheshire cat. He was so happy to hear her voice, begging and pleading for his forgiveness. He never thought to read between the lines.

"Is your mother sleeping?"

"Yeah, she's asleep. You know my back door squeaks. I don't want to wake her up, so come to my window."

"I'm on my way."

"I can't wait to wrap my lips around your big dick,

Daddy," Korea added, licking her lips in the phone, making sure he could hear her naughty slurp.

Daddy! Keith liked the way that sounded coming from Korea. He was sure he had her where he wanted her now. He'd have her packing her bags before the end of the school year.

He took a quick shower and dressed anxiously. He laughed at himself for having been worried that Korea wouldn't call him back.

"Bitches," he said out loud as he jumped into his tricked-out Mustang convertible, and drove across the bridge, headed for her place. He drove down the 580 Freeway at lightning speed and pulled off on Edwards Avenue, and then shot down the hill past the Eastmont Mall. He was making good time until he got to East 14th Street, where police and firemen had roadblocks set up around a three-alarm blaze.

Keith took the back road by the BART Station. From the street, he could see the light in her window; *His* light. Keith had been at that same window three times since they had met at her ball game. She had sized him up during the game. He could see her from the stand, eyeballing him as she ran up and down the court, hitting basket after basket, showing off. But he didn't really think about getting at the teenager until half-time, when she raised her jersey to cool her body. She had deeply defined abs, like those you only find on late-night infomercials. Her oblique muscles were as sculpted as his own, and what she lacked in feminine hips, she made up for with a rounded, muscular ass and long strong thighs. During the second half of the game he was fixated on her, carefully watching her every move— deltoids and biceps effortlessly dropping in shot after shot as sweat pushed through her smooth, chocolate skin. She could've played the game alone.

"Eighteen points in a forty-point game," he said, as she walked out of the locker room. Keith was leaning against the wall, handing her a Gatorade.

"No thanks," Korea said. "I never touch the stuff."

KOREA WAS HESITANT ABOUT TAKING A RIDE FROM HIM, but when she saw his ice blue drop-top Mustang, she had to ride. Keith told her that he was twenty-one and that he worked as a longshoreman. Korea knew better. She figured him for a baller and he had to be at least twenty-five. But she didn't mind at all. She hadn't met a dude in her short life that didn't make his money selling drugs, religion, or pussy.

"Where are you headed?" Keith asked when she was strapped into his passenger seat.

When she directed him to the notorious projects Felix Mitchell had made famous when he was killed, Keith figured he could keep her impressed simply by keeping her fitted.

She's a real dime, he thought as he drove, sneaking

glances at her. He figured she was impressed with him and his car, but she didn't let it show the way the majority of women did. Instead of cooing and giggling, she was asking him what he had under the hood. He had never met a girl who seemed as strong as a man. It turned him on.

He dropped her off and remained a gentleman that afternoon. But it only took a few weeks of conversation and a single date to get into her panties. She told him that she was a virgin, and as tight as her pussy had been, he believed her. But the way she worked her body told him she knew her pussy very well.

Like most of the girls he met in East Oakland where he had picked up young chicks before, Korea had never been to San Francisco. Keith planned a fast and immediate seduction with a topless trip over the Bay Bridge.

"Are we riding with the top down?" Korea asked when he picked her up for their first date.

"It's the only way to fly," Keith said in his most charming voice, as he shut the door behind her.

"Yeah, maybe, but I just did my hair, and I don't want it flying," Korea said.

"I got you; open the glove compartment," Keith said, starting the engine.

Korea opened the glove compartment. Inside she found a comb, a brush, a mirror, Vaseline, and something that looked like a curling iron with no plug. She picked it up.

"Is this a curling iron?" She turned it in her hand, opening and closing the lip. "How does it plug in?"

"It doesn't," he beamed, pulling away from the curb. "It runs on butane."

"Lighter fluid?" Korea asked.

"Yep. Pretty cool, huh?"

"It's really something. In fact, you're really something. You got all the tricks, huh? Pull over for a second."

"You aren't going to jump out of the car, are you?"

"That depends on your answer to my question."

Reluctantly, Keith pulled over and turned the car off. "What's up?"

"What's all this stuff in here for? Are you a pimp or is this car a chick trap?" Korea looked serious, and directly into his eyes, searching for even a hint of a lie.

"No, I told you. I have a good, honest job." Reading the disbelief on her face, Keith reached into his wallet and flipped it open. "Here is my ID, and here is my union card." He handed her the wallet. Korea examined the cards. He flashed a smile that would have made Billy Dee Williams proud and smoothed his neatly groomed mustache. "Open the billfold, and you'll find my pay stub."

Korea closed his wallet and handed it back to him. "Okay. I don't need to be all in your bank account like that. I'm going to let you know right now; I bite."

"Your point is taken, little lady." Keith started the car up and headed toward the 880 Freeway. "It's called a

Clicker," he said, nodding at the creative curler in her hand. "Keep pushing the button until it starts. It'll spark like a lighter."

Korea put the gadget inside the glove compartment and closed it. "I'm cool," she said, pulling a scarf from her coat pocket. "I don't put heat on my hair. I wrap it." With that, she tied the scarf on her head and sat back.

The engine of the Mustang roared across the bridge at eighty miles per hour while Too $hort paced the cross-water escapade with gut-wrenching bass that lay the cadence for his "Freaky Tails." It was the kind of song that you couldn't help but rap along to. Korea let her version of the rhyme spill from her Wet & Wild glossed lips.

"I met this girl, her name Korea. Korea was so vicious, she could eat cha."

Keith laughed as Korea rapped over $hort's voice. Keith nearly butted the car in front of him, trying to watch her sexy lips move. But Korea didn't notice; her eyes were closed, and she was in the trance of the hottest rap bass line to hit the scene since the Sugar Hill Gang put poetry to a commercial beat.

The faster the car moved…the more wind in her face, the better Korea felt. Perhaps it was the clean air and the ride. Or perhaps, she thought, it was just *the knowing;* the kind of knowing one cannot be taught, the thing the old folks called wisdom. In the fifteen minutes it took to cross the bay, the truth became more apparent than ever before. It was more like a revelation teaching her that leaving the squalor of her urban village would release her to an alternative future with endless possibilities. She became certain that evening that she would have money someday.

The song ended. Her eyes were open now, as they crossed over Treasure Island.

"Is this an island?" she asked, looking at him with amazement.

Korea had beautiful cat eyes that burned through Keith. He could feel Korea's spirit rise and blow through him like tiny granules of heat, lost in the wind. He had felt this way many times before, taking young girls who were on the brink of womanhood to the big city, where he used to keep a small stable of those who opted not to go home when the night was through. It used to be easy for him to impress them. He was younger and more energetic and was just as excited as they were about the possibilities of the game. Now he was thirty years old, with only one lady remaining. Korea was the freshness he needed to get his game back on point. But she was sharp. He was going to have to lock her in quick.

"Yes, it's an island. It's called Treasure Island. The bridge runs right through it. San Francisco is on the other side," he told her, smiling at her like Billy Dee Williams smiled at Diana Ross in *Lady Sings the Blues*.

Korea laughed at herself for blushing the way that she

was. She had made it all these years through high school, while her classmates fell off, one after the other, losing their virginity to losers, getting pregnant, and dropping out of school. Besides getting her pussy fingered a few times, she had managed to save herself. Here she was with this dude, she only knew through his own distorted testament to himself over a few weeks of phone calls, wondering if she should fuck him tonight. Something in his smile made her want to. In it was a smooth confidence she had never seen before in any boy her age. She loved his smile. It was radiant. It almost seemed practiced.

Korea let out a sound, something like a moan, as the topless car approached the sparkling skyline of San Francisco, feeling her pussy getting hot and wet.

"Have you been to the city before?" Keith asked.

"Which city?" Korea asked.

"This one," he said, exiting the freeway at Embarcadero. "San Francisco. That's what they call San Francisco; the City."

"Oh, like Oakland's not a city. I see," Korea said sarcastically. Then, looking up at the tallest buildings she had ever seen, she admitted, "Compared to San Francisco, Oakland is just a town. No. I've never been to San Francisco before tonight," she admitted, unembarrassed.

Keith drove through the crowded streets for a few minutes, and then into a parking garage. When the car stopped, Korea let herself out.

"Damn, you can't wait for a brother to open your door?" Keith asked her.

"Why would I do that? I have two hands," she replied. Keith and Korea walked through a courtyard and up to the door of a club. "Keith, I can't get into a nightclub. I don't have ID."

"It's cool. I got this; just chill out," he told her.

"Hey, Mo," Keith said to the host at the door of The Punch Line comedy club.

"Aye, blood, what's up?" a skinny, buck-toothed man asked, while slowly looking Korea up and down. "Hey, Miss Thing," he addressed her. He reached out to shake Keith's hand and let him slide a twenty into his. "Don't sit in the front," Mo advised. "The comedian performing tonight is a crazy bitch that loves to clown. If you sit too close, she'll make your little girlfriend cry."

Korea's different, Keith thought, as he watched her laugh at the most tasteless jokes and eat without self-consciousness. She didn't talk too much, and when she did, it was about something that actually interested him; cars, sports, her love for dogs.

"My mom would never let me get a dog," Korea complained. "She says someone might steal it." She finished her last chicken wing and licked hot wing sauce from her fingertips before picking up her napkin.

"She's probably right. What kind of dog do you want?" Keith asked her.

"A pit bull."

"Damn, girl! Yeah, your mom's right. You wouldn't

be able to hold on to a pit for long. Not in your neighborhood."

"Oh, don't trip," Korea said, with more confidence than defense in her voice. "I won't be in the 69 Village forever. I graduate at seventeen, and then I'm out. You can place a wager on it. Just because I was born in the ghetto doesn't mean the ghetto lives in me."

Keith liked her more and more. "Don't eat too much," he said. "I made dinner reservations."

"Okay," Korea said, turning her attention again to the stage to watch the conclusion of the show.

"The show was funny, don't you think?" Keith asked, helping her with her coat.

"Yeah, it was fly," she said coolly. Keith reached for Korea's hand as they left the comedy club. "Oh, that's real sweet," she said into the night air, not looking at him. "I'm not trying to clown or anything, but I'm not into public displays of affection."

"Oh. No problem," he said, a little embarrassed.

"So, where are we going for dinner?"

"The Equinox."

"Is it like Sizzler? I like Sizzler. My mom took me there last year, after we won the championship game."

Keith chuckled, and relaxed back into his manhood. "No, baby girl, it's nothing like Sizzler. But you're gonna like it."

"Just as long as the food is good; I'm starving."

"You have a healthy appetite."

"I have to. I'm a star athlete," Korea said, doing a little

dance and tossing an imaginary ball into the chilly night.

If dinner went as well as Keith expected, he would be getting a room, so Korea could show him how athletic she really was. So he had made reservations at a rotating restaurant that sat atop a nice hotel.

Keith's chest was puffed out as he walked the young woman into the hotel lobby.

They stepped into a glass elevator and shot at a speed of 500 feet per minute to the top floor, where the Equinox restaurant spun 360 degrees, unveiling one of the finest views of San Francisco and the surrounding Bay Area. It was breathtaking.

Korea devoured a tiny, juicy cut of filet mignon, sautéed vegetables, and a slice of cake, and listened to Keith lay down his pedigree for forty-five minutes. He was talking about how some guy had taken his money to put him on the list to get in the longshoreman union, and disappeared with it. "But I got in anyway. There is nothing tastier than a bite of revenge," he was saying when he realized Korea wasn't listening to him. She was kind of staring at his mouth. "Would you like some wine?"

"I don't need any wine. And you don't need to keep talking and spending all your money. Though, your lips do look good when they move. Tell me what you want, and I'll tell you if you can have it."

"Oh?" Keith stammered, suddenly feeling like he had lost the upper hand again.

"What's wrong?" Korea asked, relishing in his obvious discomfort.

"Nothing, I...."

"Umm-hmm. Pussy got your tongue." Korea lifted her foot under the table and pushed her foot into his crotch. "You didn't pick this fancy spot because it spins. That's a hotel downstairs, right?"

"Right."

"So, did you get us a room?"

Keith waved his hand in the air to call for the check. "Is it cool for you to stay out?"

"Have me back by five in the morning. My mom gets up for work at six."

KEITH WASN'T A SPECTACULAR LOVER, but his dick was small enough and his stroke was gentle enough to make giving up her virginity painless.

He snored softly in the aftermath. She stood in the hotel room window, looking down a million miles, to the San Francisco streets beneath her. Her hand slipped naturally down to her pussy.

"How are you doing?" she asked, tapping lightly around her hole. It stung a little but, to her surprise, there was no blood. "Damn, this dude is hella weak. I didn't even bleed." She looked back at him, and then at the bridge. "But I could get used to this lifestyle."

CHAPTER 5

A BITE OF REVENGE

The memory of Korea riding him had him hard already as he pulled up in front of her place.

Korea pulled her T-shirt over her head and stepped into her boxers. The hallway to the bathroom was flooded with the sound of her mother's snoring. First, she peed and then opened the medicine cabinet and looked for the peroxide. She grabbed it and a towel and went back to her bedroom where Whitney Houston was scream-ing about wanting to dance with somebody on KSOL through a small radio on her nightstand. She turned the volume up when she saw Keith's car pull up. She turned her night light on, tipped the peroxide bottle to her lips, swished, and spit into the towel. She wiped her mouth and prayed he wasn't having an outbreak as she peeked through the curtain and watched Keith get out of the car.

With a cocky swagger, Keith approached the black bars that protected her window and tapped between them on the glass. Korea looked out of the window and saw Keith standing there. She slid the window open, and smiled devilishly. She was naked already, with her T-shirt pooled around her knees as she pressed her naked breasts into the cold metal and wedged her face between two bars. Reaching through the bars with anxious hands, she released his warm dick into the cool night air. A shiver rushed through Keith as she opened her mouth and pulled his body toward it, by the seams of his pants. She took his dick into her left hand, spit into the palm of her right, and rubbed his mushroom head in a gentle circular motion with her palm. She looked up at him as he stood in the night with his hips pressed forward, his cock thrust between the protective bars of her project window.

Keith's desire expanded into arrogant expectation in her hands. She flicked his dick twice with her tongue tip and smiled when it jumped on command. "There is nothing tastier than a bite of revenge," she whispered under her breath.

She had a tight grip on his pants, pulling him toward her mouth. Then, suddenly, she opened her mouth wide, and then guided his dick inside of it. She jabbed it deeply into the back of her throat, as far as she could without gagging. No lips; just throat. No hands; just her hot mouth receiving him. There was no sucking; just deep mouth fucking. So unexpected; so aggressive that it only took a few minutes until he was on the verge of busting.

Korea gripped his dick firmly in her hand and pumped it like a shotgun. Keith's eyes rolled back in his head; his knees began to weaken. He grabbed the bars and held on tight to the metal as he plunged himself deeper and harder inside her anxious mouth. The intensity inside his dick grew stronger as his blood pumped and pulsated through it. As Korea felt the veins inside it pushing against the shaft walls, warning her of an impending explosion, she bit down hard with her teeth, locking her jaws like a pit bull, and she did not let go until she tasted blood.

The pain stilled him. Korea watched him drop like a rag doll to the ground beneath her bedroom window. Both hands on his dick, he curled into a fetal position, writhing in pregnant silence. Korea spit into her towel, rinsed her mouth with peroxide, and wiped the blood and cum away.

"Bitches!" Keith said with shallow breath.

"No, you're looking like the bitch right about now!" Korea said, wiping her mouth again. "Aw, what's wrong? I know you ain't trippin' off a little pain."

"This shit ain't over," he said.

"Oh, it needs to be. As a matter of fact, you need to get your punk ass up off the ground before I call the police and let them know there's a flasher in the neighborhood. I hear the sirens right up the street. I don't think it'll take them long to get here."

"Naw," he muttered, pulling himself up to his feet, looking at the girl he had been macking on for months in disbelief. "This shit ain't over by a long shot."

"Really? Remember, sixteen might get you thirty-two. Wait right there. Let me go get my mother real quick, so she can explain it to you!"

Keith lunged at the window. Korea slammed it shut. Keith looked up at the helicopter circling above his head. It was shining a bright searchlight over the projects.

Korea tapped lightly on the glass, and pointed up. "Here they come, Keith." She cracked her window open as he and his broken dick limped to his car. "Oh, 261.5 is the state penal code for statutory rape!" she called after him. "Look it up, you simple-ass motherfucker!"

She could hear his pretty car screeching down the street. She put her T-shirt back on and sat in the window for a few minutes and listened to the commotion in the night outside.

Gladys was awakened by a recurring flash of light flooding through her windows. She lay in silence for a while, and then she thought she heard voices. She squeezed her eyes and tried to see if they were real voices or not. But they had stopped. Her tape had stopped, too. She flipped it over and pushed play on the tape machine.

"Actions speak louder than words," the voice on the recorder began. "And remember, for every action, there is an equal and opposite reaction…"

Gladys got up and went to the bathroom. Korea heard the toilet flush and her mother walking down the hallway toward her room. Quickly, she turned off the nightlight, slipped under the covers, and closed her eyes. When Gladys turned on the bedroom light, the girl tossed in her bed and screamed out, as if she had been having a nightmare. "That's what you get!"

"Korea? Baby, are you all right?" Her mother looked at the window instinctively, and then walked over to the bed. She turned the radio off and scratched her head. She picked up the peroxide, looked at the bottle, and then at her sleeping daughter.

Her mother rubbed her hand across her daughter's dewy skin, wincing a bit at a scent she could not quite place. It had been years since she'd been with Korea's father, or any man for that matter, but the smell of a man was so distinctive, she could have sworn...

"Naw," she said, "I know better than that." Her little tomboy would never...

At the bedroom door, she looked back at her little prodigy and dismissed the thought. Not far off in the night, Gladys could hear dogs barking and men's voices on walkie-talkies. Were they getting closer?

KEITH DROVE ACROSS THE BRIDGE IN SO MUCH PAIN; he could barely see or think clearly. The flood of non-sensical ideas for retaliation would not stop flowing. He was going to have Dream Crow whip Korea's ass and bring her to him. Then he would drag her into his stable and make her work his track. He would be merciless with her. He would beat her and pull out every pimp trick he had ever read in an Iceberg Slim or Donald Goines book. He would take that bitch down so far, she would be fucking pit bulls for a fix before he even got started on his plan to make her hate herself. She would curse the day she ever spent one dime of his money. He would pull out her teeth one at a time and make her suck his dick for dinner every night.

From the street outside, Keith could see that the condo was dark. Inside the apartment building, he leaned against the door to the condo, knocking with one hand, holding his dick with the other. When Dream Crow did not answer, he fished for his key and let himself in. There was no sign of Dream Crow.

"Bitches!" he cursed out loud.

He walked over to the bar and poured a shot of whiskey into a glass and downed it, and poured another. He stripped off his clothes and walked to the kitchen, wet a dishtowel in the sink, and grabbed an ice tray from the freezer. In his room, he sat back on the bed with his back resting against the headboard. With ice wrapped in a rag cooling his wounded dick, he sipped from his glass and let the whiskey numb his mind. He was getting foggy already when he grabbed the phone off the hook and paged Dream Crow with a 9-1-1. She had not called back before he passed out.

"I HOPE YOU GOT SOME GOOD MAN PUSSY, NIGGAH." Titus was standing over his naked body. "Your bitch done snatched up one of mine's. You gon' take her place."

Keith was reaching for his gun in the nightstand drawer when something hit him in the back of the head.

IT HAD BEEN MONTHS SINCE KEITH HAD SEEN DREAM Crow. He lay in bed next to some hairy trick Titus had steered to his seedy Fillmore hotel room. He thumped the needle and stuck himself in the vein of his left arm, and let the opiate work its magic on him.

"Sweet, sweet, Brown Sugar," he whispered, turning on the television set with the remote control. He flipped through the channels, stopping when he heard Don Cornelius' voice. "That was the beautiful Dream Crow and her sister, Blue, performing their number one hit 'Unpimpable.'"

Keith watched in utter confusion as his bottom bitch cooed with Don Cornelius.

Tears welled in his eyes. He tried to sob quietly so the hairy man would not wake up. "So, are you going to give us another song?" Don Cornelius asked Dream Crow.

"Yes," she said. "This one is dedicated to someone I used to know. It's called 'Head in the Clouds.'"

Keith drew the heroin through a ball of cotton in a small dish beside his bed, and let Dream Crow serenade him with the sweetest lullaby he had ever heard.

"I got my head in the clouds, and I
Don't have a doubt, 'bout my dreams
And though it seems, you can't see

What I see, and who I want to be—
It comes so easily, when you believe…"

The most beautiful lullaby he had ever heard. Keith closed his eyes; his heart rate slowed to a turtle's pace as he listened. His stomach churned; vomit spilled over his shallow breath. Then Keith was gone.

"KOREA, THIS LETTER CAME FOR YOU TODAY," Gladys said.

"A letter came for me? Who is it from?"

"Some name I can't pronounce. Open it; let's see what it is."

Korea took the envelope and was opening it when the police kicked the front door in and took Gladys away for setting the liquor store ablaze.

IT HAD TAKEN DREAM CROW TWO HOURS TO GET A DEAL offer from Jerome, ten days to lock in on a recording contract and a few months to become Mrs. Jerome Bandarofski. She had left her whore clothes and the whore's life in Keith's San Francisco condo the night she had met the wealthy record executive who had made her dreams come true.

In his care, Dream Crow had learned to love and trust something healthy, for the very first time in her life. She loved the old man with a passion she had never felt for anyone, or anything. He had turned her into a complete human being who was capable of feeling. He was gentle, supportive, and dedicated to their marriage and to her career.

Dream Crow and Blue released three award-winning albums and a movie soundtrack under the production of their younger brother, Hartford, over the next few years, until Dream Crow retired from music when her husband, Jerome, was diagnosed with cancer. She spent the rest of his life taking care of him. She supported and loved and cared for him until he died and when she buried him, he was a very happy, very old man. He never had children. He left his entire estate to Dream Crow, including his non-profit foundation, a seat on the board of directors of Bandarofski Music Publishing, his music empire, a seven-bedroom home, three acres of land, and a few farm animals. Dream Crow and Blue retired on that beautiful unincorporated land in Blackhawk, California; a million miles away from the Tenderloin.

Dream Crow reached back into her old neighborhood only once a year, to give a scholarship to a talented, at-risk girl. The first scholarship from the Bandarofski Foundation was awarded to a promising young athlete who had a dream to go to business school.

Korea Smith had never even applied for the award, but the offer could not have come any sooner, or have been more appreciated when it did. She walked the stage on the day her mother was arraigned. Korea enjoyed a free ride at UC Berkeley, earning a degree in business management in only three years. She embarked on her career as a businesswoman and philanthropist at the tender age of twenty-one. She visited her mother regularly in a hospital for the criminally insane until a nurse called her one day to claim her body. Gladys had died suddenly, and unexpectedly, from the brain lesion that had been slowly eating away at her mind for years.

Korea never got a chance to put her mother in a fancy house in a gated community. But she developed a program that would ensure that women with no history of crime would be tested and treated for mental disorders before they were put on trial in a criminal court.

The program laid the foundation for business and philanthropic endeavors that would make Korea a respected and prosperous businesswoman.

tormy was getting sick and tired of waiting for Tom to ask her to marry him. Her engagement ring had been on her finger since she was practically a kid. She had already had it resized once and it was getting tight again, since all she seemed to do since she left her job at the restaurant was cook and fuck. She had laid out a black formal dress with a high neckline and some simple black leather Kenneth Cole shoes, but decided on a cobalt blue silk Bebe dress with a plunging neckline that draped casually over her braless breasts.

Tom wouldn't like the ensemble because it always made heads turn, but she figured that he needed to be reminded of how desirable she was. She dressed it up with the diamond necklace, earrings, and a matching tennis bracelet he had brought back from a weekend "business trip" to Brazil that lasted two weeks. She had been dressing for over an hour when he knocked on her bedroom door. She had not even started to work on her hair, which was not responding to Sebastian's curly hair solution the way that it had a week earlier.

Unless she was going to undress and get back in the shower to start her hair all over again, it was going to be downright unruly in the unexpected humidity of the Bay Area's unpredictable spring weather. It had been a rainy April, sure to bring May flowers, but to Stormy's mixed crop of Irish and West Indian hair, it brought a frizzy mane of uncertainty. Each hair seemed to stand alone in defiance as she attempted to gel, mousse, and cream it into obedience. As the minutes wore on, her hair grew bigger, seeming to define her mood for the evening.

"If I'm going to look wild, I should be wild tonight," she decided, finally letting her hair have its way in the twelve inches of space about her head.

The lipstick tube said "crimson," but looked more like Halloween orange against her golden skin, so she topped it with a true red gloss that she intended to pack in her purse for periodic touch-ups. Before she could apply it well, Tom was at her bedroom door, huffing and puffing about making him late for what could be the defining moment of his company's future. He was twenty years older than Stormy. He was a haughty passe de blanc who would be better off switching sides altogether. His perspective on the new generation of young black entrepreneurship was dated, and insulting, at a time when young boys made more in a month than some of their parents earned in a year. But she couldn't tell him that without hurting his feelings and feeling his wrath. So she let him go on for the last few months, confused as to why he was losing his accounts.

Stormy had no money and no immediate plans to leave Tom, but her time would be short if she didn't do something quickly. She was certain he had been fucking his twenty-year-old secretary, and Stormy wasn't aging backward. He was definitely the kind of man who needed to have a child to look up to him, and to boss around. And while Stormy was still very beautiful, time had found her becoming increasingly more opinionated. If it were not for the fact that she kept it hot and interesting in the bedroom at all times, she was positive it would have been over. He was, after all, always telling her that if she weren't such a good fuck, he would've gotten rid of her a long time ago. So, though her hair was a mess, as she looked in the bathroom mirror, she realized that she was definitely, undeniably fuckable tonight.

Tom pushed the door to her bedroom open so hard; it hit the rubber stopper and bounced back at him. "Stormy," he said with a false calm in his voice, "you need to come on."

"Okay, I need to do one more thing," Stormy called from the bathroom.

"I told you, this woman is a bitch. If I'm a minute late, she's going to notice, and I can kiss this contract good-bye. She'd probably much rather give it to one of her little dyke buddies anyway. Get your ass in gear, Stormy. Let's go."

"I'm coming, Tom. But don't say anything about my hair." Stormy stepped out of the bathroom and stood there for a moment while Tom examined her from her feet, up her legs, around her ample hips, arching his eyebrows at her hard nipples...

"God damn it, Stormy, what is that mess on your head? If your hair gets any bigger, you won't be able to fit your head in the fucking Porsche." He checked the time on his Rolex. "Fuck it. Let's go."

Except for some frustrated exhaling, Tom was completely silent as he drove down the hill from his Upper Rockridge mini-mansion to Broadway Terrace, and wheeled onto the freeway.

"I have a new CD. It's so, so smooth. Can I play it?" Stormy asked.

"It's not more of that rap stuff you like, is it?"

Stormy would love this man so much more if he was cool, but he wasn't. "No, baby, it's R&B. Actually, it's kind of an R&B/jazz fusion," she said, popping it into the CD player. "I think you'll like it."

"Fusion? Yeah, okay. Whatever."

Stormy sat in the passenger's seat for the next nine minutes, watching the clock and hoping the music would relax Tom as he sped down Highway 13. He'd nearly jackknifed getting onto the 580 Freeway. Relief filled her as he finally drove off the freeway and rounded the lake until he came to the Lake Merritt Hotel.

Tom's was the only car waiting for the valet guy in

front of the hotel. "Fuck!" he said impatiently. "It's ten 'til eight. Everyone else is probably here. Hey…Buddy," he said to the valet sitting on a stool, talking on his cell phone. When the young man looked up, Tom dangled his keys out of the window.

"I'm sorry, sir," the valet said, taking the keys.

"That figures," Tom muttered, stepping out of the car. "I suppose you're capable of coming to the conclusion that I don't tip incompetence."

"Of course, sir," the valet answered.

"See, baby?" Stormy said. "That's probably why your Porsche has been keyed three times this year."

"Perhaps, but that's what insurance is for," Tom replied.

He was getting so combative lately. His fiftieth birthday was approaching and she figured that was what was bugging him, but she could not be sure about anything concerning Tom these days. Stormy decided that Tom was on his period. She had read online that men have periods, too. She decided she would allow him to brew over her tardiness, until she stepped into the hotel lobby and saw all the movers and shakers who had beaten them there. The smell of money and power in the air made her want to apologize to him. The lobby was swarming with call girls and businessmen on vacation from their families, and business people who looked like they could eat his sensitive ass alive.

The clerk with long curly nails and a nametag that read: "My name is Quanisha," said, "How can I help you?"

She then directed them to the ballroom where the socializing, networking, and bidding were scheduled to begin in less than two minutes.

While it was true that she wasn't the most fashion-conscious woman in the world, or even in the room, since Tom kept her on a strict budget, Stormy possessed a beauty that was uniquely hers. Her beauty was obvious and obsession-stirring, but her confidence had been victimized by his obsessive verbal abuse, which was only aimed at keeping her humble and youthful. Stormy's wild, curly mane of red hair was her crowning glory. Her breasts were plump with promise and her hips were a pledge of allegiance to generations of strong babies and to good times that would come to any man daring to create them with her. Every one of the men in that room could feel her heat. Any one of them would have left his most loyal woman to take a ride around Stormy's voluptuous thighs. Tom knew this.

The problem was that, as weak as he was, Tom had woven a web of self-doubt so tight around Stormy's mind that she could not possibly recognize her own power over anyone. So she remained devout, true, and pure to the man she assumed would eventually be her husband; as long as she kept him satisfied in bed.

There were handsome businessmen in formal black suits and tuxedos, huddled together, talking amongst each other and clusters of classy ladies in black evening gowns with their hair brushed neatly in buns and French rolls. She paused at the door, thinking she would stand out like a sore thumb, with her frizzy hair growing by the millisecond, as Tom had predicted.

Tom surveyed the room, too. He spoke in a low angry voice. "I told you not to embarrass me. Eight o'clock means seven-thirty to people with jobs…something you would obviously not know anything about. Now, not only are you making me late, but, you look a hot mess." He grabbed Stormy's hand and squeezed it roughly, but as discreetly as he could. "Please do us both a favor and find the bathroom so you can go do something with your fucking hair, or I swear you'll feel my angst in every muscle tonight. Fuck me, for letting you walk out of the house with a blue dress on."

Stormy thought of how Tom would retaliate on her later that night. And for a moment, she thought, *that might not be too bad*. He had never hit her. Whenever she had pissed him off before, he would punish her by becoming an animal in the bedroom, remaining missionary, but thrusting deeply and talking the kind of shit men talked in movies about bad boys. It really got her excited to see him that way, but it was always short-lived.

By morning, he was always the same anal-retentive jerk he had been the day before, barking orders and passing out judgments like she was a house slave and he was her master. Stormy supposed Tom thought he had been hurting her with his penis, but the nights he was his maddest, she had come her closest to having her first orgasm. She could feel it coming…kind of hovering on the brink of something amazing…something that she could not quite describe, but it never happened. In a way, she did not want it to come. If she allowed him to take her body anywhere near the sensation that people had described to her about orgasms, she might be his sex slave for real. Tom was definitely not cool enough to deserve that kind of obedience.

"Fuck!" Tom said, snapping her out of her fantasy flash.

She assumed the position of a mistress being reprimanded and dropped her head. She froze herself into an abused woman's coma and did not move until he made her move. She wanted him to feel his strength restoring itself. She would humble herself to let him do this until the money was right enough for him to maintain a wife and a mistress, if that is what he needed. He had already lost three city contracts. If he lost another, she might become an expense that he couldn't afford.

Tom recomposed himself and nodded at a woman with a short haircut in a black suit and a purple shirt, looking curiously at him from across the room. "Go now, before I have to explain you."

Stormy walked away from him without saying a word.

"So you really gave the cigarettes up," Korea was saying in conclusion to the conversation already in progress. "Good for you."

"I get stressed. I think about smoking, but I press on," Grace Riley said.

Tom painted a smile on his face and walked toward the councilwoman, who was chatting with Korea Smith. They both watched him as he approached.

"Hello, Councilwoman Riley," he said, "this sure is a fine affair."

"It is, isn't it?" she asked rhetorically, looking over his shoulder at the woman he had left behind. Stormy was asking the woman at the coat check for directions to the bathroom.

"It's sure to get more interesting as the night progresses," Korea chimed in. Korea's eyes were following a teary-eyed Stormy as she rushed to the bathroom.

"Tom Brown, right?" the politician said, extending her hand to shake his.

"Yes," he said. "Brown Youth Services. And you are?" he asked, turning his attention to Korea, extending his hand to hers.

"Korea Smith; Project W.H.Y."

"I'm sorry; I'm not familiar."

"Oh? Don't you have a television?" she quipped at him. "I'm sorry, Grace. I see someone that I have to talk to. Will you please excuse me?"

"Definitely," Grace Riley said with a knowing look on her face. "So, we are clear on the terms and conditions of the program, yes?"

"As clear as crystal," Korea answered. "I may have to leave quickly, so I will say goodbye now. It has been a pleasure, as always. I'll have my secretary call yours, first thing Monday morning."

"Good night then," the councilwoman said, nodding her head.

"Tom." Korea nodded at him, excusing herself.

"Councilwoman Riley, if you would allow me a few moments of your time to tell you about BYS. I think our youth should be gainfully employed, staying out of trouble and learning to run a small business. So far I have plans for a coffee stand at the courthouse and a flower shop right on Grand Avenue."

BS is more like it, Korea thought. She could hear that asshole brown-nosing all the way from the bathroom door, where she was going to find his beautiful wife. "Lots of luck, motherfucker; that deal is already sealed," she said under her breath as she pulled the bathroom door open.

Stormy stood in the mirror, crying and cupping her hand under the running sink water, lifting the ounces she had collected in her palm to her hair. She seemed to be trying to twist her hair into a bun and hold it in place with a hair bow that was far too small to get the job done.

"What are you doing?" Korea said behind her.

Stormy turned around, startled. Her skin was dewy from the struggle with her hair; water streamed down her neck. Her nipples were hard and poking boldly through the blue silk.

"My guess is that you don't know what water does to silk."

Stormy looked down at her dress and saw hundreds of water spots staining her dress.

"Oh shoot!" Stormy said, "I give up."

"You won't get very far, giving up so quickly."

"So I've heard," Stormy said. "But some things aren't worth fighting over."

"I see. Do you want me to help you to do what seems impossible to you right now? Or do you want me to tell you the truth and save you the headache? 'Cause, lady, getting all that hair into that little rubber band is definitely going to give you a headache."

Korea was the most perfect thing Stormy had ever seen. She was as confident as any man, yet beautiful enough to be on the cover of a fashion magazine. Even through her handsome black suit, Stormy could see she had amazing curves. She was cool and she was fly. She had stolen Stormy's voice with a style and swagger that made Tom look like the Uncle Tom she had discovered he was.

"I…"

Korea knew the woman was not able to express what she was feeling in that moment. Korea had put that doe-eyed look on more women than she cared to count.

"Here," Korea said, "let me help you. You seem like you need the truth more than you need that hair bow."

Korea stepped quickly to her. She took the fabric-covered band from her hand, letting her finger linger in her palm for a moment. She realized that she probably didn't have a whole lot of time, but if she played her hand right, she wouldn't need very much. Korea tossed the band across the room, and then rubbed and fluffed Stormy's hair until it was something like a curly lion's mane.

Her tiny glossed lips were only inches from Stormy's as she spoke. "The truth is…you are the most beautiful woman in this building. You are perfect just like you are. You don't have to change for them. They need to change for you."

Stormy inhaled the intoxicating pheromones on Korea's breath and left her mouth open for her tongue to come inside. Korea pulled her head back by her hair and kissed her deeply, sweeping her tongue over and under Stormy's, reaching it as far down in her throat as she could.

"Umm, you ever kiss a woman before?"

"I have now," Stormy said breathlessly. "Wow, you move fast."

"I could say the same about you, couldn't I? Is that guy your husband? *Tom Brown*…" Korea mimicked the pompous way he had said his own name.

"Yes, I mean, no. We're not married but we've been together for ten years. It's just like we're married."

"Ten years?"

"Yes, since my senior year of high school."

"No. Actually, it's not like you're married. This is California, not Texas. There's no common law security for women who live with men they aren't married to in the Golden State. If your name isn't on the deed to his house or his cars, everything you own is standing right here in front of me."

"Are you serious?"

"Oh yes, it's true. You need to talk to a lawyer."

"No, I don't. I couldn't care less about that. I was asking if you are serious about this."

Stormy wrapped her hands around Korea's neck and kissed her mouth again. They kissed deeply. This time, it was Stormy's tongue that searched and explored Korea's mouth. Her lips were twice as big and covered Korea's mouth completely. Stormy was breathing heavy and getting hot all over her body. Her hips began to roll and pump against Korea's thigh. Korea could smell her pussy, a sweet and subtle fragrance of dew and raw honey that had snaked its way up Stormy's dress and spilled from her chest, flooding the steamy air between them.

"Damn, you don't smell like a straight girl."

"What?" Stormy giggled, looking away shyly. Then realizing her body was getting carried away, she backed her pelvis away from Korea's leg. "What does a straight girl smell like?"

"Dick, of course," Korea answered.

"Oh, no, I don't do that. I never have."

"You don't fuck your man? No wonder he's snatching you up."

"You saw that?"

"Huh, yeah. I think everybody did. You walked in, looking so fine in this bright blue dress, while everybody else in here looks like they're at a wake, with your hair screaming, 'Look at me!' You had every head turning; the men and their horny little wives were checking you out."

Stormy blushed. "Really?"

"Really, lady. I think everyone saw." Korea twirled a piece of Stormy's hair in her finger. "Everyone was looking at you, just like I was."

"Of course, he makes love to me," Stormy said. "I mean, he fucks me. But I have never had sex without a rubber. Not with him, or anyone else; not since my first time."

"Damn," Korea said, surprised and impressed, "so much for you being passive."

"Passive? Me? No, I'm not passive. I simply don't like confrontation." With that thought, Stormy sighed and relaxed a bit. She turned around to face the mirror again. "So, you're telling me that if I leave him, I leave with nothing after all this time?"

"Pretty much, unless he's a nice guy."

"What are you? Lawyer or something?"

"No, I'm a businesswoman."

"Oh. That could mean a lot of things."

"Don't get me wrong. Money makes my pussy wet. I love it and it loves me. I make a lot of it and I love to spend it on pretty things. But I'm a do-gooder. Part of my business is to teach youth how to become business people. I've pulled a lot of drug dealers out of the game."

"Wow, that's very cool," Stormy said, as she turned to look in the mirror to check on the mess she had made of herself. She winced at the sight of the water stains on the dress, but Korea had given her hair a confident flair. With her eyeliner smudged and nothing but orange residue left on her lips, she had a sexy coke whore look going on. "Hey, is that your commercial on TV...the one where the boy is on the corner selling crack and the woman drives up and snatches him into a van, just before the cops roll up?"

"Yes, that's it. That's my non-profit organization. We work with all kinds of children who are dealing with all kinds of shit: drugs; homelessness; poverty; sexual abuse. We even have a program to get teenage prostitutes out of the life. It's called Project W.H.Y."

"Oh, yes, that is you! I really feel your program. Oh my God, you have to talk to Tom." Stormy knew Tom hated the controversial ad campaign, but this woman was just the person to teach him what Stormy had not been able to talk to him about. This woman was sexy and smart. Surely she could get, and keep, his attention. "He could learn a lot from you."

"That may be but I don't mentor adults. Besides, we've met," Korea said, using a voice that signified she was unimpressed.

"Oh boy, judging by your tone, it sounds like you *have* already talked to him. Every time your commercial comes on, he complains. He absolutely hates them. He says they show disrespect for the law. But I think they're great. I love the W.H.Y. acronym, and the way the guy comes on at the end of the commercial and says: 'Get off the street. Get in your life. Get the Will to Help Yourself. Project W.H.Y.'"

"I hate to break it to you. Tom's a dick. And his Brown Youth Services program is some bullshit. What the fuck is up with teaching black kids how to be maids and janitors. He's probably getting funding from the KKK." Korea felt herself get completely turned on by the bright eyes and youthful enthusiasm of this woman. "I hope you're as fantastic as you seem."

"Why do you say that?" Stormy asked.

"Because, I want to take you home with me."

"Whoa...I..."

"Don't talk. Just listen. If you don't like what I have to say, don't say anything; simply walk away. I wouldn't be able to stand the rejection. Okay?"

"Okay."

"Alright, here it is. I don't waste time," Korea said, holding on to the woman who was melting like butter in her hands. "Whatever is in your closet at his house, I can replace. Whatever he's got you driving, I will upgrade. You can have your own room, and a beautiful pent-house home to run as you see fit. All I would ever ask you for is that you keep that bright smile and sunny disposition. All I would ask you for is to stay available to me. You're like a bright light. I saw you shining from across the room. I came in this bathroom to take you home."

"Wow. What's your name?"

"Korea Smith."

"Well, Korea, if you fuck anything like you kiss, we may have a future together."

"Do you cook?"

"I'm a chef."

"Are you kidding me? That Tom is one dumb mother-fucker."

"I mean, I was. I have a culinary arts degree. But Tom wanted me to quit my job so I could be home when he gets home from work. Restaurant hours can be very long. So I only cook at home. It's kind of a hobby now."

"If you haven't barebacked since your first time, is it safe to conclude you don't have any children?"

"It's safe."

Yes, Korea thought to herself. Korea had a thing for straight women. But they usually came with emotional baggage, physical luggage, or both. This chick was practically a virgin. "One more thing…"

"My name is Stormy," she answered, anticipating the question.

"Perfect," Korea said, grabbing Stormy by the hand. "Come on; let's go."

"We can't walk through the party and leave together like that."

"Oh yes, we can," Korea said.

Korea held the bathroom door open. She could smell Stormy's fear. Korea guided her out of the restroom, with a single hand placed on the small of her back. Then she grabbed her by the hand, and guided her through the party, past the coat check to the door. At the door, Korea turned to look behind her at Council-woman Riley, who was still being held prisoner by Tom

Brown. Grace Riley shook her head, and laughed when she saw that Korea had retrieved this man's woman from the bathroom and was leaving with her.

That's my girl, Riley thought.

"You know, I'm going to have to help you work on that defeatist attitude of yours, Stormy," Korea said as she held the car door open for her to get into the passenger's seat.

"Really? I thought you didn't mentor adults?"

"For you, I'll make an exception." Korea pulled away from the curb and turned onto Lakeside Drive and stopped at a red light at Franklin. She turned up the volume of the CD already in the player, Nas' *Illmatic* "Life's a Bitch."

"You like rap. Cool, very cool."

"Some. I like this. It's familiar."

"It just came out. How is it familiar?"

"Can't you hear The Gap Band under there?"

Stormy listened carefully.

"*Myyyy heart is yearning fo'or your love*," Korea sang over the sampled track. *She can't sing*, Stormy thought, *but she sure looks good trying*.

At the next light, a car pulled up next to them, thumping Tupac Shakur's "I Get Around" so loud the windows shook. Stormy looked out of her window to see the valet from the hotel smoking a fat joint, cruising the lake in Tom's Porsche.

KOREA TOOK STORMY HOME THAT NIGHT. For Stormy, it was the most fulfilling sexual experience of her life. When Korea touched her body, tiny orgasms exploded all over her skin. She sucked her breasts and her clit stood at attention. When Korea licked her pussy, she might as well have been licking her soul. Somewhere from deep inside of her, there came a rushing flood that poured like hot nectar, intoxicating them both as they shared the essence of Stormy in a kiss that seemed to last forever. It was a gentle, slow-rising high that lifted to more than six hundred crescendos of blissful orgasm for both women over the next two years.

STORMY HAD SERVED A MEAL FIT FOR A QUEEN; Linguini with lemon basil, plucked fresh from her rooftop garden, roasted garlic and rosemary, sautéed prawns with wild mushrooms, sweet yellow and red peppers, diced and marinated in oregano-flavored olive oil. There were steamed asparagus spears drizzled in a light butter sauce, waiting to meet Korea when she got home. These parts of the meal were merely side dishes to a fresh salad, made from the rooftop garden Stormy personally tended. It was an assortment of homegrown Romaine and red leaf lettuce, baby spinach, sweet plum tomatoes, cucumbers, smoked chicken, carrots, celery, and artichoke hearts, topped with pine nuts and freshly grated Parmesan cheese. The sweet French bread was served hot, and drizzled with warm olive oil, rosemary, and fresh roasted garlic, and Korea's beer of choice, MGD, was served ice cold and in the bottle, just like she liked it.

"Baby, that was great," Korea said. Kissing Stormy on her soft pink plump lips, gently but urgently then rising to remove the plates from the table. She rinsed the dishes off in the sink and stacked them neatly in the dishwasher. She could feel Stormy's arms around her waist as she stood behind her, her cheek pressed lovingly against her back. "You're too good to me," Korea said.

"I know," Stormy answered. "I figure if I give you what you need, you'll give me what I want."

"Yes, baby, just let me get cleaned up." Korea loved the way Stormy cooked but despised the mess she left behind.

"Really?" Stormy beamed. "You're going to fuck me tonight?"

"Yes, my little flower bunny, Daddy's going to fuck you tonight," Korea said, slapping Stormy on her ass. When Korea talked liked that, like she was "Daddy," it made Stormy's pussy wet, instantaneously. "Now go take a shower; you've been crawling around in the garden."

"Garden? How do you know it wasn't take-out?"

"Please. No one cooks like you. I know your cooking like I know the taste of your pussy. I could be blindfolded and pick either one of them out. Besides, your hands smell of garlic," Korea said, lifting hers from the sink to hold Stormy's to her nose. She sniffed her fingertips and curled her faced into a snarl, making a throaty sound of disapproval.

Stormy blushed. There was no greater high for her than serving a satisfying meal prepared by her own hands. She had been a food critic for an online publication for a few months and had yet to find a local restaurant that served cuisine that could even come close to her own. Her cooking was fresh, daring, and innovative, and she never sacrificed flavor for nutrition. She always replaced pork with smoked turkey, or freshly brewed chicken broth, and made sure there was roughage to complement every meal. Garlic was her special ingredient, so she often smelled of it. She imagined, it must have been hard to enjoy a pussy scented with it, but she couldn't help touching herself when Korea went down on her, as she often did after a home-cooked meal.

Stormy reached into the kitchen cabinet and pulled out the vinegar.

"You're not going to douche with that, are you?"

"Of course not, baby. You know I haven't needed to douche since…" Her voice trailed off. Korea watched as Stormy screwed off the top and poured a small amount of vinegar over her fingertips and rinsed them under the running water.

Korea knew that Stormy was going to say that she had not douched since she had made her, after what had happened at Club X. Korea wanted to bring it up, so they could start to work through it, but every time she thought about it, every time she thought about the entire night, actually, an overwhelming urge to whip Stormy's ass overwhelmed her.

So instead, she said, "That cucumber-scented glycerin soap is wonderful, but it doesn't stand a chance against the intensity of garlic. I don't know why you mess with those hippy products. I keep telling you, you should use vaginal wash."

"I can't. I tried it; it burns. I don't know how you can take it." Stormy rinsed the top and screwed it back on the vinegar bottle, and then placed it back in the cabinet. "Do you want to take a shower together in the workout room?"

"No, you know I like my privacy. Besides, you don't run your water hot enough for me. I'll be in my private bath tonight."

"Okie-dokie, but you don't know what you're missing. I had that new full body shower system installed. There are showerheads in the walls."

"Well, don't have too much fun in there. I want you to have some juice left for me."

"Alright, Daddy; last one out of the shower is a rotten egg."

"Where are we fucking tonight?"

"In the den."

"Okay, I'll meet you in forty-five minutes," Korea said. "Now go."

"I'm gone," Stormy answered, running through the house like a giddy kid on allowance day.

As she stepped into the shower, Stormy cursed herself for making Korea think about Club X. She had hoped they could do some normal pussy rubbing tonight, but realized she had better be prepared for more of the same masochistic shit, now that she had opened her big mouth. The water felt so good, she didn't want to get out of the shower. Seven heads were hitting her body from every direction. If she had thought about it, she would have had one installed in the floor.

Korea turned on the dishwasher, wiped the counter and the stove, downed the rest of her beer, and grabbed another cold one. In her bedroom, she removed her suit pants, tie and shirt, and entered the sanctuary of her bathroom. Removing her panties, she sat at her dressing table and opened her legs to examine herself with a tiny handheld mirror and smiled at her pretty, cherry red pussy, and then stepped into the shower.

She washed the world off of her body, and let her stress evaporate in the steamy mist. She lathered her pussy with feminine wash and worked her over-sized clit between her fingers for a few minutes, letting it get hard and ready for Stormy. She wondered what Stormy would do if she let her suck on her clit for once. She closed her eyes to imagine it, rubbing her clit between her thumb and index finger. She was growing larger. She pictured Stormy's full pink lips sucking on her dick, her hand gripping her big mane of hair, forcing her to suck harder. Before she realized it, her knees were buckling and she had almost cum. Her clit was very big and even harder now and she could feel it throbbing with desire. It was time. She rinsed her body, and then stepped out of the shower.

Korea looked at herself in the mirror and combed her short hair back with a fine-toothed comb. She slipped into some boxer shorts but let her perfect 34Ds hang free. She walked down the long hallway and down the stairs into the den to find Stormy waiting on the floor, naked. She lay on a black velvet blanket, massage oil, KY Jelly, two condoms, a nine-inch black dildo, a black leather harness, a blindfold, a cat of nine tails, and a pair of plastic gloves, a glass of wine and a cold beer in a bucket of ice on a large serving tray beside her.

"I know you enjoyed dinner. I hope you're hungry for dessert," Stormy said. "Pussy is served."

Without a single word, Korea was upon her, kissing her mouth deeply, her tongue sweeping over Stormy's teeth and gums, and reaching down her throat. Korea grabbed a hand full of Stormy's hair, snatched her head back, and looked deeply into her eyes.

"Who are you tonight?" she asked.

"I'm your bitch tonight."

Korea tugged a little harder on Stormy's hair. "That's not good enough. I thought you said you wanted to get fucked."

"I'm your dirty little mistress tonight."

"Have you been a bad little mistress?"

"Oh, I've been bad. I've been very bad."

"What have you been doing?"

"A little sucking, a little fucking."

"You what?" For a moment, Korea forgot she was inside a role play and was angry for real, thinking of Stormy strapped to the table at Club X, with strangers touching her…

"I've been disrespectful," Stormy said. "I've disgraced you. I gave my pussy to a man."

Korea slapped Stormy's face so hard; it shocked her, and sent a sharp pain through her temple. A single tear launched in the corner of Stormy's left eye and froze there.

"Go ahead and cry, you little slut. It makes my dick hard when you cry."

That really hurt, Stormy thought to herself. *This shit is getting out of hand.* She was thinking of a way to hurt Korea back, but she wasn't allowed to hit her. So she let out an unpredictable giggle, turning her face away, purposely fixing it with false guilt.

"What?" Korea asked her.

"I'm sorry, Daddy. That's all."

"What? What are you sorry for? Fucking some man?"

"No, I'm sorry that I liked sucking his dick so much. I liked it so much, I came before he even put his big cock between my fat pussy lips."

Stormy was so convincing, Korea wondered if she was telling the truth, or maybe expressing some deep desire.

Whispering, Korea said, "Baby, maybe we shouldn't

play this game tonight. Why don't you be the waitress or something?"

But Stormy ignored her lover. She was on a roll. She realized she never got a chance to do or say anything rebellious. Maybe there was something to this role-playing stuff. "His dick was so big that it split the corners of my mouth. I sucked it good and I liked it."

Stormy was braced for the slap this time and when it came crashing across her cheek, she did not wince and submit. Instead, she laughed out loud, releasing a cackling, nerve-wracking *Who's Afraid of Virginia Woolf* kind of laugh that enraged Korea. Stormy did not expect Korea to spit in her face. The feel of the slimy glob on her cheek and in her eyelashes silenced her laughter. She tried to roll over, sit up, and brace herself for escape, but suddenly, Korea pushed her down and stood up over her, one foot by her left ear, the other pressing her face into the floor.

"So, bitches want to suck on something," Korea said, rubbing her toes through the slime on her lover's face and forcing her big toe into her mouth. "Are you laughing at me, you simple bitch? You like sucking on things? Suck my fucking toe."

Conceding to remain *the mistress* for a game that had gone too far to turn away from, Stormy did as she was told.

"Oooh, you are a dirty fucking whore. You like that, don't you?"

"I love it."

"Stop." Korea stepped back a little and wiggled her boxers from her hips. "Take them off me," she commanded. Stormy reached up and pulled the shorts down to Korea's ankles. Korea shook them loose into Stormy's face. "Wipe your face off with my drawers, bitch."

Stormy took the underwear and began to wipe the slimy spit away. The smell of the beer and spit made her nauseous.

"Now, wipe your nasty dick breath off my foot." Stormy was getting ready to wipe Korea's foot with the boxers, when Korea screamed at her to stop, pouring beer on Stormy's breasts. "Don't you dare use those nasty things on my pretty foot."

Korea reached for the serving tray and tossed a few baby wipes down from where she stood exalted over her whore on the floor.

Korea took a swig of her beer, and opened her legs to reveal her pussy. Stormy was instantly excited at the sight of her perfect pussy with the tight dark lips, that was rarely hers to see, and never hers to savor.

"Why are you eyeballing me?"

Stormy didn't say anything.

"You want to see my dick, don't you? You want to suck it, don't you?"

Korea set her beer down and planted her feet on either side of Stormy's face. Stormy could feel her temperature rising. Beads of sweat formed on her lower back and between her thighs, as she glanced up into a pussy heaven. Stormy had never eaten pussy before, and wasn't sure she even knew how. But she knew how having your clit sucked passionately felt. She wished to herself that this would be the night Korea would completely let go. She wished she could will Korea's knees to fold so that her pussy would fall graciously onto her face and that her own natural passion and experience as a bottom would teach her what to do.

Though she knew it would never happen, she could only imagine, as she watched from below, the woman opening her tiny dark folds to reveal a very large, dark pink clit.

"Oh how you want to suck it," Korea taunted.

She lubricated it with KY Jelly and began to stroke it. Her knees folded and, for a moment, Stormy thought her fantasy would finally be fulfilled. Korea lowered her hips slowly, so Stormy could get a good look at the thing she could not have and wanted most.

When Korea was finally on her knees, her hot, wet pussy literally dripping slowly on Stormy's face, she went in for the kill. Making sure to pin Stormy's long hair to the floor so that she could not reach up and touch her pussy with her tongue, she said, "I'd let you suck me but you wouldn't know what to do with my kind of dick. So you can just watch how I make myself cum and, in another three years, maybe, just maybe, I'll give you some."

With that, the whore on the floor was defeated, and

the tear, trapped in the corner of her eye, released itself and brought a million soldiers with it as Korea's pussy swelled to insatiable heights and released twice into Stormy's stream of tears. Korea never even mentioned the tears, as she came and came again until her clitoral dick deflated into a masculine grunt. Korea rolled over onto her back, her spent pussy in her hand. She breathed heavily for a while, staring and panting into the spin of the ceiling fan.

Then Korea lovingly cleansed Stormy's face with a cool baby wipe and spoke in the sweetest voice. "How you doing in there?"

It took a moment for Stormy to swallow the lump in her throat, but it was on its way down to be digested with the rest of the evening's bullshit, so she decided to finish the game. "I'm good," Stormy whispered back. Then, out loud, she said, "Yeah, Daddy, it felt too good to get my pussy and my asshole fucked by a real man. I'm glad you taught me a lesson. I was starting to feel guilty."

"Oh, is that a fact?" Korea asked, surprised that Stormy had not had enough.

Korea reached for the tray again. She drew back a red leather cat of nine tails and quickly stung Stormy's voluptuous thigh with it. Stormy's scream aroused Korea. She hit her again, harder. Stormy screamed again, trying to cover the skin of her thigh that was beginning to welt.

"Move your fucking hands!" Korea stung her again.

The more Stormy tried to fight, the more Korea was turned on. "Turn your ass over," she commanded her.

Stormy slowly rolled over onto her stomach. She gripped handfuls of the blanket and braced herself for pain. But Korea sat on the back of her legs, rubbed her ass gently, and kissed it softly with her lips. Stormy felt the cool wetness of Korea's tongue, tracing circular patterns on her ass, and then the sting of the whip on her skin again, and again, and again. Korea was getting off again as Stormy broke down and cried for mercy. Pins shot through her pelvis, her clit hardened, and the remains of her orgasm began to ooze. She climbed up onto Stormy's ass and humped until her sticky cum shined on Stormy's stripes.

"Will you fuck me now?" Stormy asked, making her dissatisfaction known.

The pain had been too intense and Stormy was definitely not aroused. But she knew that once the game was over, she could take Korea into the rapture of her hips, and let her fuck her like the man she wished that she were.

Korea didn't think that Stormy understood that she wasn't a woman pretending to be a man. Deep inside of her, there was actually a man who needed his respect. Stormy's behavior at Club X had been anything but respectful. She was trying to stop hating her for it, but the images were always in her mind. Korea rolled Stormy over onto her back and slapped her again. Her dick was swelling but Stormy's pussy was getting dry. So instead of playing any more games, Korea opened her own pussy with her fingers and stuck her still pulsating dick between Stormy's pussy lips, and fucked her, and did not stop until she felt Stormy's waterfall washing over her.

"Why are you spending so much time in the bathroom?" Shawna asked her husband as he popped back into bed for the third time.

"I don't know. I just have to go."

"Is your stomach upset?"

"No. I just have to pee."

"I didn't hear you pee. You were in there for a long time, too," Shawna said. She lay on top of the comforter, wearing one of Hartford Crow's T-shirts; her provocative pose unappreciated by her husband.

"Well, I thought I had to pee, but I didn't have to this time," he said, fluffing his pillow behind his head and reaching for the remote control. Shawna lifted one arm up over her head and exhaled a sexy breath. "Tired, huh?" Hartford flipped through the channels. "Hey, do you mind getting off of the comforter? You've got me trapped in over here."

"Unbelievable," Shawna said, stubbornly climbing under the covers.

"What is?"

"Nothing." Shawna pouted, pushing her face into her pillow.

Hartford looked over at his wife and sipped his tea. He knew exactly why she was frustrated. But lately, he had not felt like doing anything about it.

"Hartford, do you think you can drink the tea without sipping like a British hag?"

"Sorry, Love," Hartford said softly, hoping she could hear that he was also apologizing for his lack of desire for her. He set the teacup on his nightstand and gently stroked her hair as he watched MTV.

"If you keep having to use the bathroom, maybe you shouldn't be drinking tea at this hour."

"You think?"

"Da-ah," Shawna said sarcastically, and then shooed his hand out of her hair. She needed to hurry and fall asleep to keep from pining. Her sexual desire had been building up for weeks and she was on the verge of exploding. The last thing she needed was Hartford playing in her hair.

In her dream, she stood on her father's feet as he danced around the living room with her.

"Are you ready for the big dip?" her father asked.

"Yes, Daddy, dip me, dip me!"

The man dipped the little girl and slipped his tongue into her mouth. The child smiled and wrapped her arms around his neck so he could carry her to the bedroom, where her mother lay sleeping.

"*Just lay right here on top of me. That-a-girl, that-a girl…*" Shawna could hear her father's voice echoing as she came awake suddenly and sat up in the bed.

"Call Jim," she told her husband. "Tell him you can't seem to stop pissing. It could be your prostate. My father had prostate cancer."

Shawna got out of the bed and locked herself in the bathroom. She sat on the toilet and rubbed her pussy until the pressure was gone.

EVEN THOUGH THEY WERE GOOD FRIENDS, Hartford Crow did not know how to talk to Dr. James Maddox about why his Johnson had gotten hard during his prostate exam. Both men had seen it get hard. Both men had seen Hartford's semen spill involuntarily. But Dr. Maddox had simply handed him a wad of tissue, and asked him casually about his daughters and his wife, Shawna, as he tossed his gloves into the wastebasket and washed his hands.

Damn, Hartford thought as he dressed. *I'll be forty years old on my next birthday; I should know more about my own body. How am I supposed to ask my friend about this? "Uh, hey Jim, when you stuck your finger up my ass, it sure felt good. Is that normal?"*

Hartford knew he wasn't gay. But he couldn't stop thinking about the incredible sensation as he drove home from the doctor's office. The thing that bothered him most was the fact that he was barely aroused by his wife lately, and when he was, it was difficult to maintain it.

"What did the doctor say?" Shawna asked.

"He said what you said."

"He said you have prostate cancer?"

"No, he said to stop drinking tea in bed."

Hartford was unusually flirtatious with his wife over dinner. And by eight o'clock, he was in the bed waiting for her to get out of the shower. He had seen a cobalt blue silk gown and robe hanging on the back of the bathroom door, and lay back on the bed, envisioning Shawna wearing it. But when she emerged from the bathroom, she had on the same tired houserobe she had been in for weeks. Underneath it, he could see that she had on one of his V-neck T-shirts.

"Why don't you come over here and lay on top of me?" Hartford asked her.

"No, I'm cool."

"You're cool? What does that mean?"

"Do you really want to know?"

"Yes, I really want to know."

"It means, do you think my getting on top is going to keep your dick hard?"

"Who the fuck do you think you're talking to?"

"Well, you did ask."

"You're pushing it," Hartford warned her. He watched her climb in the bed beside him. He could see that she didn't have anything on underneath the T-shirt. "Since when did you turn into a missionary maiden?"

"A what?"

"You know, a pillow princess; lying on your back all the time…making me do all the work. That shit gets old. A man needs to be fucked sometimes, too. Maybe if you changed it up, did a little dance, or put on some of that sexy shit you got stashed all over the room in boxes and drawers, it would help us out. Who are you buying that shit for anyway? You sure don't wear it for me. For me, you wear that ugly-ass houserobe and those dirty-ass slippers."

"I buy that stuff for myself."

"You buy that stuff with my money. You keep on being disrespectful, and you won't have any credit cards to shop with."

"Don't you threaten me with money like I'm some kind of hooker you're paying to be here, Hartford. I don't appreciate it. I'm your wife and the mother of your child; you need to respect that."

"Come on, baby, let's not fight tonight. Just get on top, baby, please." Hartford tried to make nice. He rolled over and kissed Shawna on her neck and then pecked each fingertip.

Shawna could feel him pressing his hips into hers, and she could feel that his dick was still limp. She was disgusted. If she didn't take control, she would spend half of the night trying to revive his flaccid little friend.

"How about this?" Shawna said, sliding her body from beneath Hartford's.

He smiled broadly and rolled over on his back as she

climbed on top of him and sat there, staring at him with her captivating Scorpio eyes for a long moment. She lifted the T-shirt over her head and tossed it to the floor, revealing two perfect breasts that Hartford had not seen in a while. She leaned forward and slapped Hartford's face gently with them.

"Remember them?" she teased.

She pushed both breasts together and rubbed her nipples against his lips. His lips parted and his tongue felt for her cinnamon mounds.

"Yes, I remember them," he answered.

He held them gently in each hand and made love to them. Hartford licked in circular motions with his tongue, sucked with his lips and mouth, nibbling and pulling gently on her nipples with his teeth.

Satisfied that Hartford was fully aroused, Shawna lifted her right breast and licked at it with her own tongue and let out an invitational moan as she sat back on his lap to feel for an erection with her ass. Nothing.

"Better yet, how about this?" She reached over and turned the lamp on and opened the nightstand drawer. She pulled out a pink rabbit dildo and turned it on.

"What are you going to do with that?" Hartford asked.

"How about I let this nice hard dick fuck me...while you go fuck yourself?"

Shawna rolled her body back over, plunged the toy inside of her pussy, and let the vibrating rabbit ears take her to an instant baby climax. Hartford watched her, feeling his nature begin to rise. She had come so quickly,

Hartford could only stare at her as she pulled the dildo out of her pussy and put it in her mouth.

She sucked the head. "Mmmm," she moaned. "Damn, I taste good. Kiss me. Maybe the smell of my pussy can get you hard."

"Yeah, alright," he said, getting out of the bed. "Don't be mad when I replace your sorry ass. Can you say pre-nup? Oh, would you look at that," he said, looking down at himself. His dick was as hard as petrified wood and pointing right at her. Hartford wrapped his hand around the shaft and stroked it from top to bottom, waving it over Shawna's face. "Ain't no good ole' hot blood pumpin' through that little toy of yours. You go on playing with your little plastic; I'm going to sleep in the den tonight."

"Wait," Shawna said. "I was just playing. I was trying to get you hard. It worked, too. Come on and get back in the bed; I'll get on top."

"Nope. I'm going to go fuck myself now."

"Damn, I swear you act so bitch-made sometimes."

Hartford's dick was pointing at her through his pajama bottoms now, as he slipped his arms through his pajama top. "I'm going to need a ride to the airport tomorrow."

"Of course, you do. How long are you going to be gone this time? A week? A month? I'm not your baby-sitter, you know?"

"It's not babysitting when they're your children."

Shawna shot him a look as if to say, *they're not* both *my children*.

"Take them to Dream Crow for the week. I'll call and

let you know when I'll be back. Somebody's got to work to pay for all those sex toys and fancy panties."

"Get off of it, Hartford. You haven't made new music in years. You make enough off royalties to take care of two families and never work again."

"Trust me, if I stopped working, and paid more attention to you, it wouldn't be long before l left you. So, you need to shut the fuck up and recognize that I'm only here for my daughter. If it weren't for her, I would've turned your ass into a pillar of salt by now."

Hartford closed the door behind himself.

Shawna let out a frustrated sigh and lay back on the bed. She turned the vibrator back on and stuck it back inside of herself and fixed her clit between the rabbit ears. She closed her eyes, trying to make herself cum again but nothing was happening.

"Damn it," she said.

She got out of the bed and went in to the bathroom. She rinsed the rabbit in the sink and grabbed a towel. She dried the rabbit and walked back into the bedroom, opened the nightstand drawer, and put the rabbit back inside. Then she pulled out her Magic Wand and plugged it in.

"God bless the entire Hitachi family," she said.

She folded the towel in half and laid it on the bed and got busy getting what Hartford never could bring her, a flood. The hard ugly back massager was the best-kept secret in the world of masturbation. She opened her legs and wedged the big fat head of the machine between her pussy lips and turned it on. The monster only had two speeds; "*Oh my God*" and "*Oh shit, oh shit oh shit.*" Shawna closed her eyes and imagined herself being fucked by a gang of men...

HARTFORD HAD A HANDFUL OF HIS SHAFT AS HE LAY ON the couch in the den watching Vanessa Blue devour eleven inches of Lexington Steele on the television. He closed his eyes as he stroked and listened to the sounds of her full lips sucking. He stroked and pumped his dick with his right hand and grabbed his balls with his left. He thought of the place Jim had found inside of him and reached down toward it...

THE POWER DRILL THUNDERED AGAINST HER PUSSY LIPS and clit as Shawna fantasized. She was outside in the woods, naked, her hands tied to trees, her knees on the ground, her mouth stuffed with two pink cocks. She had one dick in her ass and one in her pussy and she could feel them rubbing together inside of her.

"Fuck me," Shawna said out loud. "Fuck me, you fucking honkies. I'm a dirty black bitch. Nut in my mouth. Yeah, that's it. Cum in my ass. Oh yeah, that's it, cum in my pussy, cum in my mouth..." She was on the verge of busting, just thinking about the milk of life filling all of her holes. She pressed the machine harder against her clit. "Oh, that's it, that's it right there, fuck, fuck, fuck, oh God, fuck me, yeah, yeah, yeah…" she screamed, "…ahhhhh!"

Her pussy sneezed and oozed its second nut of the night. But Shawna was not done. She kept the wand in place, pressing on through her spasms, denying them the right to finish her off. She spit down her chin and imagined it was cum, and then she was back in the woods, sucking the dick that had been in her ass.

"Ooh, you make me so nasty." A few feet away she heard moaning stronger than her own. She watched one of the white men fucking Hartford in his ass. "Yeah," she said as she pumped against the machine. "Yes, fuck that niggah, fuck him good." Hartford was on all fours, his ass in the air, letting the man smack his ass. "Make him your bitch, make him your bitch, do it, AHHH! Fuuuuck!"

Shawna was cumming so hard, thinking of Hartford getting fucked in his ass, she flooded the towel as she bore down and pushed the juice out like she was giving birth, shooting it across the bed.

HARTFORD MASSAGED HIS BALLS AND LET HIS FINGERS rub the space beneath them as he jacked himself off. He opened his eyes to see Vanessa bent over a couch, getting it in the ass. He watched intently as Lex's dick pushed in and out of her tight hole. Hartford stroked his own dick harder and faster...pressing down on the meat beneath his balls, which gave him a feeling similar to the one he had in the doctor's office.

"Oh shit," he said. "Yeah, bitch, I'm going to fuck myself alright." He watched Lex pull out of Vanessa's ass and shove his cock down her mouth to the back of her throat. "Ooh, suck that dick, yeah, suck that dick..."

Hartford was pumping his shaft faster and faster, gripping his nuts and rubbing his meat until he and Lex both filled Vanessa's mouth with all man's joy.

SHAWNA LISTENED TO THE SOUND OF HER BODY as she lay in the afterglow, gently massaging her breasts, feeling the muscles in her belly and thighs contract. Her heart pounded against her chest and her pussy lips seemed to pulsate with tiny heartbeats of their own...

"Fuck!" Shawna suddenly opened her eyes wide. Outside of her fantasy, the thought of Hartford getting rammed up the ass wasn't sexy at all. "That was new. Where the hell did that come from?"

The Magic Wand had worked her so well, it was hot to the touch. She picked it up and snatched the soaked towel off the bed, and then walked to the bathroom on wobbly legs.

"If I find out there's any down low shit going on around here, he won't have to worry about a pre-nup. He'll be dead."

"BABY," STORMY SAID TO KOREA. "I DON'T WANT TO do it that way anymore, okay?"

"Okay," Korea told her.

That had been over a month ago. A lot had happened since that night. Korea had lost a couple of contracts, Stormy was working on her computer all the time, and Korea had kicked her relationship with her assistant, Melody, into high S&M gear. Her stress was mounting and her body had responded in the most unthinkable way. Now she couldn't fuck Stormy if she wanted to.

Korea was waiting for the scabs on her pussy to dry out and fall off before she fucked Stormy again. Korea never let Stormy suck on her pussy anyway. She didn't want to run the risk of transmitting the virus when their pussy lips locked and the suction of her cup drew her lovers' lips into her wetness. Korea was the wet one. So, when the two women fucked, it was Korea's juices that slicked their skin, like a man-made lubricant, giving them smooth rides to mutual orgasm. She didn't cum in a flood like Stormy did. She was constantly wet, every day, every evening, just like a man. And just like a man, Korea was always looking for a new challenge.

Korea's hot pussy cocktail was strong in scent and flowed endlessly when she fucked her woman. In the lesbian scissor position, it saturated her lover's thighs. In the missionary position it streamed down Stormy's fat pussy lips, sometimes bubbling and making little popping sounds. When she rode Stormy from behind, which she liked to do, she spread her own pussy lips apart, and let her large cherry pink clit rub the fatty flesh of her ass. She would hold herself there, in that place of blissful orgasm, feeling her juices stream between the crack of Stormy's ass cheeks and pool on the sheets beneath them. Korea always waited for her lover to cum first. Sometimes, she had no need to bust at all, but when she did, her cum was thick and sticky, bearing the smell and consistency of a man's nut. Stormy liked to suck it off of Korea's fingers. Korea liked to watch her do this, as her post-orgasmic buzz jerked her into a euphoric state of sexual satisfaction.

Korea had never told Stormy, or anyone else, about the virus. It was her own business and she was careful to keep it to herself. Until a week ago, Korea had not had an outbreak in all of the years since she had met Stormy, who gave her great loving, perfect nutrition, and kept her calm and free-spirited with her obedience and willingness to please. But lately Stormy busied herself with a new writing hobby that was turning Korea's home-cooked gourmet meals into a never-ending international food fair of foreign slop Korea could not pronounce or identify. Dinner was still on the table when Korea came home from the office every night, but it was served with a single place setting, while Stormy hid away in her bedroom clicking the night away on her computer. *This was not the agreement*, Korea agreed with herself, as she walked through the door of the penthouse down the hall past *the clicking*.

"Damn," Korea said, as she smashed her foot on the

trashcan pedal and looked inside. "This wench isn't even conscientious enough to hide the damn take-out box this nasty-looking lasagna came in." Korea left the mound of pasta and cheese on the table untouched and was showered and in bed by 9:00 P.M. She lay awake, pondering the source of her stress.

She was at the office, getting more pissed off by the second, when Grace Riley called to "informally" cancel another city grant because she had found favor in some bitch she was fucking who had developed a program for teenage prostitute decriminalization that sounded remarkably like the one Korea had developed herself. Korea had always thought her relationship with Grace was volatile since there was no sex between them. Korea was old school, so stud-on-stud romance was not in her repertoire of experimentation. But she had given Grace more credit than that. How could she destroy a strong and longstanding relationship for a hot chick right out of grad school? *Hadn't she been faithfully coughing up the sweet kick-back the councilwoman had asked for? The first contract Grace cancelled had been more understandable.* Her nephew was fresh out of the penitentiary and needed to get a foot in the political door for his B.O.B. (Back Off Da Block) project that, like hers, had promised to make businessmen of reformed ballers. Korea respected Grace, but if she got more indication that she was picking her brain for ideas, all bets were off, she told herself.

The outbreak was signaled by a persistent hot tingling

in her upper inner left thigh, a headache, and flu symptoms. The next day, when she received the formal letter
by courier from Grace, the bumps came. Korea had not
seen them in years, and barely knew what to do about
them since it had been so long. Every time she watched
the commercial for Valtrex, Korea was embarrassed;
especially when Stormy was in bed with her.

She lay alone in bed, uselessly trying to self-meditate
and relax, but the plucking of Stormy's computer keys
resounded from the next room, keeping her alert and
agitated until well after midnight.

Why won't she just come to bed? Korea thought.

She wanted to call to Stormy, but she did not want to
sound needy or desperate. The television watched her
as she tossed and turned, restlessly watching the clock
on her nightstand, thinking of her mother, of Grace, of
Stormy, and of who was on the other end of the internet
consuming her woman's time. Then she thought of
Melody, the only person giving her joy right now, until
her eyes were finally overtaken by sleep.

Slowly, a delicious flood of imagery began to overtake
her thoughts as she drifted away. Melody crawled slowly
toward her across the blue carpet of her office floor.
Her plump, welcoming breasts rubbed against one
another and pressed anxiously into the thin silk of a
turquoise camisole as her crimson-manicured fingers
reached, one after the other across the floor, pulling her
long and lean body ever closer. Her tight, muscular ass

cheeks seemed to pop to an urban beat that was not playing, drawing her panties between them. Melody's ass was nice and tight. Korea wondered why she even bothered wearing panties if her ass was going to swallow them whole. Melody's legs were bare and her feet were dressed in matching turquoise sandals that revealed her red painted toes.

As Melody crawled, she licked her lips and begged for a taste of Korea's essence. "Please, Daddy, please," she said over and over again as she tried to open the soft butch's thighs.

"You wouldn't know what to do with it, if I let you lick it," Korea said, spreading her full hand over the woman's face, pushing it away and smudging her red lipstick.

Melody laughed, a wicked, loaded laugh, smudging the remainder of her lip paint down her chin to her neck. "You would be surprised at what I can do, if you let me. All you have to do is say yes."

Melody pressed her face into Korea's crotch and blew her hot breath through her boss's pants, sending a hot sensation that stirred her to awaken.

Korea's mind opened before her eyes did, taking in the sounds and smells that changed the temperament of the room she had fallen to sleep in. Floetry crooned softly on the stereo; Stormy's favorite song.

"All you have to do is say yes, don't deny what you're feeling, baby undress...."

Warm and woody, Nag Champa incense smoke left its unmistakable impression of India in the air. A faint hint of musty Merlot, and the strong scent of China Rain, told her that Stormy had been to visit Body Time, and was nearby. A gentle and persistent light pushed her lids open. The television was silent and projected no light through the darkened room, but the curtain was open, revealing a big yellow moon; perhaps the biggest she'd ever seen. She was becoming acutely aware of the increasing heat under her comforter and the accumulating moisture between her legs.

"Stormy?" Her lover's name cracked on her sleepy voice.

From under the down comforter came a shy, little giggle. "Yes?"

"What the hell are you doing?" Korea snapped, snatching the down comforter off of her body, to find Stormy between her legs, blowing playfully through her boxers.

"I wanted to…"

"What are you trying to do? Rape me?"

"Rape? No, Korea, that's ridiculous. I'm not trying to rape you. I was just trying to wake you up…and maybe…"

"It's rape, if I'm sleeping."

"I…I'm sorry," Stormy said, instantly defeated. "But, I wasn't trying to rape you."

"No? You know the rules. What were you trying to do?"

"I was…" Stormy crawled from beneath the covers, to her own pillow, and turned her face away. "Forget it."

"I will not forget it. What were you doing, if you weren't trying to fuck me in my sleep?"

"I was trying to wake you up. I was trying to make love to you. Before I was your pillow princess, I had been known to make love to people from time to time." Then, sitting up, she looked into Korea's eyes and said, "I can, if you let me. All you have to do is say yes, baby. Why won't you?"

Korea reached for the television remote control.

"Baby, let's not watch the TV. Let's watch the moon. Did you see it? Isn't it great?"

"Yeah, it's real great," Korea said, aiming the remote at the television; she pressed the little green button.

"Sorry, I woke you up. You must've been *saying yes* to somebody in your dream; your boxers are real wet."

"Finish your wine and get the glass out of here before you fall asleep. It stinks," Korea snapped.

Korea lay with her back to Stormy. She was hot and agitated. Stormy was right; that dream of her hot assistant, Melody, had made her very wet and she wished she could finish it with Stormy. Melody was getting really kinky lately. Tuesday, she wore a dog collar and had actually barked for her and whimpered like a bad animal when she'd spanked her with a rolled-up newspaper. That bitch was freaky and innovative. Korea was getting tired of Stormy's tired old tricks. She wondered how far she could get Melody to go. Her clit was getting hard thinking about it. She squeezed her pelvis tight, trying to make the sensation die. Stormy hadn't earned her tonight. If her obsession with the fucking computer continued, she was going to find herself on the street.

I'm glad I'm not a hypochondriac, Stormy thought, watching a sad woman walking down a road that seemed to lead nowhere in an ad for some new depression pill. *I have all those symptoms.*

"Are you awake?" Stormy asked, rolling over to spoon Korea from behind. "Can't sleep, then perhaps you are depressed. We have a pill for that. Getting old, feeling tired, getting fat, getting ugly, need some pussy? We have a pill for that." Stormy laughed at herself but didn't get a rise out of Korea. She sat up on the bed and sipped her wine, and watched the screen.

Another commercial came on. "Oh no, uhn ugh. What the heck is *Restless Leg Syndrome*?" Korea flipped her pillow to the cool side and scratched her thigh. Stormy looked at Korea. "Are you okay?" she asked. "You got Restless Leg Syndrome? We have a pill for that."

"Anyone ever tell you that you talk too much?" Korea said into her pillow.

"Only you."

"I'm going to say this to you again and I trust it'll be for the last time. I would appreciate it if you don't get on top of me when I'm sleeping. Don't attempt to insert anything inside of me; no fingers, no tongues, and no inanimate objects, of any kind. If I wanted a man, I would have one."

"Okay, Korea. I promise that I'll never, ever get on top of you when you're sleeping," Stormy said, rolling onto her back. "You didn't touch your lasagna. Weren't you hungry?"

"Did you make it?"

"No, I..."

"Then why would I eat it?"

"I guess you wouldn't."

"This relationship isn't a guessing game, Stormy. All I asked you to do for me when we met was to keep yourself available to me and to take care of home. I promised to do the rest. I'm handling my business, but lately you haven't been fulfilling any of your promises. It's like I'm taking a back seat to your computer. This isn't working."

"Tell me about it," Stormy spoke through a sigh. "But really, baby, I don't want to fight," she said, resigning before the fight even began.

Stormy got out of the bed, picked up her half glass of Merlot, walked to the sliding patio doors, stepped through them, and onto the balcony. In silence, she sipped her wine and seduced the big yellow moon with her naked body until her sadness was beginning to inebriate itself away.

Stormy's glass was getting empty when she began to slowly sway her hips through the cool night air. Her eyes were steadied on the moon that seemed to be winking at her like an exquisite quiche. Way up there on the penthouse balcony, no one could see her. No one could touch her or hear her thoughts. Her eyes swept over the stars as she sipped and pondered upon the source of their dazzling lights and of the clever hands that put them in their places. Stormy was embarrassed, thinking of what the God that designed this midnight sky must have thought of her now. She was ashamed that she was so unworthy to even talk to Him. Even her nakedness, she thought, must have insulted Him.

But looking down, at the beautiful body God had given her, freed her spirit for a moment. In a sudden burst of confidence she had not known in far too long, she tried to pray. She tried to pray to see if she could get that feeling she had gotten as a child; the feeling that he was listening. Naked on the balcony, full of wine, she prayed.

"God, most merciful Father, and creator of all, please take a moment to forgive me for my sins. I ask that you make me pure in this moment of magnificence, so that I may be worthy of speaking to you again, after so much time. I understand that with the new life I have chosen, I have strayed far from your plan for me, but I am listening now. Speak to me. I don't ask of You riches and fame, only for peace and happiness. You know my heart, dear Lord. Please send me someone who appreciates me for more than my subservience, but one who respects my talents. Send me somebody who sees my light and doesn't try to put it out. Send me somebody with a light that shines as brightly as those stars of yours. I hope you can hear me. If you can hear me, if you can forgive me, if you ever loved me, help me now. Hear me now. Amen." Stormy waited for a sign; a twinkle in a star, a flash of light or the butterflies she used to feel when she prayed. But nothing happened.

"Sometimes a good fight is exactly what I need, to get me going," she heard Korea's voice state behind her.

"Funny, all it takes for me is a little respect," Stormy answered without turning around. Stormy's eyes gazed into the moon and glazed over.

Korea gazed at Stormy. "Look at that big ole' moon," Korea said, looking at Stormy's full tan ass. "Isn't it great?"

Stormy didn't respond. She was in a faraway place, nearly dreaming, as she stood there in the moonlight. She had almost forgotten Korea was there, when she felt her ass cheeks gently being pulled apart and a warm tongue sliding expertly between them. Her knees buckled, a shiver ran the course from her feet to her shoulders, and her crystal wine glass fell eighteen floors, from the penthouse balcony. Stormy bent slightly forward, resting her arms on the garden wall, and spread her legs open, allowing her flower to part for Korea's apologetic tongue.

Korea and Stormy lay on the bed with their down comforter and silk sheets disheveled around them. They listened to the sounds of Oakland, California after dark. A helicopter hovered persistently above them. A car door slammed. A car alarm sounded off and a kitten shrieked on the street below the high-rise building. In the distance, birds of the sanctuary in Lake Merritt squawked.

"Are you getting bored with me?" Stormy asked, staring into the dark of Korea's bedroom.

"Why do you ask me that?"

"Because you didn't cum when you were eating me out."

"No. I'm not bored. I have a lot on my mind. I mean, I like change; things can get boring sometimes."

"You mean people can get boring sometimes."

"Them, too."

"You want to go again? You can fuck me with your pussy, until you cum. I don't need to get off anymore."

"No."

Stormy thought about how the last erotic encounter she planned for Korea had changed their love-making style forever, but she asked the question anyway. She knew this thing was slipping away fast, but she wasn't ready to leave yet.

"What is your fantasy, Korea?"

"I have a lot of them."

"I know that. I mean, which one have you been thinking about lately?"

"You sure you want to know?

"Yes."

"I want to fuck a man in the ass."

"You do?"

"Hell yes. That shit would be so fun."

"You want to fuck me in the ass?

"No."

"Good. I'm not into ass play," Stormy said. "Why don't you want to fuck me in the ass?"

"Why don't I want to fuck you in the ass?"

"Yes."

"What fun would that be? You're a woman. I can do anything I want to you already. It wouldn't be a challenge."

"Oh. I didn't realize sex needed to be a challenge."

"Baby, anything worth doing needs to be a challenge. That's your problem now. Nothing seems to be a challenge for you. Everything comes too easy for you. You don't have to work for it. People simply give it to you."

"That's not true, Korea. You sound like Tom."

"Please don't compare me to that sorry excuse for a man."

"Damn, baby, you sure you don't want to bust on me real quick? You're cranky."

Korea did not respond to that.

"What you're saying about me isn't true at all. Do you think taking care of you and this penthouse is easy?"

"For you, it is. It should be anyway. You don't have anything else to do."

"I do. I happen to have a job."

"Do you call that little article you write on the Internet a job?"

"I hate it when you do that. Why do you have to be so mean to me?"

"Because I can. You need to think about why that is."

"I'm not responsible for how you treat me; you are."

"No, you are. Just like you were responsible for how that sorry-ass man of yours was treating you. You're a fucking muffin, Stormy. You need to get a backbone and start standing up for yourself. Maybe I would respect you more."

"Oh yeah?"

"Yeah."

"Okay, how about I start right now."

Stormy got out of the bed. She slipped into some underwear, pulled her favorite dashiki from the night-stand drawer, and slipped it over her head. Korea rolled over and hugged her pillow. Stormy's defiance came at a price; her heart was pounding hard in her chest and her hand was a little shaky as she pulled Korea's bedroom door closed behind her. She sat down at her computer and logged into her email account. She had ten un-opened emails.

"*Dear Miss Talbert, this is Paul Moon, head chef at Blue Restaurant. I want to thank you for your glowing review of our cuisine in The Cutting Board. Our business is booming thanks to you. If you ever want to come by for dinner, consider yourself my guest.*"

Stormy smiled, and typed a response to him. Then she opened the next email. It was from T. Calloway, her editor.

"*Hey, Stormy, T. Calloway here. You are doing a great job! Check your PayPal account.*"

There was a smiley face blowing a kiss at the end of the message. Stormy logged in to her PayPal account and beamed when she saw her new account balance. She opened the Yahoo window and opened another email.

"*Dear Miss Talbert. You probably don't remember me. I was your waiter at the Torrent Café on Grove Street. I wanted to write to thank you for being such a nice customer. I didn't even know who you were, but when I realized you had been there to review us, I thought, wow, she could have been a real bitch (excuse my language), but you weren't. We get some real nasty clients sometimes because our place is always so crowded, but you were graceful and patient, even when I brought you the wrong order. And, I might add, you are beautiful. I hope this isn't inappropriate but I have to try.*"

I have never met a woman like you before. Your natural beauty is stunning. I noticed you weren't wearing a wedding ring. If you would consider letting me take you out sometime, I would be a very happy man. Call me at…"

"What the fuck do you think you're doing?" Korea's voice startled her, and she jumped.

"I'm checking my email," Stormy replied.

"You've been in here all night already. Bring your fucking ass to bed."

"I'm only doing what you said."

"Don't try me. Come to bed now. And take that stupid-looking dashiki off. That shit ain't sexy. You've got me feeling like I'm sleeping with Angela Davis."

"Awe, baby, isn't that one of your fantasies?"

Korea didn't find her amusing. "Hurry up," she said. "I'm getting sleepy."

Stormy took that to mean that Korea wanted some more pussy tonight so she logged off without responding to the sweet young man, who had been so nervous in her presence she had forgiven him instantly for bringing a strawberry and walnut salad instead of the roasted pecan mixed green. He couldn't have been more than twenty. She laughed at the thought of herself as a cougar as she logged out of her email account and shut her computer down.

Korea's eyes were closed when Stormy walked into the room. She slipped her West African shirt over her head and let it drop to the floor.

"Is this better?"she asked in a deep, sensuous tone

that forced Korea's eyes to open, and to see her. Under her square-cut ethnic garb there had been a tight little half-tee and tattoo-designed spanks from Christian Audigier's Ed Hardy line. Stormy spun around so Korea could see how the panties clung to her phat derriere, letting just a little escape from the lacey hems. "You sure you don't want to stick your dick in there?" she said, slapping her cheeks with her hands. "You haven't fucked me with your strap in a minute."

"Naw, just make it bounce for me, baby," Korea said softly. "Make it clap."

Stormy obliged, raising herself on tipped toes, pivoting her feet in and out, her thighs followed obediently, opening and closing, pulling the cheeks of her ass with them until they began to clap. Korea slipped her hand down under the covers to touch her own pussy. She rubbed her tiny dick and watched Stormy's ass open and close.

"Bend over. Slide your panties to the side so I can see."

Stormy climbed up on the bed so Korea could get a good look at her pretty golden pussy. She slid her panties to the side and opened her pussy so Korea could look inside. She opened and closed it with her muscles, and made it pop for her daddy a few times. Passion was flooding Korea's eyes but no moan escaped.

"That's it, baby, don't stop," Korea said, pressing and rubbing her button until she came in a faint grunt.

"That was good," Korea said. "I could almost forgive that fucked-up dinner after that. Get in the bed."

Korea fell asleep, holding Stormy tight and pinning her down with two arms and a thigh. It made Stormy uncomfortable to be wrapped like a hotdog this way, but she stayed there, basking in the affection. She lay awake a while longer, picturing Korea's fantasy of fucking a man with a dildo, wondering how she was going to make it happen. Maybe this new fantasy would get her off of the old one. Maybe it would make her forget about what happened that night, at Club X. Maybe Korea would forgive her and they could start fucking normally again, like they used to.

IN THE LIGHT OF DAY, STORMY MOURNED THE PASSION-ate sexual relationship she once enjoyed with Korea. Stormy was naturally submissive, and had been straight before she met Korea. She was groomed by her Southern-raised mom to be a housewife and a supporting cast member to her leading man, traits she continued to live with, and abide by, even when she chose a woman to play the part of her leading man. But it had been more difficult than she imagined, to please someone who was every bit of the woman she was. Stormy felt there was little she could give Korea that Korea could not provide for herself. Men, with their childish neediness, had been much easier to handle. All she had learned from Tom was how to coddle. But what she had learned from Korea was an addictive independence that was becoming the root of their problems.

Stormy wasn't the neatest person, but struggled and managed to keep Korea's two-level penthouse condominium clean and organized, although she thought it was a job for a professional. Between two levels, there were two master bedrooms, a guest room, three-and-a-half bathrooms, a huge living room, a massive dining room, a den, and a workout room. Korea generally spent most of her time between the state-of-the-art workout room, perfecting her beautiful androgynous body, and her private master bedroom.

Stormy was expected to maintain the entire condo alone. It was easy enough to do, when it was all she had to do. But her newfound career as a food critic, with her own weekly column, "The Cutting Board," was gaining momentum and she didn't have as much time to handle domestic matters. Besides, she thought to herself, as she looked at the clock on her computer, hoping Korea would be grossly late coming home again, with sex getting so sporadic, she didn't really feel like cooking or cleaning a damned thing.

Stormy grew her own vegetables and spices in a rooftop garden she had planted herself. "From way up here on the eighteenth floor, you can almost see God," she often told Korea, when she was trying to lure her away from the television onto the balcony, where she loved to make love.

But Stormy took most pride in her gleaming stainless steel decor kitchen, which was big and beautiful enough to set the stage for her own erotic fantasy cooking show. The night the beautiful kitchen was complete, Stormy created a sensuous Punany Experience, personalized for Korea to thank her for the stunning treasure.

"Hi there," a naked woman said softly as Korea stepped through her penthouse door one evening. "I am Sam. All that you desire is all that I am. Anything less than your perfect satisfaction, I cannot understand. Anything that is not beautiful or delicious is not in tonight's plan. I will be your hostess for the evening. This is my beautiful assistant, Pam. We welcome you to your Punany Experience."

A broad smile was all Korea's mouth could manage as Sam and Pam took her driving gloves and rain-soaked coat, and then guided her to a fireside seat where each woman unzipped and removed a boot from each foot and placed both of them on a towel that lay on the floor between a steaming bowl of water and a bottle of olive oil. The scent of eucalyptus wavered through the warm air as Sam squeezed the water from a cloth and washed the businesswoman's feet with the gentle attention that womanhood is made of. Pam rubbed the olive oil between her hands while softly explaining its healing properties. Sam now worked on Korea's head, neck and shoulders, expertly massaging from her nape to her temples, back again, and down to her shoulders. Korea could feel the stress in her body dissipating.

"Breathe," she told Korea.

It had been an unusually stormy season, especially for California, and Korea was most definitely glad to be in from the cold. She felt her eyes close and her back sink into her favorite chair. "This is the life," she said.

"I am Starla," a third woman said softly into her left ear, awakening her from her dream state. Korea opened her eyes to find an olive-skinned Italian woman with a long, thick, jet black ponytail standing before her, wearing only an apron, tied loosely around her waist, revealing well-trained abs and a hint of a neatly groomed black bikini hairline.

Starla served Korea a hot toddy of tea and brandy and a small dish of chocolate truffles. "I'm your sous chef tonight," she said, dismissing the women with a wave of her hand. The women took the water and oil away. "We take great pleasure in serving you in The Palace of Eros tonight, where your Punany Experience was written and produced by Stormy Talbert. You will find your dining choices inside of this program." Starla handed a small black program to Korea, and continued her introduction. "Ms. Talbert has directed us with regards to your dietary needs and personal appetite. Should you crave anything that is not on the menu, please do not hesitate to let us know. On the back of your program, you will find a catalogue of merchandise that may be used for romance, persuasion, coercion, or force." Starla flashed an award winner at Korea and concluded her introduction with, "Light seafood appetizers will be served in twenty minutes on a petit platter of Betty."

"Betty?" Korea asked curiously.

"The house specialty," Starla said with a faint smile. "The head chef will greet you shortly. You may relax here, or choose to follow your servants to your private bath."

Sam and Pam returned with a purple silk robe and matching boxers.

"Huh, yes, I think I would like to get a quick shower, and then I will be back for those appetizers," Korea said. "Um, I would like to order these for now," she added, pointing to a pair of purple latex gloves.

Korea showered, standing over Sam and Pam, who lay grinding each other on the shower floor. She turned the water off, stepped from the shower, and commanded Sam to lay on the chaise and to open her legs to receive her gloved fingers.

"Come here," she said to Sam. "Kiss me."

Sam opened her mouth and pushed her hot, wet twisting tongue into Korea's mouth. When she found Korea's tongue, she grabbed gently with her teeth, pulling it into her control, and sucked it like she was sucking a dick. Now the two women were both staring into Pam's open legs. Korea went in, fucking Pam slowly with two fingers for a few minutes, and when she felt Pam's pelvic muscles relax, she slipped two more fingers inside of her. She turned them slowly, and pushed in and out.

Sam leaned in and kissed Pam's pussy and sucked on her clit as Korea forced her hand deeper and deeper inside until her thumb slipped easily into the slippery cave. She carefully pulled her fingers together and balled them up inside of Pam, fucking her deeply with her fist. Pam screamed in ecstasy and pain.

"Oh, oh, I'm next, please!" Sam said.

"Do me a favor and shut her up."

"Okay."

Sam climbed up onto the chaise and sat on Pam's mouth, and silenced her with her hot muff. Korea could feel Pam's muscles contracting and releasing as her orgasm built up around her whole hand. Her muffled cries and moans were caught in the hot sticky nut of Sam, who was fucking her face like a rodeo champion, and coaching Korea to thrust deeper inside of the woman.

"She likes that. Ooh yeah, fuck her deeper. Her pussy is a bottomless pit." Sam egged her on.

Korea thought her arm would be ripped off as Pam pushed her pelvis back for a long moment, and then suddenly pushed hard with her pussy muscles, giving birth to an orgasm that forced Korea's fist out of her body in a flood of sap. Her body irked and jerked and continued to emit juices, as Sam joined her in orgasmic release, cumming in her mouth and falling to the floor. Korea climbed on top of Sam and busted one good long time, releasing all of the day's stress onto Sam's pussy.

DRESSED IN THE PURPLE ROBE AND BOXERS, Korea was escorted to the bar, where a human platter was adorned with a fine selection of seafood. Tiny portions of shrimp, scallops, oysters, clams, and lobster had been baked, broiled, boiled, sautéed, simmered, chilled, grilled, smoked, pickled to perfection, and served on a platter of…

"Don't tell me," Korea said to the petite Asian beauty lying on the bar, "you have got to be Betty." She paused. "Well, ladies, care to join me?"

Sam and Pam helped Korea devour the appetizers while they watched Starla prep the kitchen.

Stormy was a flawless beauty as she emerged from her bedroom and sashayed down the hall toward the kitchen. Korea almost choked on a shrimp as she jumped to attention, examining this woman from her feet to her hair. Stormy wore cobalt blue three-inch pumps, the diamond anklet Korea had given her for Christmas, and a very short, very sheer, blue silk apron that left her thunderous thighs and hips exposed on each side. Her midsection was merely highlighted by a thin strip of fabric that branched around her breasts, leaving the stubborn impression of two perfect nipples. Her apron was draped from her neck by a crystal sling and fastened in the back by only two crystal straps. Stormy's ass and back, in their entirety, were exposed. The tiny triangle top on the back of her G-string read "Head Chef."

"Are you enjoying yourself, Ms. Smith, in The Palace of Eros?" Stormy asked her patron.

"My God, yes, baby, I'm having a good time; the best time. Thank you. I love the entertainment. The kitchen is amazing and I'm looking forward to the meal. Would the head chef be obliged to give me a kiss before we begin?"

Stormy blushed and the women "ooed" and "ahhed" their encouragement and approval as Stormy and Korea embraced and kissed.

Assisted by her topless sous chef, and her two fully nude assistant cooks, Stormy created a simple but magical meal around Korea's favorite meat, filet mignon, medium-well and well-seasoned. Korea enjoyed watching the full and perky breasts and buoyant asses bouncing around in the kitchen as the women whipped potatoes and poured cream and melted butter to produce the most perfect twice-baked potatoes. The asparagus was tossed in roasted garlic and ground sea salt. The women moved playfully around the kitchen making purposeful spills for Betty to bend over and clean up and every time something was spilled, or broken, there was an ass to be swatted, whipped, or spanked with the big wooden spoon that was passed around the room.

Korea and Stormy ate together while the women cleaned. After dinner, they lay on the floor in front of the fire, Stormy with her wine and Korea with a cold beer.

"Before we discuss the rules of engagement for tonight, I want you to sit on my…" Before Korea had completed her thought, her mouth was full of Stormy's pussy. She rode her mouth like it was a dick, and came until Korea choked on juices that shot from deep within her. It was

Stormy's first flood; the first time she had ejaculated. But it wasn't her last. For the next year, she didn't want to come at all, if she couldn't cum that way.

The Palace of Eros closed at sunrise in a crescendo of moans and orgasms as six voices, and twenty-four limbs, twisted and convulsed in the morning light, on the floor, before a dying fire.

STORMY CHECKED HER EMAIL FOR THE THIRD TIME, looking for the invitation she had been waiting for to join the Food Critic's Guild. An invitation to join the guild was an honor that would entitle Stormy to unlimited writing assignments and international travel opportunities.

She wasn't sure how Korea would take it if she decided to start traveling for her newfound career, but she didn't really care anymore. What used to be an alluring mysteriousness that kept Stormy intrigued with Korea was beginning to look like secrecy, and Stormy didn't like secrets unless they were her own. Until now, she hadn't kept anything from her lover. She had always been an open book, sharing her every desire and concern with Korea, even when Korea didn't care to listen. But there was no invitation from the guild yet. There was a new notification from PayPal and an email from her managing editor at *The Cutting Board.*

She logged into her PayPal account…"Whoa!" she exclaimed with a bright smile. "What is going on here?"

She quickly transferred the money into her bank account and returned to her email and clicked on the name "T. Calloway."

Stormy,

T. Calloway here. Did you check your PayPal? (I put a little bonus in it.) Nice, huh? Just my personal way of saying thanks. You're really bringing us hits now. I'm checking in to see how you are doing. I also want to compliment you on your latest work. Your style is incredible and getting better every day. "Cooking with Love" is amazing…No edits this week beyond your standard typos (start spell checking, sweetheart.)

My favorite lines:

"The chef was obviously tired, rubbing his eyes and yawning…It was clear to me after the appetizer that he did not feel like cooking, and after the main course of a sleepy and sloppily plated chicken lasagna, I suggested the manager send him home." —Cutting edge stuff…

"In all fairness, I waive this week's review of "The Food Council" in Emeryville, CA, until the chef has had a good night's rest. There is one thing that has become more clear to me than ever: When you do not feel like cooking, "Love" is definitely not on the menu." —Powerful…

Your romanticism is intriguing. You're even getting fan mail now! I really respect your passion. (Are you this passionate about everything you do? If that is the case, I can't wait to meet you.) —T. Calloway.

"Bing!" An instant message popped up on the screen.

T.Calloway: *T. Calloway here. Do you have time to talk?*

"Wow, is he psychic?" Stormy said aloud, typing a response.

TheCutB: *Hey, boss.*

T.Calloway: *Great news, Stormy. The Cutting Board is going to print.*

TheCutB: *You mean it will be a physical publication?*

T.Calloway: *Yes. It will open at least 20 new positions. I need you on board.*

TheCutB: *I don't understand, I already work for you...*

T.Calloway: *The Cutting Board Website would be a different entity. This would be a daily gig. We need a full-time staff to produce a weekly. Relocation would be required.*

TheCutB: *To...*

T.Calloway: *Washington, D.C.*

Though she had thought of leaving often over the last year, Stormy wasn't sure she could give up the lifestyle she had with Korea. That, and the fact that she was addicted to her, had kept her there; unsatisfied, but present.

TheCutB: *Let me think about it...*

T.Calloway: *I'll give you 30 days. You need to know, the new publisher is leaning toward a bigger name for your column. She's a critic from the DC Post who is well-respected. She's established and on the board of the Food Critic's Guild.*

TheCutB: *I see.*

T.Calloway: *Starts at $120*

TheCutB: *Are you kidding, I make $300 now.*

T.Calloway: *Don't be silly, you make $300 a column. I*

am offering you $120K a year with a two-year contract. But you would be working every day, not whenever you feel like it.

THECUTB: *I'll think about it.*

T.CALLOWAY: *Think fast.*

THECUTB: *Thanks.*

T.CALLOWAY: *One more thing. Think you could fly down to L.A. to cover a new spot?*

THECUTB: *L.A.? Sure, no problem.*

T.CALLOWAY: *Good then. Southwest, Friday 2pm. Make a reservation at "The Ethiopian Sea" on Sunset. This is a review with a public interest twist. Pays $500 + RT Air and Hotel for 2 days. I want to see what you've got, so be creative. Some homeless guy's suing for food poisoning. Check your email for details.*

THECUTB: *OK, bye.*

"Oh my God! Oh my God! A hundred twenty thousand dollars a year! Oh shit!" Stormy screamed out loud. "Korea is right. There is something very sexy about making money. I think my pussy just got wet."

KOREA SAT SILENTLY AT HER OFFICE DESK, WONDERING what the issue was with Stormy. She had to know that once you pass a sexual plateau, there is no going back. They had already reached far beyond mundane fucking. That night at Club X was proof of that. Korea still got excited whenever she recalled the last sexually deviant tryst she'd had with Stormy in public. It had been Stormy's idea of a birthday present, and Korea had never gotten over it. She loved it. She loved it too much. It had been good to be so bad inside that San Francisco dungeon of swinging, swapping, and sadomasochism. Visions of Stormy strapped to a table, or getting eaten by strangers, sometimes played in her head when she was getting ready to fuck or punish Melody. But she hated what it had done to her respect for Stormy.

It had happened on her birthday, last year. Korea had taken off work early to get ready for what she thought would be a romantic night on the town that would include dinner, a sexy theater show, and salsa dancing. She drove to San Francisco and darted into Nordstrom to pick up her suit and a gown for Stormy. Korea had planned the whole thing, with a little help from Martha, her former secretary. On her way back across the Bay Bridge, Martha had called to remind her to pick up flowers from the The Blossoming Flower Shop on Grand Avenue. That was where she met Melody, the first time. There was electricity between them, and they both felt it right away. Korea had left her card in the lottery bowl marked *"Win a Bouquet, We Give Away One Every Day."*

Korea was pulling into her parking space before dark. She was proud of this unusual accomplishment, and beamed as she greeted Charlie O, the doorman.

"Hey, Miss Korea," Charlie O said, relieving her of all but the flowers as he held the door for her.

"Hey, back at cha," Korea chimed, with a wide-toothed grin. "How has the day treated you?"

"Well, Sister Korea, I'll tell you; I'm too blessed to be

stressed." Charlie O called for the elevator while Korea checked her box for mail.

"Amen to that," said the voice of Darlene Davenport, the front desk clerk. "Miss Korea," she stated plainly, holding an envelope on the tip of her fingers. "Message for you."

"Thanks," Korea said, taking the small pink envelope, smelling it, and smiling.

"Happy Birthday," Darlene Davenport said to Korea's back as she followed Charlie O into the elevator.

"Thanks again," Korea said, ripping the note open with her teeth. Inside the elevator, she read anxiously over a set of six instructions, written in red lip liner, feeling her heart race faster and faster. She stepped out of the elevator into her penthouse, thanked Charlie O, and sent him on his way with a ten-dollar tip. When the elevator doors closed and descended with the doorman inside, she dialed Martha.

"Martha, change of plans. Cancel all of my reservations for tonight."

"But Korea," Martha began with the usual personal interference that drove Korea nuts.

"Martha…"

"You really should spend tonight with Stormy, she misses you so, and…" Martha continued.

"Martha…" Korea attempted again.

"…it's been so long since you've treated her to anything…"

"Martha! Just do what I tell you to do!" Korea shouted into the phone before disconnecting the line.

Korea felt bad about having to fire Martha on Monday morning, since she was probably too old to find other work easily. But she was too nosey, and too involved in her personal affairs. But when Melody popped in with the winning bouquet, Martha had been replaced.

Inside the penthouse, Korea hung the dress and the suit in the coat closet, took the bouquet of flowers into the kitchen, and called out to Stormy. Hearing no answer, Korea smiled, ran some water into a large vase, and squeezed the stems through its tight neck.

Korea flipped the little note open again and read the first instruction.

#1. Don't attempt to find me. Until you have completed instructions 2 and 3.

#2. I have drawn a bath for you; submerge yourself in it.

#3. Dress yourself in all of the items that have been selected for you, for your erotic birthday evening.

#4. There is a limousine parked outside. Go to it. Get inside.

"Damn," Korea said to herself, remembering how she had found Stormy sitting in the limousine tied in rope with bondage knots.

Korea realized it had been hard to have sex without a little sadomasochistic action ever since that night. Stormy wasn't into it anymore, she could tell. But Melody liked it just fine.

It was Fantasy Friday. Every Friday morning before the office was open for business, Melody and her boss both arrived by 7:30 so they could jump-start their day and have at least a half-hour for role play. Melody never knew what to expect; Korea always came up with something new and innovative. She would dress in something hot and change into work clothing before the switchboard could forward her first call of the day.

Melody was wondering if her relationship with Korea would stay pure like it was now when she became her woman and her partner in the company as she stepped out of her white lycra panties in the office ladies' room to dress for today's fantasy. She spread them neatly on the baby changing table, pulled a red Sharpie from its top, and inscribed them *"Korea, you are the master of my fate, I am 4ever your slave—Melody."* She let them dry while she liberally applied red lipstick to her lips. Beside her name, she sealed her panties with a kiss. She smiled at the love note and stepped back into the panties.

Korea put her finger on the intercom button. "Melody?"

"Yes, Ms. Smith."

"Have you finished drafting that letter to the council-woman?"

"I'm putting your signature on it now."

"Do I have any appointments?"

"You have a one o'clock with Sally in Human Resources and a three o'clock with Mrs. Paris from the Council for the Prevention of Human Trafficking."

"Alright, come on in here. Leave your laptop."

Melody loved to hear those words: *leave your laptop*. She knew that when she did, she would be handling other business for Korea Smith. Melody had never been into women before, but Korea had her completely turned out. After their first time together, Melody had quit her fiancé of two years. She didn't give him a reason; she moved into the apartment Korea found for her, and got an unlisted number.

Theirs was the strangest and most interesting relationship Melody had ever had. Korea never asked her anything about herself and because of it, Melody never had to lie. Everything in this business was forthright because it had to be. Like the proposal she was typing now. Melody knew when she sealed it in the envelope and mailed it to Councilwoman Riley, it would generate another $650,000 contract for Project W.H.Y., but she also knew only part of that money would touch the community because the councilwoman would get her cut. But, as Korea had explained, if it weren't for Riley, Project W.H.Y. would not be able to provide any services at all.

So just like in business, Korea made sure their sex life together was as clear as crystal. There was not one thing that Melody would not do if Korea commanded her to. What she had with Korea was pure and honest. She respected that. When she had been with her man, it seemed that they were both always lying about something. Where they had been; who they were with; how much money they spent. It was one pile of crap after another. Melody knew as long as she kept the fantasies coming, she would have Korea Smith for herself in no time.

She walked into Korea's office wearing a low-cut red blouse, a white mini-skirt and red patent leather pumps.

"Didn't I tell you that kind of attire is completely in-appropriate for this office?"

"Yes."

"Yes what?"

"Yes, master," Melody said, dropping to her knees, keeping her eyes fixed on the floor.

Korea walked around her desk and sat on it. She lifted her cowboy boot off the floor and used the pointed tip to raise Melody's chin. "Lick it."

Melody opened her mouth and trailed the edge of Korea's boot with her tongue.

"Good girl. Now take off my boot." Korea was getting hot watching her. Her unquestioning obedience was a real turn-on. "The sock, too. Lay down, take off your panties, and give them to me." Melody did as she was told, holding back a smile. She lifted her skirt slowly so Korea could read what she had written to her. "Oh, isn't that sweet," Korea said. "Just take them off." Melody wiggled the panties down her hips and handed them to her Dom. Korea lifted the panties to her nose and inhaled as she inserted her toe into Melody's mouth. "Suck it."

Melody moaned and she sucked Korea's big toe, pushing it in and out of her mouth, licking the tip and then reaching with her tongue for the other toes. She opened her mouth wider until they were all inside, sucking and licking between them. Her hips were pumping against the air.

"Oh, you want something inside your hot little pussy, don't you?" Korea asked.

"Yes, master. Please fuck me."

"I'm not going to eat your stinky little pussy when you look like you've been on the stroll all night."

Korea walked to where Melody's feet lay and kicked her legs open. Stepping up to her hip, she ran her bare foot up Melody's thigh and slid her big toe down her slit until she felt her hole and pushed her toe inside of Melody's hot little box, and let her fuck her foot until she came.

"Thank you, master," Melody said gratefully.

"It's almost eight-thirty. Okay, go put your suit back on; we've got business to do. Pull the file on the Council for the Prevention of Human Trafficking and bring it to me. And call Sally from HR and find out what she wants to waste my time with now."

"Yes, Miss Smith." Melody lingered for a second too long.

"What is it?" Korea asked.

"Ugh, do you want me to help you with your boot?"

"That's over." Melody looked down at her panties in

Korea's hand and pointed. Korea looked down at her hand. "Oh, I'll keep these. They have my name on them."

"Got it," Melody said, scooting out of the door.

Korea took a long curious whiff of the panties again. She could tell by the scent of them that Melody had given up men. She hoped she wasn't getting serious.

KOREA'S CELL PHONE WAS BUZZING IN ITS HOLSTER. Korea answered. "Hey, baby, I was just thinking about you." She opened her desk drawer and dropped Melody's panties inside and closed it.

"Hey, guess what?" Stormy asked.

"You're making filet mignon, baked potatoes, and steamed broccoli for dinner?" Korea guessed.

"No. Well, not no, but, I mean, I will if you want me to, but that's not why I called."

"Okay, why don't you just go ahead and tell me?"

"Well, I got my first out-of-town assignment."

"What? No, you don't," Korea said.

"Yes, I do, isn't it great? Mr. Calloway offered me five hundred dollars, a hotel room, and an airline ticket and everything."

"I hope that Calloway guy, whoever he is, wasn't too disappointed when you explained to him that you won't be going, because you have a very busy, and a hard-working wife that you're responsible for taking care of, because she loves you and takes care of you so very well."

She paused for a reply, but none came. "Where did this guy want you to go flying off to anyway?"

"Just Los Angeles," Stormy said sadly. "It's only a forty-five-minute flight."

"Well, if that's the case, why didn't you just go, and come home before I did?"

"Because, I respect you, Korea, and I love you, and I wanted to share my good news with you."

Korea could hear the disappointment in her voice, but this hobby of hers was getting out of hand. "Look, Flower Bunny, you can't be this gullible. You can't go flying off to another city on some writing assignment you got over the Internet. That's as bad as answering an ad on Craigslist. You could get killed out there. You don't even know this person. If you need a holiday, take my car, take a friend, go shopping, go to the hot springs… I don't get you."

"You used to."

"You used to take care of me. Now I'm competing with your fucking computer. We need to discuss this when I get home. Thank you, Stormy. Thanks for calling me at the office and fucking up my day with some bullshit." Korea hung up before Stormy could even say goodbye. "Melody?" Korea said through the intercom.

"Yes, Ms. Smith?"

"Start me a file called Calloway. My wife writes an online food article for this guy's E-Zine called *The*

Cutting Table, or *The Cutting Room*, or something. Get me everything you can."

"Yes, Ms. Smith."

Melody typed: Cutting, Stormy, Food, Recipe, Cook, Calloway, into her Google search box and up popped "Stormy Talbert, The Cutting Board Critic."

Damn, Melody thought, *that bitch is fine*.

After reading a few of Stormy's articles, Melody realized that the lovely woman peering back at her through the computer screen was also talented and smart. Melody figured she would have to make herself indispensable, somehow, if she was going to snatch Korea from her.

She picked up the office phone and dialed the Human Resources Department. "Sally, please."

"This is Sally."

"Sally, this is Melody Toggle calling on behalf of Korea Smith. Ms. Smith's calendar is filling up so quickly that she asked me to move some things around for her. Perhaps your business with her is something I can handle for you."

"Well, I don't know," Sally said hesitantly into the phone. "It seems Martha, the woman who had your job before you, has filed a wrongful termination suit against Ms. Smith, and the lawyer contacted me just yesterday about turning over Martha's employment history records."

"Oh," Melody said, "I see. Allow me a half-hour to get back to you."

Melody hung up the phone and Googled: "Grounds

for wrongful termination." She read up on the topic before requesting permission to enter Korea's office.

She could feel an unfamiliar pining in her veins and a pounding in her heart as she stood before Korea in the simple black suit they had shopped for together at the Hilltop Mall. Korea had paid for it and the Kenneth Cole shoes on her feet. Melody was sure there was more to come, if she could just make herself very important to Korea's program.

"Well?" Korea asked. "Cat's got your tongue?"

Not yet, Melody thought, *but I'm working on letting your kitty snatch my tongue clean out of my head*. The thought of herself licking between Korea's chocolate thighs nearly knocked her off of her heels. She composed herself and explained the situation that Sally had described.

"Wrongful termination! What the fuck? That old bag was all in my business. Is this for real? Is this something she can win? Call my lawyer for me, Melody. Find out if this is something she can win."

"I don't think there will be any need to, Ms. Smith. I've done a little research and found that California is an 'at-will' employment state."

"What does that mean?"

"It means that you have the right to fire anyone you want, for any reason you desire."

"Good," Korea said, satisfied. "Then call my lawyer anyway and tell him that we know this, and we need him to prepare a response now, for whatever Martha plans on throwing at me. His number is in the Rolodex."

"Okay," Melody said. "Will that be all?"

"Yes, that will be all."

Melody wasn't sure what she was hoping for, but "that will be all" could not have been it.

THERE COMES A TIME IN EVERY SEXUAL LIFE, WHEN orgasm is not enough. In the beginning, Stormy's relationship with Korea was great and was guided by their mutual desire for, and commitment to, pure sexual satisfaction. Stormy knew nothing of giving head to women, and Korea was committed to keeping her ignorant. So Stormy settled comfortably in the downy soft palace of The Pillow Princess, finding comfort in the luxury of doing little more than cumming on the command of Korea's fingertips, tongue, lips, thighs, and fist.

For a while it was enough. But after a few years, she decided that if she was going to sacrifice her reputation by publicly claiming to be a lesbian, she was certainly not going to sacrifice her sexuality. Giving up this lover was not an option, so Stormy committed herself to keeping the bed heated with fantasies. But after their trip to Club X, Stormy feared she had awakened a brutal instinct in Korea that would never sleep again. They hadn't had sex without pulling, spitting, slapping, and name-calling in so long, Stormy regretted introducing her to the whole scene. Still, she blushed when she remembered the look on Korea's face when she got into that limousine and saw her in there all tied up in white cotton rope.

"Can you get yourself out of those knots?" Korea had asked her.

"No. Even if I could, I couldn't take them off unless you told me to. Tonight, you will be my master and I will be your slave."

"Oh? So that means you will do everything I ask you to?"

"Yes, master."

This is going to be fun, Korea thought as she tested the waters with a few commands to see if Stormy was going to truly be down. The driver took off and headed for San Francisco.

It was a smooth ride, full of giggles and games. Korea had removed all but the ropes on Stormy's hands by the time the limo came to a stop at the mouth of a dirty San Francisco alley. Korea walked the damp pathway decorated with garbage cans and sleeping bums, tugging on a leash that pulled Stormy along behind her. In front of them there were two huge red doors marked with a big X.

Could it be that what had gone down between the red walls of Club X had changed them both forever? Stormy thought, as she pulled the filet mignon from the broiler.

Stormy spread a smile across her face when the elevator arrived at the penthouse. She had decided to take Korea's advice and give her some tender love and care. She spent the afternoon cleaning the house and washing clothes. The penthouse smelled great and looked spotless when Korea stepped off the elevator into it.

"What's all this about going to L.A.?" Korea said as she hung her coat.

"Hi, honey!" Stormy called from the kitchen in a happy, bubbly voice.

"I repeat, what's all this business about going to L.A.?" Korea shouted over Michael Jackson on the stereo as she walked down the hallway to the kitchen.

"I want you to know that you don't have to worry about that anymore. I listened to you this morning and you're right. I should be about taking care of you. If I was taking care of you more, you would be fucking me more. Now, why don't you wash up for dinner? I just pulled your steak out of the oven."

"Can we talk about this some more over dinner?" Korea asked, suspicious of the woman's bubbly disposition.

"If you would like to, honey bunny, but really, there's no need. I understand that you're only trying to protect me. Besides, I thought you might want to eat alone in the den. The game's coming on. Your newspaper is in there waiting for you, too."

"Okay, what are you going to do right now?

"Me? I'm going to take a shower. I've been running around this house all day, cleaning and preparing for your arrival. I didn't make time to shower and I'm funky."

"Really, let me smell you. I like it when you're funky." Korea grabbed Stormy playfully, trying to smell her armpit.

"No, baby, I stink. Go to the den; I'm going to bring your plate to you."

"Okay, but don't get any of your funky armpit juice in my food," Korea joked.

Stormy plated Korea's meal and took it to her with a cold Miller Genuine Draft beer. Korea was already screaming at the referee.

Good, Stormy thought. *She'll be in there for hours.*

Stormy rushed to the shower, washed, and quickly dressed for bed. She ran into her room, and logged into her computer.

THECUTB: *Change of plans…I'll arrange my travel. Just drop the expense funds into my PayPal account*, she typed, then logged off, went to the kitchen, loaded the dishes into the dishwasher, and poured herself a glass of merlot. She expected to be asleep or carefree by the time Korea came in, either wanting rough sex or none at all.

When the game was over, Korea took her plate to the kitchen, rinsed it, and put it in the dishwasher. She had just dropped her beer bottle into the recycling bin when her cell phone rang. The name on the screen was "Melody Toggle." Korea didn't answer.

"Damn," she said out loud. "When will I learn? That bitch is out of pocket."

Korea could see that Stormy wasn't asleep yet when she walked through the room to the master bathroom, so she took an extra long time preparing for bed. Stormy wouldn't be down for continuing what Melody had aroused in her that morning. That sweet, missionary lovemaking shit didn't turn Korea on anymore. But Stormy was a good woman. Stormy was the best woman she had ever had.

CHAPTER 9

CALLING CARD

hawna couldn't help but to snicker when she looked at Hartford sitting in the passenger's seat of the SUV. The image of him getting fucked in the ass by a dirty white guy in the woods was still flashing in her head.

"What's so funny?" he asked, but the question went unanswered.

"Why does Daddy have to leave, again?" Raven asked her mother, as if Hartford wasn't even in the car.

"Because, baby, Daddy has to fly to Los Angeles to work, so that you can keep all of your nice things." Shawna pulled up to the curb at the Oakland Airport. "Girls, say goodbye to your father."

"Bye, Daddy," Alex said, reaching over the seat to hug her father's neck.

Alex had always been a charming and delightful girl. Hartford's first wife, Magenta, Alex's mother, had died nearly ten years ago. Through her long illness and hospitalization, Alex had been the rock that kept Hartford grounded. As Hartford held his daughter's arm, he realized it was hardly the arm of that small child who had sung "The Lord's Prayer" and prayed the 23rd Psalms over her mother's grave. No, she wasn't a little girl anymore. *Not at all*, he thought, as he squeezed her forearm to his neck and smelled his dead wife.

Momentarily startled, Hartford turned around and really looked at her for the first time in a very long time. Underneath immaturely applied makeup, there was a sad fifteen-year-old girl wearing a dead woman's perfume. But she smiled for him anyway. She always had a smile for her father.

"Anaïs," Alex said.

"Release me," her father answered.

It was a cherished and private moment for the pair, one that pre-dated everyone else in the car. It was their private ode to an endearing memory of Magenta floating around their brand-new house in one of her flowered dresses, leaving the scent of Anaïs in every room.

Hartford had given it to her when they had celebrated his first big break. Alex was still in diapers then. He took his first big check of $500,000 and put a down payment on their dream house on Monday morning. By Friday, they were on a weekend flight to Washington, D.C., aboard a private plane on loan from Jerome Bandarofski. Friday night, they had dined on one another. Saturday, it was French cuisine, *Henry and June* on a big screen, followed by another long sweaty celebratory romp at a quaint little bed and breakfast in Adams

Morgan. On Sunday morning, they had renewed their vows at Haines Point, near the statue of The Awakening. They had been struggling together since high school, living hand-to-mouth on two part-time jobs and a musical dream.

Anaïs Nin had been Magenta's favorite author. Magenta was the most supportive and most sensual woman Hartford had ever known. She gave all of herself to him; body, soul and imagination. During their brief life together, Hartford wanted for nothing outside of his family. He swore himself to her. He never once betrayed her. Not once. But, now here he was, leaving Shawna and his children to do just that, he hoped. His unhappiness was becoming more apparent in his house every day. And his last song, "You Only Love Once" said it all for him. It had earned ten times that first check. He owned his own foreign film theater and a chain of bed and breakfast inns that spread from Sonoma County to Santa Clara.

Shawna didn't care if Hartford was making the trip to have an orgy at Prince's mansion with Madonna and the Pope; she was still going to stay. As long as his mess didn't wind up at her house, she told herself, she could live with it. Besides, whenever she was really lonely, she had Peter, a little piece of her own that kept her quite satisfied with gifted hands that gave the most orgasmic yoni massages. Peter was only nineteen years old and still trying to pay back his student loans, so he worked very hard for the scraps she gave him from Hartford's table.

Shawna broke their tender father-daughter moment with the clearing of her throat. "You know, they're like vultures at this airport. I still have a ticket from the last trick you pulled on me in this very same spot." Checking her watch, she added, "Around this very same time." She flashed a knowing grin, noting the sloppiness of his pattern. Then, gesturing at Raven with a head nod, Shawna said, "Someone's got daggers for you."

"I'm just working," he said.

"Yeah, working me."

"You really ought to work on your insecurities, Shawna; they can be lethal. I keep telling you to start a business; get some hobbies. Maybe you wouldn't be so unhappy."

Hartford kissed his wife's hand, and stepped from the car onto the airport curb at passenger departures. He got his bag from the back of the SUV, then walked around the SUV to Raven's passenger window and knocked.

She hesitated at first, and then rolled it down. "Were you going to let your daddy leave without saying good-bye?"

"No," the little girl lied, squinting in the sun flooding past the dark tinted window into her eyes.

"Do you remember what I told you?" he asked.

Raven pretended to think about it before she answered solemnly, giving into the failure of her defiance. Hartford's youngest child, Raven, who would be eight years old on her next birthday, stood five feet tall, had budding breasts, and was spreading into teenaged hips. Her last visit to the doctor put her at a hundred twenty-five pounds. Hartford had grown up in a house full of women. His sisters, Dream Crow and Blue, had both become women very early. *And living with three bleeding bitches is nothing to take lightly*, he reminded himself. He would have to remember to tell Shawna to have the *girl talk* with her real soon. In comparison, Alex was petite, like her mother had been. She had gotten her period just last year.

"Always make your first words and last words your best words. Those are the ones people remember most," Raven quoted her father.

"Good girl." He kissed her on her soft red hair. "Now, this morning, I think your first words to me were…Oh, that's right. You didn't speak to me this morning, my bad. So that would make the first thing you said to me today, the word 'No.'"

"Hey, that's not fair, I…"

"I'm just making my point, sweetie. You know Daddy loves you. Be good to your sister, you hear? I'll be back soon." Hartford had noticed the tension growing between them, but he had no idea what it was like for Alex when he was away.

Raven seemed to perk up. "Have a safe trip, Daddy," she said cheerfully.

"That's so much better, baby," he said, stepping away

from the window. "Those are my girls!" Hartford said to the car as he walked away, waving with the back of his hand and disappearing behind automatic doors.

"Who does that?" Raven mumbled. "Who waves with the back of their hand and expects you to take them seriously?"Alex rolled her eyes at her little sister and put her headset on. "What the fuck is so funny?"

"You."

"Hey, no cursing," Shawna said.

"Is that all you are going to say to her? No cursing?" Alex asked.

"Oh, Alex, be patient with your little sister; she's going through so much emotionally and physically. You've been there. I was patient with you."

"Yeah, bitch, I'm just emotional," Raven said under her breath, but loud enough to be heard.

"She just called me a bitch," Alex complained.

"She's hormonal."

"Then again maybe she wasn't talking to me. Hmm. She's not going through anything; she's just bad, Shawna."

"And just when did you start calling me by my first name, young lady?"

"At least I didn't call you a bitch," Alex snapped. "...Mom," she added for effect.

"Raven, baby, won't you get out and come around and take your father's seat before this policeman comes over here and gives us a ticket."

Raven darted her eyes at her sister who was tuning

her out, raising the volume of Bob Marley in her ears when Raven suddenly snatched the iPod. "Let me see that, it's my turn."

The older girl stared at her younger sister like she had gone mad. "Are you crazy?"

"Raven, honey, hop in the front seat and give the iPod back; that cop is going to come over here."

"Why does she get all the good stuff? It's my turn! You've been using it all morning."

"Give it back to me, Raven."

"No, you are too goddamned stingy with everything, I'm sick of you. You're a terrible sister." Raven held the iPod in the air, trying to keep it away from Alex who refused to play the childish game that had once amused her.

"I don't have to take what is already mine," Alex said, snatching it back. "It's my iPod; you don't get a turn. You don't get a turn with anything that's mine."

"I hate you," Raven said. "I really hate you." The young girl's green eyes were becoming brown and glazing over.

"Yeah, I know. Just leap, little tadpole, if you're feeling froggish. I think what you need to do is hop your wide ass in that front seat, before I start to whooping on it. Don't think for one second, because I'm not all bloated with fast-food chain hormones, that I can't hurt you."

"I don't have to fight you to hurt you."

"What are you talking about, you little demon?"

"You just be careful what you eat."

"Hey! Stop it, you two!" Shawna screamed. "Put your seatbelts on, right this moment, so we can get out of here."

Raven opened her door slowly.

"Close the door, baby; just put your seatbelt on," Shawna said.

Raven stepped from the SUV, and then slammed the door.

In the few loaded moments from the time the door shut, the police officer who had been eyeing Shawna and her children stepped from the curb, headed directly toward the SUV.

Shawna welcomed the flood of nervous excitement as she watched the tall, handsome man stepping toward her in his Oakland Police Department uniform.

What is it about uniforms? she was thinking when Alex interrupted her naughty thoughts.

"You should pull off and leave her," Alex suggested.

Shawna looked back at Alex angrily. "I don't leave my children," she said with her teeth clenched and her jaws tight.

Alex was taken aback momentarily as a thick, choking kind of silence filled the vehicle; she swallowed hard, looking for air. Then, rolling her window down, she said, "Wow, really? Bite my tongue out, why don't you? I only meant for you to circle the airport, to teach her a lesson. She's going to make you get a ticket on purpose." Alex knew that Shawna's mother had abandoned her as a child, but it wasn't something they talked about. "I promise that's all I meant. I wasn't trying to say anything about your mother, or what happened to you, or anything like that; I swear."

"Don't be ridiculous," Shawna said. "I don't even know what you're talking about. You need to shut up, now, okay? Just shut it up." The mood of her eyes had suddenly turned from anger to sadness. She was avoiding eye contact with Alex, but Alex could see them in the rearview mirror.

"I'm sorry," Alex said.

Shawna didn't say anything; she searched for Raven in her rearview mirror and refreshed her lip gloss for the handsome cop headed her way.

RAVEN HAD WALKED SO SLOWLY AROUND THE SUV that the cop beat her to it. "Driver's license and registration," he was saying into Shawna's window as Raven climbed into the passenger's seat. He was already writing the ticket. He was fine. Just looking at him was making Shawna feel a whole lot better.

"Officer, I was just pulling off." He kept writing. "Come on, have a heart for a struggling mother." This time he looked at her, paused, and then kept writing. "My, you're so big. Are you any relation to Paul?" she asked coyly into his monstrous chest, reading his badge. "Officer Robeson?" Her movements were slow and animated as she shifted her shoulders toward him and touched his arm.

"Don't touch me, ma'am; I could take you in for assault."

He spoke so robotically, Shawna couldn't tell if he was one of those anal retentive asshole cops, or a fag, but he was pissing her off. "I don't know a Paul Robeson," he said. Then the tall milk chocolate-colored police officer answered her flirtation with a slowly enunciated, "Driver's license and registration, please."

Alex watched from the back seat as Shawna regressed into erotic protest. Opening the single button that concealed her cleavage, she huffed and reached for the glove compartment.

Maybe marrying a musician was a bad idea for a woman with abandonment issues, Alex thought to herself as she watched Shawna self-medicate with attention. They weren't close at all, but Alex was learning a lot from Shawna.

"Oh, please, Officer Robeson, you're getting me all upset. You can see these girls are giving me a hard time. I know you were watching." Shawna readjusted herself in her seat, pushing her breasts forward, and handed the cop her documents.

"Girls?" Officer Robeson inquired, not sure if the woman was referring to the voluptuous breasts bulging from a shirt that strained to hold them in place, or the two young girls in the car, who were now silent and pretending not to be paying attention to their mother.

"I know you're not going to give me a ticket when I simply couldn't pull away from the curb without having them in their seatbelts."

"It's all about discipline. It comes with the job," he continued, pompously adding, "at least that is what I hear."

"Oh, you mean to tell me a handsome man like you doesn't have children?"

"Not unless you count whiny traffic violators." Shawna laughed a little too long at his joke. "I'm a lawman," he said to Shawna, ripping a ticket off the pad, and handing it to her. "I'm not cut out to be a...what do they call it these days?" He searched insincerely for the urban term, *"baby daddy."* "There are rules that must be adhered to in every circumstance when it comes to that. I only have one rule, and it's non-negotiable."

"What rule is that?"

"Safety first."

The officer poked his head into the SUV and looked at Raven and then at Alex. "Hey, ladies," he said, "give your mom a break. You could make her wreck. You girls strap up and have a nice day."

"Uh, thank you, officer, but..." Shawna stopped him in his tracks. "I need some advice. I mean, in cases like mine, for example; a traveling husband, ungrateful children, and this stress and tension in my shoulders. Perhaps I could not safely pull away from the curb? I have so many tickets. I'm not asking you to fix them or anything, but if I was to dispute this one, and you didn't show up to court, it would go away, right? That's what the last officer who gave me a ticket told me."

"Oh, another officer told you that, huh? Did you get his name?"

Shawna opened her wallet and pulled out a card. "Officer J. Davis. Do you know him?"

"Very, very well," Robeson said, smiling so brightly his face became new.

"I couldn't afford for my husband to ban me from driving, because of all of these tickets. Maybe the three of us can talk about how to clear up all of them. I'm just a housewife, so the most I can offer is a little civil service."

"I'll mention it to him at our next ball game, and see what he says."

"Really? Oh thank you," Shawna gleamed. "Are you on the same team?"

"You can definitely say that."

Who do they think they are fooling? Alex thought. *Is that supposed to be code talk?*

"I'm a full-time homemaker, like I said. I don't have a business card, but here's my calling card. Call me with your ideas."

When Shawna pulled away from the curb, Raven watched the cop slip the number into his wallet. "Mommy, we have plenty of money to pay those tickets. Why do you need him to help you?"

"Baby, ever since nine-eleven, they've gotten carried away with security. It's a plot to rob people. If they didn't want you parking here, they simply wouldn't allow you to. There would be a place to stop yards back, and a controlled shuttle service or a tram for travelers. I absolutely refuse to pay airport tickets. It's a matter of principle."

"Or not," Alex muttered, sticking her earphone jack back into her iPod and returning to Kingston.

CHAPTER 10

THE HOUSE OF CROWS

Hartford stood in baggage claim at the Burbank Airport, reading a text message from the woman who was supposed to be doing him a favor right now. She was forty-five minutes late.

I thought about what u want. No can do. Not into reverse ass play. Let's just stay friends. I have an idea for u though. I shoot at the Playboy Studio 2day. Come through. Don't fake, I'm leaving your name at the gate.

Damn, Hartford thought. He had figured that since she was a porn star, Sweet P would be down for a rim job and a little finger action. He had told her what happened in the doctor's office, and she seemed to know exactly what he was talking about. Over the phone, she had said she knew plenty of guys that liked getting their asses played with. But shoving her finger in his ass had obviously freaked her out. *Damn*, he said to himself as he flagged down an idle Town Car.

"3030 Andrita Street," he told the driver.

It was a long ride in bumper-to-bumper traffic. Hartford stared out of the window at the smoggy Los

Angeles sky, thinking about Shawna. She was going to have to make some changes quick, or he was going to divorce her; even if he didn't find another woman first.

Hell, I can always hire a nanny, he told himself.

Playboy Studios was a den of adult amusement. A parade of half-naked women skipped down the hallway as he walked through, following the sexy receptionist who led him to the set, where the show would be filmed and broadcast live. Sweet P and five other women were doing a run-through as the director warned them that they were not to actually put their tongues on each other's private parts, or they would be dismissed immediately. The bunnies looked like nuclear wives, fresh out of the 50's, in their slippers, robes, and gigantic rollers as they rehearsed for the show. There were six bunnies on a platform and two naked hosts on the couch behind them, laughing and playing like giddy teenagers at a sleep- over.

Hartford was nibbling on cheese and crackers at the catering table when the sultry voice of Sweet P spilled over his shoulder. "What's up, Hartford?"

She was six feet tall, standing two inches above him in her platform boots. Her face was an experimental canvas of blues, pinks, and reds. All that had not been sharply contoured away from her fleshy baby face was the famous pink pout that pedophiles jacked off to.

"It's all good," Hartford said, wanting to address the text message, but not wanting to dwell on it.

"I want you to know, I'm not judging you. It's just not my thing."

"Yeah, yeah. I can dig it."

Sweet P sighed. "We tape for half an hour. You're going to stay and watch, right?"

"That's what I'm here for. Oh, and uh, were you able to set up a meeting for me with Playboy Radio?"

"Yes. Farrell has some time to meet with you after we shoot. You can talk while I get dressed, and then I have a surprise for you."

"What kind of surprise?"

"A good one," Sweet P said with a giggle. "I called a friend of mine. She's a massage therapist. She has a slot open this evening. I can go there with you right after this is over."

Hartford didn't really know what she was driving at, but he didn't have any appointments until the next day, so he had no objections.

"It's all good," he said again.

"It will be," she said, dismissing herself to a group of Playboy Bunnies who had been transformed from nuclear wives to sex kittens, ready to paw and lick on command for horny callers who masturbated over televised phone calls.

Hartford relaxed into his front row seat and watched the beautiful bodies climbing all over one another, licking and nibbling, spanking and stroking. Men and women, young and old, called in with true confessions and fantasies. Some pleaded desperately with the hosts to lick each other's titties; others wanted to be talked dirty to or ordered around. All of them gave detailed descriptions as they brought themselves to climax.

Hartford wondered how the cameramen managed to keep their dicks down; he was definitely hard. He adjusted himself.

"First time, huh?" a blue-eyed young man holding the boom microphone asked, and winked suggestively. "It's easier if you look at it as art. Porn is art, you know?"

"Uh, yeah, I know. I can respect it," Hartford said, not sure that he could.

His dick was beginning to leak and he wasn't sure how much more he could take when, thankfully, the directly yelled, "Cut! That's a wrap, ladies!"

There were six or seven men waiting patiently by the entrance door at the end of the hall. They were boyfriends or husbands of the playmates who quietly talked among themselves as, one by one, the little bunnies popped out to greet them. Hartford wondered how these men could be with women who made their living by fucking other men.

Just then, as before, the blue-eyed boom boy read his mind and answered, "It's easy if you look at it as art. I have some incredible pieces in my office. Would you like to come inside?" Beyond the door the boom boy held open, he could see a blue light flooding the room and illuminating the mounted image of a man with a bullwhip shoved up his ass. "It's Mapplethorpe," he said. "It's widely respected art, I promise," young blue eyes said with a fading glimmer of hopefulness as his nemesis stepped into his scene.

"Are you after one of my men again?" Sweet P asked, wrapping her hands around Hartford's waist from behind.

"Bitch!" the boom boy spat, disappearing to his room with a snap of his finger.

"Hey, let's get you over to the radio station, before Farrell's next program starts," Sweet P said, grabbing her friend by the hand.

"Cool."

"Hey, do you have some music in mind? He's really serious about making a splash with Playboy Radio. You should hear the lonely truck drivers who call in."

"I have some fresh new producers who may have some music that he'd like to throw in rotation. I'm meeting with them this weekend to check out their stuff. Maybe you'd like to come along. I need to make sure their heads are on straight."

"Sure. You need me to fuck somebody?"

"No, not this time; I just need you to meet me there."

"I HATE IT AT AUNT BLUE'S HOUSE," Raven complained as she packed an overnight bag with two nights of clothing.

"It's Dream Crow's house. The whole place, even the animals, are hers. Aunt Blue just lives there," Alex informed her.

"So what? It stinks."

"That's sage."

"What's sage?"

"The smell in her house."

"You mean she makes it smell like that on purpose?"

"I guess. It's supposed to be for cleaning."

"She needs to get some bleach for that."

"Not that kind of cleaning. It's kind of like to get rid of evil spirits or something."

"I don't like it."

"Maybe you're an evil spirit," Alex said, zipping her laptop into its case. "It doesn't bother me."

"Maybe you're stupid," Raven snapped back at her sister, grabbing her jacket. "I think she's weird. I don't like her, or the way her house smells."

"She probably doesn't like you either. Let's go. Your mom is waiting for us."

"I don't need you to tell me what to do. Don't you think I know that *my* mommy is waiting?"

Shawna honked the horn again. She couldn't wait to get rid of the kids. She had some hot cop ass to get, and those fussy little wenches were moving too slow.

Raven and Alex came out of the house. Alex locked the door and Raven headed down the stairs. From the top of the stairs, the little girl could see her impatient mother in the running SUV, her knuckles white as she gripped the steering wheel and revved the engine.

Raven walked deliberately slowly down the stairs. "We're coming, Mommy!" Alex pushed her to get her to move faster. "Stop before you make me fall down the stairs," Raven whined.

"Walk faster. You see that she's waiting."

"Make me."

"Why do you still call her 'Mommy?' You aren't three years old anymore, you know."

"You're just mad because she's not your mommy," Raven said.

"That's a laugh," Alex said.

"You're just mad because your mother's dead."

"I hate you."

When the little girl reached the bottom of the stairs, she turned around and looked at Alex with cold, old eyes. "You should hate yourself. You should hate yourself because you're weak and stupid, just like your mother was!" Then she turned around and ran to the back door of the SUV, swung the door open, tossed her bag in, and jumped inside, slamming the door behind her. But before she could lock the door, Alex was on her, pulling her hair.

"Take it back! Take it back!" Alex screamed.

"Stop it, Alex!" Shawna said. "Get your hands off of her!"

Alex felt Shawna smacking her head. "Ouch, that hurt," Alex said, releasing her grip on the younger child.

"Good," she said, "now you see how it feels to have someone bigger than you hit you."

"You don't even know what happened."

"I don't need to. Just get in the damn truck. I don't have time for all this nonsense today."

"But you don't know what she said."

"And I don't care. Get in the truck," Shawna said.

Alex tightened her eyes, looking at Raven as if to warn her that there was a whole lot more where that came from. She picked her suitcase up off of the ground and threw it the back seat, hard, landing it smack into the side of Raven's head.

Raven started to cry. "Mommy, she threw that bag at me."

When Alex got into the front seat, Shawn back-handed her. "Didn't I tell you not to touch my child? Don't start that shit. Not today. Shut up! Both of you just shut the fuck up!" Shawna revved up the engine of her SUV, turned on the radio, and backed out of the driveway. She was speeding down the hill to the freeway. "I can't wait to drop you little heifers off! I need a damn break."

THE CROW SISTERS SAT ON THE BACK PORCH of the Bandarofski estate overlooking the farmland that spread as far as their eyes could see. Dream Crow seemed to have aged quickly after her husband died. Her beautiful light brown eyes had weakened over time and now she needed glasses to see two feet in front of her. She was still a beautiful woman, underneath her sadness, but the zesty excitement that had once made her the belle of every Bandarofski Ball had been buried with her husband. She moved slowly now. She spoke carefully now. She sipped sweet tea while Blue nursed an afternoon Bloody Mary.

Blue had always been an old soul. She had seen more than her share of bad things, and didn't mind at all that her eyes were clouding over. The doctor had told her it was probably caused by her diabetes, and dehydration. Their mother had been completely blind when she died.

"Sister Blue, do you miss your old life?" Dream Crow asked her.

"Working at the hospital, you mean?"

"Yes. Do you miss it?"

"Sometimes I do," she answered her sister. "Then again," she said slowly and thoughtfully, "sometimes I don't."

"What do you miss the most?"

"I used to miss caring for people. But now that Jerome's gone, I have you to care for."

"What don't you miss?"

"Well, Dream Crow, you can put it like this, I couldn't have been more ready to leave San Francisco General when you called to bring me to L.A. to sing with you. I wasn't out to be a star or anything, but entertainment was a far cry from all the ugly I saw in the streets of San Francisco. You know, they had me nursing on children who had been beaten and abused and mistreated so badly, Jesus would have jumped off the cross to whip their parents' asses, and the world be damned."

"Sister Blue, you're a mess. Now you know the good Lord wouldn't do any such thing."

"For a while, there was a wave of some really weird stuff going on, too," she continued remembering. "It was like people had gotten hold of some crazy drug that was completely distorting their sense of right and wrong. In a year's time, I treated at least seven of the same kinds of cases. They were severely malnourished children who had been locked in their rooms and bathrooms for months, sometimes years, at a time. They had lesions, lice, and worms from where they had been left in filth. They smelled from the inside out, like their insides had rotted. You would think people would need to pass a test to have children, just like you have to pass one to drive a car, or to graduate college. That's why I never thought twice about having children of my own. There's just too much ugly. Who knows what their husband or wife might do to their children for kicks?"

"Sister Blue, you have to have sex before you have children."

"Oh, don't you start in on me now; I've had sex." Blue sipped and stirred the celery stick in her drink to remix the red potion that was beginning to separate in her glass. "Well, I've almost had sex; plenty of times."

The women laughed for a moment, and then Blue became suddenly serious.

"Sex is just plain over-rated. And it's misused. You should know that better than anyone, Dream Crow."

There was a moment of somber reflection as they both thought of Seth.

"Sister?"

"Hmm?"

"You know me and Hartford always knew about you and him, right?"

"I realized that Hartford knew. He'd seen us together. I did try to keep it from you, though. How did you know?"

"He told me."

"Hartford?"

"No, Seth."

"Why did he do that?"

"Why do you think? So I'd feel all right about replacing you. It was just a few days after you were gone. He was missing you bad. He cried a lot and stayed high. Hartford was worried that if he made Seth leave, the county would come for us, so we let him stay." Blue sipped her drink and continued to speak. "He wasn't trying to rape me or anything. He just tried to get me to agree to be with him, is all."

"Did he ever…"

"Hold your tongue! I wasn't having it. I told him the only way I would have his dick was in a jar. It wasn't long before he left on his own."

"I'm glad he didn't do anything to you. I never thought he was a bad man. I loved him, as sick as it sounds. Not the way I loved Jerome. It wasn't pure like that. I loved him for taking care of Momma and making sure we didn't end up on the street. You know, if it weren't for Seth, we'd have probably ended up split apart in foster homes. You were too young to remember all the men who were taking advantage of Momma when Daddy died. She was lonely back then. They were taking her money, fucking her, and taking food right out of the refrigerator to take home to their own children."

"Imagine that," Blue said. "No, I didn't know. Did Momma know about the two of you?"

"Not at first. When she figured it out, she just stopped talking." The sisters were silent for a while, sipping and remembering.

"You want me to make you another drink?" Dream Crow asked.

"No, I'm okay," Blue said. "I want you to know that even though I didn't understand it, I never judged you for it. Still, it kind of soured me on the whole idea of sex. Even when I became a woman and finished the nursing program you put me through, I still didn't want to give myself to anyone. It seemed to me it was more trouble than it was worth. Every last one of my nursing school friends dropped out because they were either pregnant or their man wanted them to take a job, move in, shack up, be in love... Sex was a damn disease in my book."

"What about love?"

"Love? Ha! What about it? Truth be told, I might've been less afraid of the sex than I was of love. Sex is a byproduct of that contagion. Now, if I had been out there like you were for a time, dealing with sex like a business, I might've been all right. But with love comes all the rest of the symptoms."

"You mean butterflies and that nervousness that makes you feel kind of out of control. That's why I say I didn't love Seth like I loved Jerome. Jerome made my hands sweat. He made my whole body catch on fire sometimes."

"That old man?"

"You'd better believe it."

"It sure will make you hot all right. Hot enough to kill a man," Blue said.

Dream Crow laughed. "I guess."

"Did I ever tell you about my VOYA theory?"

"VOYA theory? No, I don't think so."

"Love is a virus," Blue said. "It's a deceptive virus that works in conjunction with the object of your affection. See? VOYA, Viral Object of Your Affection. When you're first infected, you don't know that you're sick at all. You actually think you're feeling suddenly great. You have more energy, you're happier than you had been before, and it's easier to breathe now that you have VOYA. But what you think has been the antidote to your former condition is actually the venom of a virus that can be fatal if it isn't treated properly. There's no cure for it and once it's inside you, it must run its course.

"Now this is the important part, because your resistance to love and your recovery from the viral infection will depend on the interactions that occur between the virus and you, the host. The host cells are primarily located in the brain and the reproductive area and are carried through the nervous system to the heart, where it is spread throughout your entire body. For women, the symptoms start to show soon after the virus gains entry and binds to vaginal receptors. How quickly it spreads from there may depend on the frequency and intensity of her orgasms, but the virus has been known to spread rapidly; even when no orgasm has occurred. The first indication that the side effects have begun is the patient's acute inability to recognize logical fallacies, erroneous statements, or to do background checks. Your cerebrospinal fluid, the fluid your brain floats in, has been completely infested with the virus so you feel dreamy and are dazzled and short-sighted, not being able to see further than your VOYA. It's during this period that most patients begin to form several psychoses such as general ignorance, jealousy, confusion, stupidity, and paranoia. You may experience peevishness, becoming quick to anger, or fight with family and friends who recognize your condition and try to offer advice for treatment of VOYA, or quick to forgive and excuse your VOYA. Those who survive the infant stages of the viral contagion, especially those with good credit, may suffer from something called Cosignatory. This is the worst side effect that may bring your Credit Cell count down to poverty levels. Some hosts may also get an extreme outbreak of UHaulism, which is not all together bad because it increases the speed at which you are likely to recover, putting VOYA at a closer range for observation.

"Usually the virus begins to dissipate as binding to vaginal receptors ceases. Following this period, a condition called Infidelity sets in. Some of the side effects that will indicate you're entering the Infidelity phase of VOYA may include, but are not limited to, denial, weight gain, weight loss, skin rashes, loss of hair, insomnia, irrationality, feelings of self-worthlessness, alcoholism, drug use, drunken calling/texting, depression, acts of vandalism, and covert operations. In some cases, hospitalization is necessary. In the worst cases, death occurs.

"The Infidelity phase can be one of the most painful phases of VOYA, but it's often the final phase, and when treated with the CO Solution, recovery is eminent. The CO Solution was actually created with antibodies from VOYA and spliced from one of its less common side effects, Covert Operations. Of all of the side effects that will or may occur during the Infidelity period, Covert Operations is the least harmful as it can bring clarity where there had been only speculation. The term 'Seeing is believing' is the national campaign slogan for the VOYA Recovery Project. Our program encourages patients to move their condition to the CO stage as early as possible to reduce infection time. It is important to note that CO should not be performed alone as it can worsen your condition causing Blind Rage—an onslaught of many or all of the other side effects combined. When performed with companionship, CO can create a great support system. Bonding with lost friends and loved ones who are happy to assist you in your recovery as you spy together under the cover of night can be the first step to a happy life after VOYA."

Dream Crow was laughing her ass off the entire time Blue was speaking. "Now you know you don't have a damn bit of sense," Dream Crow said. "You missed your calling. You should have been a comedienne."

"You asked me if I miss my old life and I have to say, I got tired of seeing those children like that. I got tired of bandaging streetwalkers from the Tenderloin. They were getting younger and younger every day. I don't miss looking at all the ugly; ugly things can make your eyes hard. It's probably why I'm half blind now."

"You can say that again," Dream Crow said, pushing her glasses up on her nose, thinking of the little girl she had brought in with needle marks all over her body.

"Remember your little friend. What did you call her?"

"Pillow."

"Yes, Pillow," Blue said. "She was a real pretty little girl under all of that makeup. We did what we could for her, you know."

"I knew you would."

"They didn't know a lot about AIDS back then and

there was hardly any money for medications, if you were poor. It was a shame, the way she went out. It would've hurt your heart. Her hair fell out, until there were just patches left. She had purple lesions all over her body and looked like an old woman in the face. When they lifted her dead body off the bed, there were pieces of her skin stuck to the sheets."

"Oh my God," Dream Crow said. "I'm so sorry you had to see that. God rest her little soul."

"So, I guess the answer is no, Dream Crow, I don't miss it at all. I don't miss any of it. And I thank you kindly for getting me out."

"I am your sister. I practically raised you. How could I even think of leaving you there?"

"I'm glad you found love in the old man. You really deserved it."

"So do you, Sister Blue. It's not too late, you know."

"I'm fine, right here with you. Right here with you and that pig over there, and the horses, and even that ornery old goat you have."

"That was Jerome's goat. He sure loved that stubborn thing."

"Well, now it all makes sense."

"What do you mean?"

"A man that could love an old stubborn, stinky goat wouldn't have any trouble at all loving you."

"That's so cold, Sister Blue. Are you trying to say I stink?"

They laughed together and talked a while longer until

Dream Crow broke the devastating news that sent Blue into a tizzy. "I guess we better get ready then," she said.

"Get ready? Get ready for what?

"Hartford's children are coming over."

"What!" Blue screamed. "Both of them?"

"I'm afraid so. Hartford called last night. He's in L.A. The wife called this morning."

"I'll take you up on your offer now."

"What offer?"

"You can mix me another Bloody Mary. Lord, have mercy," Blue said, getting up out of her seat. "I've got to go clean this house."

BLUE HAD FINISHED CLEANING THE HOUSE and two more cocktails when the security guard phoned with news of visitors.

"Well, well, well. Who do we have here?" Blue said, looking at her brother's children standing in the foyer. "Dream Crow, come see your little nieces," she called to her sister in the kitchen.

"Don't leave them outside, Sister Blue; let them in. I'm making an early dinner. I hope you guys are hungry!" Dream Crow shouted from the kitchen.

"It smells great," Shawna said.

"No, it doesn't," Raven said under her breath, but Blue heard her.

"Hello, Shawna," Blue said absently. "What did you say, Raven?"

"Nothing."

"Yes, you said something. What was it?"

"I think I'm allergic to that stuff you burn."

"The sage? Oh, yes, you probably are. Well, girls, you look lovely. Take off your shoes and coats, wash your hands, and help your aunt set the table. Okay?"

"Okay," Alex said. "Bye," Alex said in her stepmother's general direction as she stepped out of her shoes, took off her coat, and hung it on the coat rack.

"What, no hug?" Shawna said to Alex.

"Not right now; I have a headache," she snapped and turned on her heels. "Auntie Dream, I'm coming to help you!" She disappeared down the hall.

"Okay, baby. Stop in the bathroom and wash your hands," Dream Crow called back to her. "I've got cabbage in the sink for you to wash."

Blue watched carefully as Shawna helped Raven wiggle out of her coat. "Umm-hmm," Blue began humming an old gospel hymn to herself and walked over to the little table just inside the door. She uncovered her sage, pulled a lighter from her bosom, and put a flame to the leaves until the embers burned hot.

"Come on in," she told Raven. Blue went in for a closer look. "Let me look at you," she said, raising the little girl's face so that their eyes met. Raven looked away. "Don't be frightened of me, girl; I'm your blood. What is it? Do my eyes scare you?"

"No," Raven said, finally focusing on the woman's eyes. "I'm not afraid of you."

"Well," Shawna said, in a high-pitched superficial tone that broke the pregnant silence in the smoky doorway. "I'll be back to get them Sunday."

"Bye, Mommy." Raven hugged her mother's neck tightly.

"Well," Blue said, "go on and get washed up for dinner." Then to Shawna, she said, "Please stay by your phone."

CHAPTER 11

AN ACQUIRED TASTE

Korea may not have been thinking clearly after an unforgettable session of Fantasy Friday with Melody, but she was certain that she would be sending Stormy packing before Christmas if things didn't get spicy between them soon. The exotic dance the young woman had performed for her would have been enough to keep the voyeur's interest for a few more weeks, but when Melody lay down on her office floor and pulled six feet of pearls from her pussy, Korea had been hypnotized. So, she had accepted Melody's dinner invitation, to see if she had the other stuff it would take to be her woman. She definitely had heart and had proven she could be an obedient little bitch. Korea figured it couldn't hurt to check her out. She was, after all, in complete control when it came to Melody.

But something in her gut was gnawing at her belly walls as she lied on Stormy's voicemail. "Hey, beautiful, don't wait up for me; I have a meeting that could last for quite a while tonight."

Stormy was on a southbound plane when the message came.

Melody couldn't believe how nervous she was, waiting for Korea to come over. She had made dinner as soon as she had arrived home from the office. She had showered and douched twice, just in case Korea decided to put her lips and tongue to her cat. After the morning they had had together, she was sure Korea was considering her a contender for the role of Mrs. Smith. She had carefully strategized every moment of their weekly rendezvous. The look on Korea's face as she watched her slowly inching a long string of pearls from her pussy was priceless.

"I bet the old bitch came in her boxers," Melody said as she primped in the mirror.

Melody looked delicious in her tight shorts and half-tee as she opened the door and led Korea to the living room.

"Have a seat," Melody said proudly. "Dinner is ready. I just have to make you a plate."

Korea sat down and looked around at the cluttered little apartment. There were candy wrappers balled up on the couch beside her, fingerprints on the television screen, and ashes piled up in the fireplace. There were pictures in paper frames on the mantle of Melody and other young women at various nightclubs. There was a large collection of music CDs and a modest library of romance novels.

"I'm so glad you're finally here," Melody said from the kitchen. "When you got this place for me, I thought it meant you were going to be coming over a lot."

"Is that what you thought?" Korea said coolly. She had walked to the kitchen door and was watching Melody's round tight ass as she bent over and pulled a pan from the oven.

"Oh, you startled me," Melody said. "I didn't see you standing there. Oh well, you might as well have a seat here at the table." Melody prepared Korea's plate and brought it to her with a proud bright smile. "Whew!" she said, turning off the oven. "I haven't cooked like that in a long time." She pulled a beer can from the cabinet and returned to the table with a glass of ice. "You want me to pour that for you?"

Korea was speechless. She had to taste it to believe it. She sat at the kitchen table, poking a rubbery turkey wing with her fork. Next to it was a lump of gummy white rice. Both the turkey and the rice were covered in a lumpy white gravy that tasted like raw dough. The only thing on her plate with any color was the frozen chopped broccoli that had not been left in the micro-wave long enough. It was unseasoned and still cold in the center.

"I like to make sure my vegetables keep their vitamins," Melody said, sitting down with a saucer of broccoli across from Korea. "That's why I don't overcook them like some women do." Melody fed herself some broccoli. "Don't be shy. Dig in," she said. Korea looked at her plate in disbelief. "Oh snap, I almost forgot the garlic bread."

Melody made a trip to her toaster oven and returned with two toasted slices of white bread that had been seasoned with margarine and garlic salt.

"This is the worst food I've ever tasted," Korea said. "I can't believe you had the nerve to serve this."

Thinking they were beginning a role-play game, Melody said, "I'm sorry, master."

"I have to go," Korea said. "What the hell was I thinking? This shit is ridiculous."

"No, don't leave. Please, don't leave." Melody followed her to the door. "I can order a pizza. Please stop. I can do better; I'll do anything." Melody snatched her T-shirt over her head and flung her body against the front door, blocking it so Korea would not leave. "Listen," she said, squeezing her nipples. "You can do anything you want to me if you stay. You can punish me if you want to. You can beat me," she said in a throaty tone.

She grabbed Korea's wrist and struck herself across the cheek with her boss' hand. "You can do the nastiest shit you can think of and I will only ask for more. Trust me, Daddy, you don't want to leave. I've got rubber sheets on my bed, and a taste for a golden shower."

"Melody, all that sounds good, but I'm a little disgusted and hungry right now. I'm going home to get a real meal. So, I'm going to have to get with you another time."

"Your wife can cook, but is she going to let you piss in her mouth?" Korea became still for a moment. "I didn't think so," Melody continued. "She's probably not back yet, anyway."

"What are you talking about?"

"Your wife is probably not back from her writing assignment." The stunned look on Korea's face told Melody that she hadn't known. "You told me to keep track of her. I talked to one of the editors this morning. She's in Los Angeles."

"Fuck that!" Korea said, attempting to open the door.

Melody threw herself at her feet. "You should stay. Teach her a lesson. Please don't go, master," she said, holding her ankle. "Teach her a lesson. Come on!" Melody unzipped her shorts. "Come on, Daddy; teach her a lesson. Use me!" She stuck her hand down in her shorts and rubbed her pussy. "Use me," she repeated as she fucked her fingers. She could feel Korea breaking down.

Korea looked at the woman groveling on the floor. She pulled her cell phone from her pocket and dialed Stormy's number.

"Oh shit," Stormy said, looking at the incoming call. She was already in line at the Southwest counter. The PA system was spouting off every few minutes, so Stormy jumped out of line and headed for the door, unaware that she had already pressed the answer button.

"Hello?" Stormy said when she got outside.

Korea listened to the sounds of an airport in the background. "This is a homeland security advisory notice."

Korea hung up the phone. "Bring your nasty ass in here, bitch," she said to Melody, grabbing her by the hair.

Melody held on to her wrist and let her pull her into the bedroom by her hair.

Korea stood over Melody on her bed. "I bet your nasty ass can suck some pussy, can't you?"

"Yes, master."

It was the moment Melody had been waiting for. She had never sucked pussy before, but she was going to do this shit like a veteran tonight. She laughed inside, thinking, *that bitch Stormy has fucked up now*, as Korea squatted down and covered Melody's lips with her black cherry tart. At first scent, she was jolted by the unfamiliar hot mustiness between Korea's legs, and found herself hesitating. But then Melody closed her eyes and let her tongue move naturally through her crevices until she found Korea's small hot pink dick hardening under its hood. She flicked it with her tongue tip and made soft, circular motions around it until it began to pulsate against her tongue. She thought she heard a moan.

Korea couldn't believe she was letting this bitch suck on her pussy. Maybe she was just getting back at Stormy for disobeying her. She wasn't sure, but she knew one thing. Melody could suck some pussy. She wasn't doing any of that extra shit girls tried to do when they didn't know what to do. She was on the spot, listening to her body and responding to it.

Korea lifted her hips a little. "Stick out your tongue," she said.

Melody stuck her tongue out as far as she could and lay her head down flat so Korea could ride her tongue like a dick.

"Unngh…" Melody's muffled moan urged Korea on.

"Yeah, yeah," Korea was saying. "Fuck that pussy. Yeah…" She was getting so hot, she wanted to explode. *What the fuck am I letting Melody do to me? Damn*, she thought, *I've got to get in control.* "Suck it," she said. "Suck my fucking dick." She was bouncing her clit hard again Melody's mouth.

The taste of Melody's blood on her tongue excited her. She wished Korea would hit her. She had her own fingers deep in her pussy, pumping her palm with her clit and was cumming hard. "Hit me, Daddy; slap me. Slap me hard. I'm cumming." Korea slapped her hard across her right cheek. "Again, Daddy; I'm almost there."

Korea slapped her again, trying to control her own nut…then Korea felt the familiar quake of her love slave. Melody's body was still convulsing as Korea stood up over her, jacking her clit off until she came hard and then pissed all over Melody's face and chest. Melody sat up to collect the golden shower in her mouth. She swallowed as much of it as she could. She loved the hot salty taste of Korea's pee and she loved the pleased look on her master's face. She must have smiled involuntarily.

"What are you smiling about?" Korea asked.

"Nothing," Melody answered timidly.

"Don't lay they're gawking at me like a fucking teenager. It's not that kind of party. Do you understand me?"

Melody didn't answer her. Korea took her head by her hair and smashed her face into the wet rubber sheet and held it there. "Do you understand me now?"

"Mmmm," Melody moaned, sticking her tongue out to lick up some more pee.

"You're so nasty."

"Only for you, Daddy. Only for you."

Korea felt herself getting hard again. She rolled Melody over and straddled her ass. "Don't you go getting ideas," she whispered into the younger woman's ear as she humped her. "I'm the boss, at all times. Say it."

"You're the boss."

"Again."

"You're the boss."

"I can't hear you," Korea said, shoving two fingers into her asshole.

"Ahhh," Melody winced, as Korea shoved them deep into her. "You are the boss! You are the boss!"

"That's right. And you will do whatever I tell you to."

"Yes. Yes, I will," Melody said breathlessly.

Korea was wet and sliding easily over Melody's round ass as her body built up to a climax. She had three fingers digging deep inside of her little freak's ass. Melody humped wildly against the pissy bed. Something inside her was stirring her to an insatiable longing. She had never felt this way before. She wanted all of her holes filled up with whatever Korea gave her.

"I, I, I'm cumming!" she screamed, bearing down until her pussy shot over every inch of space beneath her.

Korea's climax came seconds later, and Melody convulsed and shuddered under her. Korea slipped her fingers out of Melody's ass and fed them to her. Melody sucked greedily, moaning and basking in orgasmic aftershock.

"You are such a nasty little freak," Korea said, climbing off of her. "I'm leaving now. Don't think about taking a shower either. You just lay there tonight and think about how fucking nasty you are. I hope you don't think I would ever make a bitch like you my woman."

Oh, but you will, Melody thought, rolling over onto her back. She closed her eyes and smiled at the possibilities. *Her uncle had been right about lesbians. A few more weeks, and she would be packing a UHaul and signing checks.*

"There are towels in the linen closet in the bathroom," she called out to Korea, who was running shower water.

Korea stepped out of the shower and put her suit back on. She stood in the mirror in the bedroom, looking for a comb on the dresser. There was a bunch of cheap jewelry, and even cheaper perfume, a toothbrush with brown gel on it, weave glue, a curved needle with thread in it, and loose weave tracks of various colors and lengths. Korea picked up the only thing that looked safe to touch; a small pile of business cards. She thumbed through them. Underneath the business cards there were several ID cards, three for check cashing centers, two California ID cards and one Nevada ID. They all had Melody's face on them. They all had different names and dates of birth.

Korea looked at Melody sleeping carefree on the pissy

rubber sheet with shit breath. "No," she said. "Just no."

On the way down in the elevator, Korea thought of how nervous Stormy must be right now, thinking she was in trouble. Korea laughed a little, thinking of how cute it was that she was trying to get a little career going. She would have to let her know she had forgiven her already.

STORMY WASN'T THINKING ABOUT WHERE KOREA MIGHT be going on Friday night after work. She was just happy that she would be able to have more time in Los Angeles and that she could still be home before she was missed. Korea left the house at seven o'clock in the morning. Stormy was on a nine o'clock flight.

Stormy planned to arrive at The Ethiopian Sea at five P.M., and to be on the eight P.M. flight back to Oakland. First, she went to visit Sam, the man who lay in the hospital claiming to be sick from food poisoning, and threatening a lawsuit.

"He's homeless," said a voice behind her. Stormy turned around to see a woman holding a bottle of honey wine.

"I'm Amira David," she said. "I own The Ethiopian Sea. The nurse outside said you're some kind of reporter."

"I'm Stormy Talbert. I'm actually a food critic. I don't know what I expected to find here, but, here you are. I'm reviewing your restaurant tonight."

"Oh? We didn't poison him, Mrs. Talbert."

"Miss."

"He ate from the trash sometime between Sunday night and Wednesday morning. We're closed Monday and Tuesday. So you see, Ms. Talbert, the last time we threw any food away was Sunday night."

This article is going to be a fine human interest piece, Stormy thought as she listened to the entrepreneur explain that the man in the bed was just using the hospital for a clean place to stay. She said that the man sometimes did crazy things right in front of the police to get himself arrested for a clean cell to spend the night in. But to her dismay, some opportunistic personal injury attorney, who regularly visited the hospital looking for clients, had coerced him into making a bogus claim against her.

"I cannot believe Sam would do this to me, when I've fed him so many times," Amira said nervously. "I only want to live the American dream, Ms. Talbert. Make sure you write that in your article, please. Say what you must about your meal this evening, but make sure that your readers know that this lawsuit could destroy my dream. No one knows what life is like in my country for women. In America, you can be a single woman without being frowned upon or thought to be a lesbian. You can be a woman who owns her own business."

"I will find a way to include your feelings in my review, Amira. It was a pleasure to meet you."

"Likewise," Amira said, reaching for Stormy's hand. "I won't be at The Ethiopian Sea tonight, Ms. Talbert.

I have to meet my attorney for dinner. But my staff will take good care of you." Amira was still holding Stormy's hand.

"Call me Stormy."

"Stormy, I like that. Maybe I will. Can I?"

"Can you what?"

"Call you?" The unexpected flirtation caught Stormy off guard, and made her blush. "I'm serious. I know a dark little place that serves the finest Godiva and coffee. Perhaps we could meet there later."

"Actually, I have to be back in Oakland immediately after dinner. But I have your number," Stormy said, finally, freeing her hand from Amira's to fish for her business card. Stormy handed it to the smiling woman, who searched her eyes intensely.

"And now I have your number," Amira said. She leaned over and kissed Stormy on the cheek and whispered in her ear, "They kill us back home."

The hairs on the back of Stormy's neck stood up. Amira's words left an eerie feeling with Stormy that followed her out of the hospital and was with her for most of the afternoon as she meandered around West Hollywood until the restaurant opened.

Stormy was the first customer inside The Ethiopian Sea restaurant. Hartford was the second. It was a fateful meeting that would change both of their lives forever.

"I'm Berta; I'll be your server," a big-hipped woman covered in white said to Stormy as she led her to a lidded basket table and a small wicker stool, situated in a private area, framed by wooden beaded curtains. Incense burned, music played, and Stormy was instantly seduced by the tranquility. The waitress placed a red cloth napkin, a finger bowl, and a menu inside the basket table. "Can I start you off with something to drink?" Berta asked. "Our honey wine is very respectable. We make it ourselves, from local beehives. It's unfiltered, organic, and great for allergy prevention."

"Alright then," Stormy said, "I'll have a glass of honey wine."

Berta probably has fifty pounds of pure ass under those loose layers of white cloth, Stormy thought, as the woman turned her bodacious hips around and released a curtain of wooden beads that boxed Stormy inside her private dining space. She pulled out a notepad and pen and began to write. She was thinking about Amira when Berta returned with her wine. "*It is a shame,*" she wrote in her little pad, "*that many women have to hide some of their best features to appease the insecurities of men. Amira David came to this country for one thing…*"

Stormy did not see him come in, but she felt him watching her. She looked up to find Hartford staring at her between the strands of beaded curtains that divided them. His face was clean-shaven, except for a slender mustache and two thin lines of sideburns that led to a neatly groomed goatee. She noticed his manicured fingertips as he popped Dabo Kolo in his mouth. Her mouth dropped naturally open as she watched him suck spices off of his fingertips with his full sexy lips.

"How are they?" Berta asked him, of the spicy pan-fried snacks, when she brought his wine to him.

"Addictive," he answered. He smelled the sweet honey bouquet and sipped from his glass. "It is very good. Will you bring me the bottle and ask the lady to join me?" Hartford said when he caught Stormy returning his gaze. His smile was brilliant and white and he was...*out of his damn mind*, Stormy thought when he asked Berta to set them up *family style*. The term was common to Ethiopian dining and meant he wanted to eat off of the same plate with her.

"I can open the curtain between you," Berta chimed.

"That would be fine," Stormy said gratefully.

Hartford and Stormy both watched Berta's ass as it shuffled around between them when she pulled the beads open and fastened them to the wall.

"What are you writing?" he asked.

"My thoughts," Stormy answered, smiling. "I'm a writer, a restaurant critic, actually. How about you? What do you do?"

"I make music. I'm a producer."

Stormy had come to the restaurant to taste the food and to write a review of it, she told him. She was determined to bring an international taste to T. Calloway's online magazine that had, before her intervention, seemed content in collecting praise pieces on classic Southern cuisine. She wasn't sure if Hartford had heard a word that she was saying. He was starting to undress her already, so Stormy decided this would be a good time to let him know she was in a lesbian relationship.

"So, do you cook, or do you just write about other people's cooking?"

"I love to cook. My girlfriend says I do it very well... Cook, I mean?" she teased.

He smiled. "Girlfriend, girlfriend?"

"Yes, Girlfriend, girlfriend." Stormy looked away and sipped her wine.

"Oh, I wouldn't have thought..."

"You wouldn't have thought what?" she said, surprising herself with her instant anger.

He was giving some stupid reason for his response, but she wasn't listening. In a second, she was going to have Berta drop the beads. For the first time in her life, Stormy knew her worth and it could not be measured in gold alone, nor could it be measured by one man's opinion. So if Hartford planned to cripple her because of her sexuality, he could just forget it.

"...so don't be mad, lady. Like I was saying, I'm just disappointed that you're taken."

"Isn't that a wedding ring on your finger?"

"What? This old thing? I might be having this thing melted down into a big fat X real soon."

"Oh?" His words reminded her of Club X, and of Korea and her new fantasy, and she wondered...no, she could not go there. She changed the subject. "Thanks for the wine. What do you think of it?"

"You're the critic. Tell me what you think."

A recent article in the local paper she had picked up at the airport said The Ethiopian Sea was a "quaint little Bohemian favorite" because the wine was made from local honeybees whose sugary potion was good for your health. And unlike the California Napa Valley Chardonnay Stormy usually preferred with meals, that tended to make her tongue and lips pucker. No matter how much butter and oak flavoring the menu claimed, the honey in the homemade wine relaxed her tongue and warmed her cheeks with an incomparable natural sweetness that melted into the flesh of her cheeks with a pleasing ease. Still, it was hard to imagine consuming this wine with anything other than the food from the Motherland or a semisweet dessert. But she didn't say any of that. She had learned that people were more comfortable with her if they thought they were smarter than her, so as she had with Berta, she acted uninformed, simply responding, "This wine is very sweet."

"It is good," Hartford said, sipping a freshly poured glass of the foggy topaz-colored brew.

After their food arrived, they ate in silence for a while. Stormy struggled to keep her notebook clean as she jotted down notes, and Hartford struggled not to eat too fast.

"So, what kind of music do you make?"

"I'm actually an executive producer. I used to do R&B,

jazz, and contemporary stuff you might hear on the radio, but now I handle music scores and soundtracks for major motion pictures."

"Umm," Stormy said, swallowing. "Anything I might have seen?"

His mouth was full of boiled egg and she giggled, sipped her wine, and waited.

"Have you seen *Tatiana's Revenge*?"

"Have I? I loved *Tatiana's Revenge*. It reminded me of an old school movie called *I Spit on Your Grave*. It was about a woman getting revenge on some wild woodsman who raped her."

Hartford's eyes lit in pleasant surprise. "Yes, yes, though the writer and producer would never admit it publicly, *Tatiana's Revenge* was ripped off that movie."

"Hmm," Stormy said. "Well, the music was the shit."

Stormy and Hartford dined and drank wine and talked for more than an hour, about music, movies, cooking, and his family.

"Well, I guess since you're considering melting that ring into an X, you aren't real happy with your wife."

"To be frank," he said, his speech slightly slurred from the wine, "my wife is spoiled and boring."

"Is she socially or sexually boring?"

"Both. It's not a good look for the wife of a music man, if you know what I mean," Hartford countered Stormy.

"By that you mean?"

"I mean, I get all kinds of play, all the time, from

women, and some men, trying to break into the entertainment business. Not just singers and musicians either, but actors and producers as well. Most of them are willing to do most anything to get a token to play the fame game."

"Oh?" Stormy heard herself ask in a little girl's voice that made him look at her funny.

"Just the other day I got an invitation to a Calistoga Springs Nature Man Spa from a client's agent."

"Is that unusual?"

"I usually welcome the opportunity to get away from my wife for a few days, but when I checked the place out, I discovered it was clothing optional."

"Why did that make you uncomfortable?" Stormy asked. "Are you uncomfortable with your naked body? It looks like you're in shape."

"The invitation came from a man."

"Oh."

"So I had to wonder, what kind of man wants to conduct business with champagne springs bubbling up his ass?"

"Oh, so you've never been with a man?"

"No."

"No?"

"Hell no."

"I don't mean any offense. I'm only asking because the invitation seemed to stir you so much. I don't find the idea repulsive at all." Stormy chased her last bite of beef tips with her final swallow of honey wine. "You know, there's a magic button in your ass that only gay boys and old guys seem to know about."

Hartford shifted nervously in his chair, and for the first time since they had begun speaking, he didn't look into Stormy's eyes when he spoke again. "I don't know why I'm telling you this. I don't even know you."

"That's because it can be easier to talk to people you don't know. Don't worry about it. Go ahead; I'm a good listener."

"Well, I know about the button you're talking about. I had a happy ending massage recently," he confessed. "A friend of mine took me to a massage therapist. First, she gave me a massage, and then she jacked me off. Only this chick had one hand on my dick and one hand in my ass."

"You mean her finger, right?" Stormy asked, laughing. "I mean, if she got her whole hand in there..."

"Yeah, man, yeah. It was just her finger. But it relaxed the fuck out of me. I've never come so fast. I'm sorry if I'm being too blunt. This wine really creeps up on you."

"So would you let a woman go there with you?"

"I told you, I already have."

"No, I mean, *go there*. I mean, strapped up and everything."

Hartford laughed out loud and looked around the restaurant nervously. "Check, please!"

"Aw, don't be shy now. This conversation is for grown-ups. It's not like it would make you gay or something, if you let a woman please you in that way. If you like it, you could get your wife to do it."

"Now that's never going to happen." Hartford cleared his throat, and then sat back in his chair. "Have you done it before?"

"Me? No. It's just a fantasy; something that's been slipping into my shower thoughts lately. I only want to watch. I think watching a woman and a man in reverse position would be such a huge turn-on. Just talking about it now is making me really hot, really wet," Stormy said, shifting her hips back and forth in her seat.

"So if you're watching, who is fucking?" Hartford inquired.

"Oh, I'm fucking. I rarely pass up the opportunity to fuck. I love to fuck, but I especially love to be fucked. In my fantasy, I'm on my back, there's a big strong man thrusting his dick deep inside of me, I'm holding his back and ass, and pushing him deep inside of me. When I was fucking men, I always liked it like that, deep and missionary, sharing heartbeats. I suspect that your wife and I have that in common."

"You can say that again," Hartford said, laughing. "You mind if I order us another bottle?"

Stormy nodded and continued with her verbal seduction of the man she had targeted to fulfill Korea's fantasy. "You know, Hartford," she said, touching his hand softly. "There is something hot and intoxicating about breathing in the same sex-filled steamy air between two people. I can close my eyes now and feel it." Hartford watched her full mouth as it opened and closed, expelling imagery of her fantasy so vividly, he was living it. "...his tongue is in my ear, he's sucking my lobe and whispering secrets, his sweat is in my mouth and eyes, my hair is bunched in my fists and his dick is so deep inside of me, I can almost feel it in my throat. Oh, yes, honey, you can best believe I'm fucking." Stormy paused to check Hartford's face. "Are you blushing?" she toyed with him.

"I don't know. Am I?"

"Yes, shall I go on?"

"Wait," he said. Berta brought them another bottle of honey wine and cleared their trays. "Go on."

Stormy closed her eyes again. "In my fantasy, while this man is fucking me, a beautiful woman slides upon him from behind, rimming him with her tongue. When she does this, I can feel him growing stiffer inside me."

Her mouth is fantastic, Hartford thought.

"She oils his back and glides her breasts across his body, massaging him. Then she mounts him from behind; she's gently pushing into him, forcing him deeper inside of me. I can feel the weight of the two of them pressing into my clit and I'm on the verge of exploding. He's whispering in my ear, telling me to instruct her when to back it up and when to go deeper, his dick is getting harder, she's deep in his ass...Aaagh," Stormy gasped as Hartford slipped his tongue inside her mouth. "Whoa!

I've got to go!" Stormy said, interrupting his probe. "We're getting carried away here."

"Not as carried away as they are," Hartford said. He nodded his head toward the booth next to hers where a man's hand had disappeared up a woman's dress.

"Oh…" Stormy said. "Now I'm embarrassed. Do you think they were listening?"

"Let's get out of here before you get cited for starting a riot." Hartford dropped two hundred dollars on the table and led Stormy to the door.

"You are quite the storyteller," he said when they were outside. "You sure you haven't done that before?"

"No. I think my lady wants to, though."

"Listen, it's only eight o'clock. You want to get a nightcap?"

"Oh shit! I'm supposed to be on the nine o'clock flight back home. It was nice meeting you. I have to find a cab."

"Wait, not so fast. Where is home?"

"Oakland."

Hartford smiled. "And you thought you could get away from me."

"Do you live in Oakland?"

"Yes, I do. I have a car waiting. Why don't you let me give you a ride to the airport and you can tell me all about your lady friend? What's her name?"

"Korea."

During the ride, Stormy told Hartford all about Korea.

She arrived at the airport just in time for her flight. She thanked the driver and jumped out of the car before Hartford could get out and open her door.

"I'll be back home in a few days," he said through the window. "Here, take my card. You know, when you were telling your story, I couldn't help but to see myself in it. Tell Ms. Korea I'm down if she is."

STORMY CAME HOME TO AN EMPTY HOUSE. In all these years, Stormy had never disobeyed Korea and Korea had never spent the night out. It was a true sign that their relationship was ending. She didn't spend the night moaning about it. She used her time to crank out the article. By the time she finished and emailed it to T. Calloway, the sun was coming up.

Korea came in smelling of pussy at five in the morning. She didn't say a single word to Stormy. She got in the shower, put on her suit, and left again.

All afternoon Shawna cleaned, shaved, picked, plucked, and planned in anticipation of the two men in blue to arrive. Her mind had been flooded with the most insane imagery all day. While she washed her hair, the thought of being handcuffed and fucked with a cocked gun possessed her. When she shaved her pussy, the thought of having one in her ass and one in her pussy at the same time; their dicks rubbing together, with only her thin skin separating them, was so intense she had nicked herself. When she closed her eyes and wet her face to wash her mask off, the image of both men ejaculating in unison all over her face could not be rinsed away. Today she was going to live out as many fantasies as she could think of. And she knew just where to start. She wanted to live out the fantasy that had been getting her through all that boring sex with Hartford—water play. All of these thoughts sent an unbearable throbbing to her clit.

She looked out of the living room window again. "They're late," she said, disappointed.

She was lying on her bed with a bullet on her clit, just giving in to a tiny quake when Robeson called from his cell phone, to make sure it was still alright to stop through.

"Yes. It's cool," she said, sounding a little breathy.

"Good, then come to the back door; we're already here."

"Shit!" She sat up, hopped off the bed, and went to the door. "Well, would you look at The Officers Friendly," Shawna said to the two uniformed men standing in front of her.

Robeson smiled when he saw Shawna standing in a short silk robe and fuzzy glass slip-ons. "I told you," he said to Davis.

"So...uh, how is this going down?" Davis asked.

"Well, first, I've got to get you guys as wet as I am," Shawna said, stepping boldly to the two men to grab hands full of their crotches. Without any words, Robeson and Davis followed Shawna to the master bathroom, stripped themselves, and stepped into the shower with her.

It was Davis who surprised her with the size of his dick. He couldn't have been more than 5'8" but the dick he owned should have belonged to Robeson, who towered over him but only had about seven inches to offer.

"You want to frisk me?" she asked Robeson, turning her face to the shower wall to let him know he would be on ass detail. Shawna had a deep, wide pussy that needed girth and length. She wanted Davis' big black nightstick inside of it.

Robeson lathered his hands and washed her ass cheeks, letting his hands slide up and down her crack. Davis slipped himself between Shawna and the shower wall. He took the showerhead off of the hook, rinsed underneath his dick and balls, and then he aimed the pounding flow at Shawna's pussy, sending her clitoral sensations that nearly crippled her. Her knees buckled and her legs shook. If not for the two strong men holding her up, she would have hit the shower floor.

Robeson stepped from the shower. He dried his dick and searched his uniform pockets for a condom. Davis took the opportunity to test the pussy out. Spinning Shawna's back against the wall, he bent his knees, aimed his dick at her center, and ripped past her pussy lips like a bolt of thunder through a stormy sky.

"Uhnnngh," she grunted. "Wait, wait," she said in phony protest.

"I'm not going to nut in you," he said. "I just want to see what I'm getting myself into." Davis' dick was so fat, that her pussy hole was stretching to receive it, as he thrust in and out of her. His dick was so long she could feel it poking her cervix. "I'm going to put a condom on in a minute," he whispered desperately. He reached under her arms, lifting her a bit, putting his hand on her shoulders, and then pulled her down hard on his dick. "I'm real modern about these things," he whispered into her ear, digging deeper, this time. "But my dick is old school."

"No," her mouth said as her thigh slid up his leg, exposing even more of her throbbing cunt to him. Feeling the dangling showerhead bouncing off her leg, she reached for it and handed it to him. "Okay," she whispered back, "you can hit it a couple more times, then you have to strap up, okay?"

"Okay," Davis said, getting even more excited. Davis quickly pulled out, flipped her around, pushed her face to the wall, and dug so deep inside of her, his dick seemed to grow another inch. And when he put that shower-head to her clit again, Shawna could not feel his nut for her own.

"No parking," Robeson said through the shower door. Shawna's legs shook involuntarily as she stepped onto the tile floor. "You can't get tired yet," Robeson said, picking her up, and carrying her to the edge of the bed. "You have some tickets to work off." He bent her over the edge of the bed and twisted the top off of a tiny tube of lubricant and squeezed it on her asshole. He rubbed the lube around and ran his finger in and out of her.

Davis found his rubber and placed it, unopened on the nightstand. He sat back on the bed as Robeson positioned Shawna on her knees, and hung his big dick out for the housewife to suck.

When she didn't move fast enough, Robeson gave her ass a smack. "Don't just stare at it, crawl up there and put it in your mouth." Robeson followed behind her on his knees, sliding himself into her tight ass, as she took Davis into her mouth.

"Yeah, suck it," Davis said, pushing the back of her head down, forcing his dick to the back of her throat until she gagged.

Robeson moved slowly, easing his way into Shawna's ass. His short, fat dick massaged her walls and her body began to rock slowly back and forth. With his hands, he guided her hips; with his thumbs, he massaged her hipbones. Davis got up on his knees in front of her. With both hands on her head, he massaged the base of her skull and pushed his dick in and out of her mouth. The men found no need for conversation or commands. They were a silent team, communicating though eye contact and body language. Shawna felt her tension drain from her. Her clit even calmed down as the rest of her body made its presence known and appreciated in ways she had forgotten about since she had become a wife and mother. Shawna felt as light as a feather, floating back to the comfort zone of passivity she had enjoyed before her husband and children came to steal her joy. The three hovered there in that space for a while until both men came together; Robeson into his condom, Davis down her throat.

"Good girl," Davis said, pushing his tongue into her mouth, sucking anything remaining of himself off of her tongue. "You didn't spill a drop."

"That felt so good," Shawna said. She could still feel her back and hips and head tingling with tiny muscular orgasms.

"You like that, huh?" Robeson asked, smacking Shawna's

ass softly as he pulled out to change his rubber and to choreograph the next scene.

Davis spread her legs wide so Robeson could get a good look at his handiwork. "Look, partner," he said. "You got her little hole stuck open."

Robeson strapped up again and lay on his back on the bed. Davis picked Shawna up and placed her on Robeson's lap so she could swallow Robeson's dick with her ass again. Davis pushed her back against Robeson's chest and shoved his diamond cutter inside of her. A deep moan escaped her lips as the cocks pushed against one another inside of her.

There, wrapped between these strong cops who risked their lives every day for a city that hated them, she surrendered control. She let Robeson and Davis bite and beat and fuck and suck whatever they wanted to and was not about to apologize for any of it. Shawna wanted to make sure she had some real men in her life. I'll bet getting *them* on all fours would be impossible, she thought, as visions of Hartford getting fucked by the dirty biker flashed in her mind. Her pussy was so wet, Davis was swimming in it as her walls seemed to collapse and give way to a river of her juices. She began to cry and to buck wildly, making both dicks slip out of her body.

"No," she cried. "Give them to me; give me those dicks."

Davis nodded at Robeson. "You heard the lady," he said.

Robeson rolled his condom off. The officers presented their dicks to the insatiable woman, who lay begging for them on the bed. Shawna grabbed their cocks and slid her hands up and down their shafts, licking, sucking, and milking the men until they both spilled on her face.

Shawna lay with her eyes closed, and her hips still pumping gently against the air. "I could cum a thousand more times," she said. "You don't know who you are fucking with."

"No, you don't know who *you're* fucking with," Davis said as he leaned in and kissed her on the lips, and gathered a little juice for himself. When Shawna opened her eyes, they were kissing.

THECUTB: *So what did you think?*

T.CALLOWAY: *I think you're very special. I think you're going to make a great addition to our team. If we're going to take our chances going to print in a digital world, I can't imagine gambling on a more talented writer.*

THECUTB: *I really enjoyed writing the article. You should have seen Bill; he was so happy to be clean and in a bed at the hospital.*

T.CALLOWAY: *You describe him so well. I was standing in the hospital room with you. I never would've thought of putting a human-interest piece on a homeless man together with a food review. You even managed to tie in to the restaurateur's American dream.*

THECUTB: *Well, at least now, her business should pick back up when people find out that her food isn't contaminated with salmonella.*

T.Calloway: *You're building a very nice portfolio. You should start backing up your work on our server, in case anything happens to your hard drive.*

TheCutB: *OK. I will do it right away. I've been thinking about your offer. It sounds better and better to me all of the time. Can I call you to talk about it?*

T.Calloway: *No, I really don't do phones. Put it in an email. Got to fly.*

Blue stood in the hallway outside of the kitchen listening to Alex and Raven talk. Alex finished stacking the dishes in the dishwasher and Raven swept the floor.

"I don't know why we have to clean up whenever we come over here," Raven complained. "Don't they have maids?"

"No," Alex said. "It's just the two of them. They don't need maids."

"Then they need to do whatever they do when we aren't here," she said, putting her broom down. She had swept lint and crumbs into a small pile on the kitchen floor. "I'm not picking that up."

"Don't start," Alex said. "Please, we can have a nice time here. Tomorrow, I'll take you outside. You can ride the horse."

"That horse doesn't like me."

"I wonder why?" Alex said, holding the dustpan on the floor near the trash for Raven. "Just get the broom and sweep the trash in it and you can go watch cartoons."

"No," Raven said, crossing her arms. "I ain't a maid."

Alex was getting frustrated with the girl and wanted to go lay down, so she grabbed the broom and held the dustpan down with her foot.

"What are you doing?" Blue asked her.

"I'm sweeping this up so I can go to bed. I'm tired, Auntie, and Raven's getting on my nerves."

"Dump it out."

"But, Aunt Blue…"

"Dump it out. I told Raven to do it and that's just what she's going to do; even if it takes all night."

Alex did as she was told and handed the broom and dustpan to Raven. "I tried to warn you." Raven stuck her tongue out at her sister. "Good night, Aunt Blue."

"Good night, sweetheart," she said, receiving a peck on her cheek from Alex, who happily trailed off down the hall and up the stairs to her designated bedroom. "Well?" Blue said, looking at Raven. "Is this going to be a long fight or a short night?" Raven dropped the dustpan and let the broom handle fall to the floor. "Have it your way," Blue said, taking a seat at the table. "Stand right there and don't you move a muscle unless you're moving to do what I told you to do."

How Hartford could have such an unruly child was beyond her. "Is he paying any attention to what's going on in his house?" Blue wondered. She wasn't going to beat the child, and she could not really make her stand there, but Raven was as stubborn as any Crow had ever been so she wouldn't budge until she couldn't stand anymore. Blue hummed gospel hymns while she waited for Raven to stand down. It took nearly three hours for Raven to break down and finally sweep the trash up and put it into the can.

"Okay," Blue said. "Put those things in the closet. Then you can go to bed. But don't turn on the TV, or we'll have round two."

RAVEN KNEW THAT BLUE WOULD BE DOWNSTAIRS for another couple of hours, drinking. She rolled out of bed and crept into Blue's master bedroom. The carpet was soft under her feet. She stopped for a moment, squishing her toes in it as she looked around to see what she could do damage to without getting caught. The nightlight in the bathroom was on.

"Oh, yeah," she said when she had figured it out. "Round two."

"This is what you get, you evil bitch. You want to make somebody a maid. I'll clean up for you, all right," Raven said, pulling Blue's toothbrush out of its holder on the sink. She knelt in front of the toilet and dipped the brush in the water and swirled it around. "Oh, my goodness," Raven said. "Oh, my, is that a stain? Shame on me." Raven scrubbed the stains from every corner of the toilet bowl with the toothbrush, until the bowl nearly sparkled. "There, the toilet is as good as new. Now let me get the shower." She was inside the tub, behind the shower curtain, when she heard Blue coming.

Blue had to pee so bad, it seemed like her lungs were filled with vodka. She stumbled through her room and into her private bathroom and plopped down on the toilet. She seemed to pee forever. "Oh, what a relief," she said. She wiped and was ready to get up, when she felt Dream Crow's cabbage and vinegar taking her stomach over. "Uh oh," she said.

Her asshole sounded off like a foghorn and expelled a scent that made Raven slide to the floor of the bathtub. Raven remained trapped in her own funky prison for a good fifteen minutes. It was torture but it gave Raven an idea.

The next morning, Raven was transformed; she was positive and engaging. She woke up bright and early and helped Dream Crow feed the chickens. She played Scrabble with her sister and her aunts in the afternoon and volunteered to clean up by herself after dinner.

Raven had even suggested the family movie Dream Crow should pick up from Blockbuster. "Oh, you're going to just love *Happily N'Ever After*," she said, singing praises of the film until Dream Crow and Blue left to go find it.

Alex was very suspicious. "What gives?"

"What do you mean?"

"I mean, why are you being so nice, all of a sudden?"

"I just feel like it," Raven said.

"Really? Aunt Blue must've had you standing on your feet for a long time last night. Shoot, if I knew that would work, I would've done it years ago." Raven smiled at that, but did not laugh. "So, are you really going to clean the kitchen by yourself, or do you need me to help you? I will; I don't mind."

"I'm for real. I'm going to clean the kitchen."

"Okay, then. I'm going to go take my shower and stuff. Let me know when they get back with the movie."

"Okay," Raven said, rinsing a dish and placing it neatly in the dishwasher.

"Hey, Raven?"

"Huh?"

"It's nice to see you like this. Maybe tomorrow we can get the horse to let you on his back."

"Okay."

Raven turned the oven on to 350 degrees, like the tube of cookie dough instructed. She got a cookie sheet out of the cabinet and spooned the dough onto the cookie sheet, making three neat rows of four. From her pocket, she pulled the chocolate bar she had found in Blue's bathroom medicine cabinet.

SHAWNA WAS STILL WALKING ON AIR FROM HER TRYST with the Officers Friendly when Blue called her to come get Raven. "I'm telling you, she's the devil and you need to come get her. She's got every one of us over here sick, shitting all over the place."

"I'll just take them both," Shawna said anxiously.

"That won't be necessary," Blue said, grunting into the phone. "There's no sense in punishing Alex for what Raven has done. Alex wants to stay and we love having her. Besides, she's sick too."

"Fine," Shawna said. "I'll be there in the morning."

"No, honey, if you want her back in one piece, you need to come right now," Blue demanded.

She had Raven packed, prayed over, and waiting at the front door when Shawna arrived. Blue fanned sage smoke around with a church fan that had an image of Dr. Martin Luther King Jr. on it and said, "Anything not here for the highest and best of good, be gone!" and pushed Raven out of the door.

CHAPTER 13

WHEN STRANGERS COME TOGETHER

Korea hadn't spoken to Stormy all weekend and Stormy's attempts at apologies were futile. But when Stormy told her about Hartford, she was all ears.

It was funny, Hartford thought, how things always work themselves out for him. Here, he had come all this way to L.A. to experiment with a little ass play, but had found out that what he was looking for was actually already available at home, just minutes away from his own uneventful bedroom. He read the email from Stormy again, feeling his heart beat faster.

"I've been thinking about what we discussed. Have you? This is my email address, use it to contact me, I'm online every evening until about 9. When are you coming back home? Let me know if you need a ride from the airport. Korea would like to meet you."

Hartford had been thinking about Stormy's fantasy. The taste of her tongue was the most delicious thing he had savored at the restaurant the night they had met. He wanted more. If her lady friend looked and tasted anything like her, he could not wait to get back to Oakland. He was done with Shawna. He would stay married to her for the kids' sake, or until some real wife material came along. But he was through with her. She was selfish, inconsiderate, spoiled, lazy, and superficial. He hated that he had been pressured by the music game to get with a woman like her. She was fine and all, but besides her good looks, there was nothing there. He really missed Magenta. His first wife was a real lady. Alex was so much like her.

Hartford picked up his phone and called his sisters. "Hey, Dream Crow. How's it going?" She told him all that had happened, with Blue interjecting a few choice words in the background. Hartford was shocked and embarrassed. "I'm on my way home."

"What for?" Dream Crow asked. "There's nothing you can do here, besides bring us some toilet paper. We are just shitting all day, that's all. Come to think of it, you should stay in L.A. as long as you need to get your out-of-town business finished. That way, when you come back here, you can be present and let these girls know that they have a father. You know, when you leave a house full of women together, there's going to be drama."

Hartford talked to his beloved daughter for a while and promised her that he would not leave town for a long time once he got home.

"I miss you, Daddy," Alex said. "I can't wait to see you."

"I love you, baby girl."

"I love you more."

"That's impossible."

HARTFORD HATED TO ADMIT TO HIMSELF THAT SHAWNA was right about his career. The moment he laid ears on the future sound of Bandarofski Music Publishing, he knew he was a has-been producer. His smooth jazz-funk signature sound had been reduced to samples that lay the cadence for much more aggressive mechanical drum patterns, gnarly electro synthesized sound punctuated with pop culture punch lines and catchy rap hooks. The worst and best part of it: his managing director had hired ten young producers for the cost of one Hartford Crow.

There were four on duty the night he entered Band Studios with Sweet P on his arm. She wore a sheer black A-line dress with a royal blue panty thong and bikini top underneath, but the young producers barely acknowledged her.

"Hey, yawl! It's him!" one of them said when he walked into the studio. "It's Hartford Crow." The boy, who could not have been more than eighteen, checked his face against the big picture on the wall of the music icon, who was shaking Jerome Bandarofski's hand, and holding a Grammy music award. "It's him," he told Hartford. "I mean, it's you!"

The other young musicians didn't have to be told to

stand; they simply did, talking over each other to introduce themselves. There was "Barry Bond, not Bonds with the s but without it, as in James." Then there was "Ocean and Atlantis, like the lost city," who always produced as a team. And finally, there was "Tommie with an i-e not a Y, aka Fayze," who was the team executive and had more than twenty-five Hartford Crow samples in use after only two months.

"*Mr. Crow, it's such an honor…Mr. Crow, you're the best,*" Sweet P teased as he walked her to the studio door after the boys had ignored her for nearly an hour. "I'd bet anyone of them would consider tapping that prostate for you, if you asked."

She was joking, but taking potshots at him at the same time. Hartford let it slide, knowing she was just jealous, though he wasn't sure if she had anything to be envious about.

Hartford listened intently for the next few hours to the innovative usage of his most popular and classic works. They had even made use of some obscure music he had never released, but all remained a part of the Bandarofski catalog. He walked out of the studio, not sure about how he felt, but certain he needed to find something besides music and Shawna to occupy his time.

MORE THAN A WEEK HAD PASSED since he had seen any of his girls, but Hartford couldn't stop thinking of Stormy and her wild fantasy, so instead of calling Shawna, he called Stormy to pick him up from the Oakland airport.

"I'm on my way," Stormy said. "Southwest?"

"Yes," Hartford said.

Stormy called Korea to let her know they would be having a guest for dinner and possibly dessert. She dressed quickly, hit the 880 Freeway, and collected the man before he had a chance to change his mind.

Hartford would not have guessed by Stormy' free-spirited, hippie-flared style that she was living, as his grandmother would have said, "so high on the hog." But the penthouse was undeniably phat.

"Damn," he said. "If I was a bachelor, I wouldn't mind this. I wouldn't mind this at all."

He accepted a glass of chardonnay from Stormy, who promised that the object of his ambitions would be arriving soon. In the meantime, she showed him Korea's state-of-the-art workout facility, her garden, and stainless steel gourmet kitchen. She gave him a quick peek at the designer master bedroom they might be experimenting in later that night and then led him to the east balcony of the penthouse where they sat and talked.

As soon as Korea saw him, she wanted to fuck him. Korea did not believe in awkward moments, so when she arrived, all conversation stopped and the pair immediately got physical with a telling kiss.

Stormy was right, Hartford thought, *Korea's beautiful*. Hartford was digging her swagger from the moment she had said hello. She had actually looked him up and down, like he was a piece of meat. *Now that was new*, he thought, hoping he hadn't blushed like the bitch he felt like in the moment. Except for her obvious attraction to designer clothes and footwear, Korea wasn't anything like his wife. *She really has her shit together*, he thought.

But he couldn't figure out what was going on with Stormy. From the moment Korea walked in the door, she was a nervous Nellie, dropping things and stuttering. There wasn't even a hint of the confident woman he had met in Los Angeles. It wasn't until she started running down her dinner menu that she even started making sense.

"Stormy, what's for dinner?"

"Uh, I um, I wasn't sure what you had a taste for tonight, and I knew we had a guest coming…Hartford, I hope you like chicken and fish…"

"Stormy, get on with it. What did you cook? You *did* cook, right? Because if I see another take-out box…"

"Your choice," Stormy finally said, confidently. "Smoked chicken with caramelized onions and Shiitake mushrooms or fresh Atlantic salmon cured with salt and sugar and perfumed with lemongrass. There's some wild rice and Lyonnais potatoes with sweet cream butter and fresh Romano cheese, just like you like them, baby. Your vegetable choices are Sicilian cauliflower with capers and sage or zucchini bacon fritters with basil-mayo dipping sauce."

The sound of it made Hartford's mouth water. The only thing Shawna knew how to make that was anything close to gourmet was her "special vegetarian, not really beef, beef nachos."

"Didn't you make a salad? I told you I wanted a salad," Korea quipped.

"Of course," Stormy answered, unfazed by her attitude. "I made a spinach salad, made of baby spinach from my garden."

"Oh yeah? What's in it?" Korea asked nicely, after realizing Hartford would need to see some softness in her if he was to agree to be her bottom.

"Well, baby, the garden is doing so well. The salad is made up of sweet cherry tomatoes, English cucumbers, fire roasted red onions, and garlic. I topped it with a sliced boiled egg, pecans, and crumbled blue cheese. The dressings are homemade. There is a warm bacon dressing and red wine vinaigrette with pomegranate."

"That sounds mouthwatering," Hartford said.

"Well?" Korea said to Hartford. "Are you going to wash up for dinner, or are you one of those men who doesn't wash his hands until after he touches his food, or his dick?"

He liked her sense of humor. Though, he admitted to himself, it was hardcore coming from a woman. But if he was going to let her inside him tonight, or any other night, she would do well, he agreed with himself, to stay just like she was.

"MY GOD, WOMAN," HARTFORD SAID, RUBBING HIS belly after dinner. "You are blessed."

"Yes, baby, it's true; you outdid yourself tonight," Korea interjected into the line of emotional fire between them. She wondered for a second, but quickly dismissed the idea, that they had been intimate. Then turning to Hartford, she said, "I want you to be comfortable and clean tonight, so use the master guestroom to get ready. I have to work out. Stormy will come for you in a couple of hours. Is that cool?"

"Yes, that's cool," Hartford said.

Korea deliberately kept a straight face at all times when talking to him, just as she would have if she had been shopping for a new car. There were no discernible inflections of any kind that he could use to judge her attraction. But inside, she was a giddy kid.

Fucking, shit, hell, damn, she said to herself as she watched his tight little ass follow Stormy down the stairs. "We're all going to hell tonight."

EXCEPT FOR THE FACT THAT BOTH KOREA AND HARTFORD completely forgot Stormy was in the room, the fantasy played out much as she had described to Hartford when they were in Los Angeles, with Stormy on the bottom, Hartford in the middle, and Korea behind him, riding him like a prize bull. Korea gripped handfuls of his Afro-like horns, thrusting her big black dildo inside of his ass, and came more times that Stormy could count.

Stormy, who had immediately gotten into the shower when the episode was over, could hear Hartford thanking Korea through the bathroom door.

"Thank you, thank you, thank you," Hartford kept saying to Korea as he removed his condom and got dressed.

Korea couldn't say a word at first. She was too cool to say what she was feeling. All she knew was that she was still coming. Her pussy had saturated the black leather harness and her pussy juice was trailing down her legs, as she walked Hartford to the door, raping his ass with her eyes. And when he turned to say goodbye, she grabbed him by his hair and shoved her tongue in his mouth. They both pulled tight against the other's head, trying to get their tongues in deeper. He breathed heavily, as she sucked his tongue. He wanted her inside him again so badly, he was salivating. A stream of spit escaped the corner of his mouth, and Korea licked it away. She could hear his heart pounding in his chest.

"You need to get the fuck out of here," she said.

"Why?" he asked. "Don't you like me?"

"I want to throw you against that wall and fuck you again. I want to fuck you right, without that little bitch in the way."

"Just tell me when," Hartford said, "I'm yours."

"THAT WAS SOME NASTY SHIT," STORMY SAID TO HERself in the bathroom mirror. "I can't believe I orchestrated the whole thing. The entire room smelled like ass. Correction, the room smelled like shit. I couldn't even focus on sex. How do gay boys do it? Didn't that motherfucker use the enema I gave him? I'm just glad it's over. That's one fantasy that would've been better left a fantasy."

Stormy went into her room and logged into the Good Vibrations website. She surfed through the vast selection of mock cocks. "They would be in alphabetical order," she said. "Anal. No." She continued reading the list, "Bull's eye Silicone, Double…Glass, G-Spot…Realistic, okay, there's my baby." Stormy selected an updated version of the dick Korea had stuck up Hartford's ass. She didn't care if they had used two rubbers, that dick was not going to touch her pussy ever again.

Before she climbed in bed, she made a little trip to Korea's master bathroom, and dumped the old dick in the trash. The television was off. The lights were off. Korea was naked and sound asleep, actually snoring! Now there was a sound Stormy had never heard before.

In the morning, the dick had been boiled, oiled, prepped, and put right back in its silk bag. Korea was pissed off that she found it in the bathroom trashcan. But, instead of saying so right away, she said, "I don't want a fucking omelet; I don't even eat omelets. Make me a smoothie. Don't use banana either."

Stormy knew that Korea had eaten a bacon and sharp cheddar omelet a few days before. She was confused and she didn't know what to do at all.

She filled the blender with strawberries, blueberries, a banana, half a cup of apple juice, and a couple of ice cubes, put the top on, and pushed chop, and then puree. She poured breakfast in a glass and sat at the kitchen table across from Korea. "I know you like my omelets. This isn't about omelets. What's up?"

"What's up? Look at you, talking to me like I'm one of your homies. I'm not your homie. But since you asked, I have a question for you. Who the fuck do you think you are? Why did I wake up this morning and find my dick in the motherfucking trashcan?"

Stormy opened her eyes wide. She couldn't believe what she was hearing. "Are you kidding me? That thing is contaminated."

"Don't you ever throw away anything of mine."

Oh, shit, Stormy thought. *She's serious.* Okay, she said to herself, *let me think.* She quickly ran through her head, all that she knew pertaining to this, and came up blank, except for…"Oh, baby, no, no, I wasn't mad about it or anything. I'm just saying, we need to get a new one. I ordered one already. It will be here tomorrow."

Korea shook her head. "The more I school you, the dumber you seem to become. You know what your problem is? You're spoiled; that's what your problem is. You don't know what to do when shit doesn't have anything to do with you."

Uh oh, Stormy thought. *New fantasy, anger, irrationality… it's happening again.*

"Ouch," Stormy said.

"Ouch? What the fuck is that?"

"Just ouch."

T.CALLOWAY: *The board is convening next week to make our final staff selections. I have to have you here.*

THECUTB: *I haven't made up my mind.*

T.CALLOWAY: *Don't waste your talents. I'm not just offering you a chance. You will be offering The Cutting Board a chance, too.*

THECUTB: *I have to talk it over.*

T.CALLOWAY: *Explain.*

THECUTB: *I'm in a relationship.*

T.CALLOWAY: *Explain.*

THECUTB: *My partner doesn't want me writing…She says it's a waste of time.*

T.CALLOWAY: *I'm booking you a flight. Be on it.*

STORMY'S HEART WAS BEATING SO HARD IN HER CHEST, she thought Korea might hear it, so she stood in the doorway of her bedroom when she asked, "Korea, do you think it would be alright if I went on a kind of working vacation for a while, just for the weekend?"

"This weekend, sure."

"Sure?" Stormy asked.

"Sure," Korea repeated. "Do me a favor. Can you cook

up a couple of meals so I can put them in the microwave?"

"Sure," Stormy answered. *Absofuckinglutely*, she thought.

If Stormy hadn't asked to leave town, Korea was going to find a way to send her away. Her timing could not have been more perfect.

CHAPTER 14

THE LONG RIDE TO SODOM

"Damn, he makes my dick hard," Korea said to herself.

Now that Stormy was gone, Korea was going to be able to fuck Hartford the way she really wanted to. She had cleared her entire calendar from Friday afternoon until Stormy was scheduled to be back on Tuesday. She was going to turn that motherfucker inside out over the next five days. But first, she needed to get rid of this bitch.

Fantasy Friday was uneventful for Melody that week. Korea hadn't arrived at the office until ten o'clock. All of Melody's advances had gone unnoticed, though she tried to make her issues known by the way she carried a noticeable attitude with her around the office as she performed duties she had not been required to since she was hired.

"Is there a problem?" Korea asked her when she dropped the file marked "The Cutting Board" on her desk.

"No. Of course not," Melody said.

"Of course not," Korea replied. "That will be all. You can go home early, if you'd like."

"It's only two, Ms. Smith."

"So it is. Don't worry about it. I will be out of the door by three o'clock myself."

"Oh, is there some meeting I don't know about?" Melody asked.

Korea replied only with a glance in her general direction. At first, she didn't even notice that Melody had put her Fantasy Friday gear back on.

"Don't embarrass yourself, Melody. And please don't embarrass me," Korea said when she noticed the green shorts and fishnets she was wearing.

Melody sulked and closed Korea's office door. She was failing in her assignment.

"Shit!" she said when she got back to her desk. Not sure what to do, she picked up the phone.

"Hey," she said. "It's me. It's not going well. I think she's tired of me already. It's either that, or she has another woman. No. If she has someone else, it's definitely not her wife. What should I do?" Melody listened carefully to her instructions, deciding to follow them to a "T" this time.

Before she left the office, she called Sally in HR and set up a lunch date for three.

KOREA TOOK TWO FROZEN MEALS THAT STORMY HAD prepared for her from the freezer. The Tupperware containing a buttered lobster tail, sweet corn, and couscous was marked *Friday*. The smoked salmon, fresh garden snap peas, and brown rice was labeled *Saturday*. "*Do not microwave*," Stormy had written. Korea put them on the counter and let them thaw while she got her bedroom ready for Hartford. As she ripped the sheet off the bed and replaced the fitted Egyptian cotton with a rubber sheet she had stopped off at a little specialty shop to pick up, she wondered if Stormy had arrived in Washington, D.C. She checked her messages, but there had been no call. She wondered why Stormy had lied about T. Calloway. The thought of Stormy's punishment ran through her hair and eyes as she showered.

"Bring a couple days of clothes," she had told Hartford.

He was nervous, speaking under his breath. "I can't stay over," Hartford was saying to her on the phone when Shawna walked up behind him and kissed him gently on the neck.

"Come to bed," Shawna said, intending for whomever was on the other line to hear her. When he didn't seem affected by her tenderness or her aggressiveness, she stepped around the La-Z-Boy, blocking his view of the game so he could see her. Shawna was dressed in a sheer nightgown and glass slippers. Her hair draped around her shoulders and framed her face.

"I've missed you, my love," she said. "Come to bed. I'll get on top this time; I promise."

Hartford couldn't deny his attraction. The thought of watching his missionary bride ride him suddenly stole his tongue, and he was silent on the phone.

"Hello? Hello?" Korea searched the line.

"Yea, uh, I'll be there, but the meeting will have to be short. I have some business at home," he finally answered.

"Don't be ridiculous," Korea charged, pushing him into reality. "What can she do for you now that she hasn't done since you've known her? Wake up, mothafucker; this is a real booty call." Korea did not stay on the phone waiting for him to respond; she hung up and put the food in the oven.

"Who was that?" Shawna asked as she straddled his lap.

"An appointment; an appointment I shouldn't have forgotten about," Hartford said.

"But..."

"Get off my lap."

When Shawna rebelled, he stood, letting his wife fall to the floor.

"STORMY REALLY CAN COOK," HARTFORD SAID, amazed that his salmon had ever been frozen.

"You can say that again. My lobster tasted like she broiled it today. But knowing Stormy, she probably did. Her food is great but that's enough about her. Why don't you and I get to, *you and I*?"

"By that, you mean..." Hartford said playfully.

"By that I mean, we should stop eating Stormy's dinner and eat each other."

Korea did not wait for Hartford to say anything. She pushed him down on the kitchen floor and ravished him with every ounce of the man inside of her. She tackled him like a linebacker. His head hit the kitchen floor and his dick got hard and he felt the urge to push it inside her, but he had not anticipated a struggle. There, spontaneously on the floor, Korea had no tools, no toys, no devices to advise her, or force his submission, so she gave in. She gave in to an urge on a whim and let her pussy glide down his dick.

Her pussy is like a virgin file, Hartford thought. It was as though it had been locked up tight in a vault long ago, but her fragrance let him know she was not green at all as he drove his manhood between her walls, ready to explode already.

"Oh no, honey, you need to put a condom on," she whispered on a desperate breath, not wanting to stop but making herself.

"But, baby," he said. "I've just been tested; I'm clean."

"You sound like a fool," Korea said, standing on her feet. "Follow me."

Korea led Hartford into the bedroom, where the incense had burned out, leaving a husky scent of sandalwood in the air. There was a glass of wine waiting for him on the nightstand on Stormy's side of the bed. Next to it, Korea's strap and cock already wrapped in a condom, and lubed for a long ride to Sodom. Stormy's big moon, as brilliant as it had been the month before, was shining through the balcony window.

"Put this on," she said, handing him a condom. "I've

never felt like equals with anyone in my bedroom before," Korea said, "until now."

Hartford wasn't sure what to do with the gentle moment Korea offered, but he was sure she was not a gentle woman. What was more, he had not come to Korea for anything gentle, and he wasn't about to let her bitch up now. So he lay down on the bed and rolled the rubber over his dick, and then he flipped himself over, offering his ass like the moon offered its midnight shine.

"Your choice, little mamma; top or bottom."

Korea stared at him in silence while she stepped into her leather harness and positioned her dick over her clit, pressing down to make sure it was on target. Korea lay down on Hartford's back, her heart racing through him. She kissed his neck, and then nibbled on his earlobe. She slapped his ass, and then bit his shoulder, hard. His hips began to roll an invitation for her to come inside. It was easier than it had been the first time. Korea's dick slipped right in.

"That's it," Hartford said. "Come and get it."

Korea reached under him and grabbed his dick, stroking it as she pumped inside of his ass. Hartford's dick was getting harder and bigger in her hand. His moans urged her deeper inside of him, as she squeezed his dick and pumped it like a shotgun.

"That's it, sweetness, give me that ass, give…it…to… me…"

This time it was Korea who could not hold on. Her clit was so hard behind her strap-on, it throbbed, almost painfully.

"Fuuuck!" she screamed, nutting all over herself. She peeled the condom off his dick and let her hand spill over with his hot cum.

Sometime during the night, Hartford had removed her strap, and was sucking her sap in her sleep. Korea dreamed of Stormy, raping her. "I told you, not to ever get on top of me," she was telling Stormy, when all of a sudden, Stormy stuck her big black dick inside of her pussy, shoving it hard against her back wall.

"You got some good tight pussy," Stormy said. Korea opened her eyes. "Yeah, you got some good pussy. Fuck me back, bitch. Come on; fuck Daddy back."

Korea couldn't help it; she rolled her hips, lifted her ass in the air, and fucked Hartford back. She opened her mouth for his tongue and even let him pull her hair and, for the next twenty-four hours, they took turns being bitches in a war between tops and bottoms that they never wanted to end.

Now that Korea had finally found the sexual high she had been looking for her entire life, she didn't have time to placate amateurs or gross people. So when Melody came into her office with a pair of handcuffs, she didn't just send her away. She fired her. Korea had found the thing she had been yearning for and no one was going to stand in her way.

SHE WAS LOOKING FORWARD TO MEETING T. CALLOWAY, so Stormy was disappointed when she saw that he had sent a woman to pick her up from the airport. The woman was waving a sign with her name on it at Ronald Reagan Washington National Airport. She smiled and was courteous when she greeted her.

"Hi, I'm Stormy."

"I know that. We've been running your picture with your column for a while now. Tisa..." The woman reached out to shake Stormy's hand. "I hope your flight was comfortable."

"Oh, yes, it was fine. I signed up for the frequent flyer program."

"Oh? That sounds like good news, then? No pressure to talk about it now. But between us, the board will make a formal offer to you tomorrow. So you should get a good night's sleep."

The women walked to a black sedan in the parking lot and Tisa loaded Stormy's bags into the car.

Stormy exhaled to release some of the pressure she felt mounting, as she considered the magnitude of the move she was making. It would be her first real job in a decade, if she took it. She imagined an entire row of T. Calloways sitting at a long table staring at her, throwing questions out. *What can you bring to this magazine? Why should we choose you? What's so special about you? You've never even had a real job?* The sound of the engine starting invited Stormy back into the car.

"Oh my God, I'm nervous," she said out loud.

"Don't be," Tisa said. "Those guys will look like a bunch of D.C. stuffed shirts. But underneath they're a bunch of marshmallows. Charm them." She smiled and placed her hand on Stormy's shoulder. Her touch sent a little unexpected shock straight through Stormy's body.

Damn, Stormy said to herself, wondering how long she was going to still be attracted to women once she started dating men again. Tisa was very pretty with smooth, sun-kissed, reddish-brown skin, long black hair, full lips, and Asian eyes. Stormy felt her eyes dropping down on their own to check out the woman's breasts...

"Are you hungry?" Tisa asked, catching her just as she was picturing silver dollar areolas.

"Yes."

"Good. Let's get you checked into your hotel room and then I'll take you to dinner. This town may seem like it's all about politics, but it's all about food. I know a place that's only minutes from your hotel."

"Oh...okay," Stormy said, sounding a bit confused.

"What's wrong?" Tisa asked. "You sound skeptical, or disappointed, or something."

"It's nothing."

"Don't lie. What's wrong?"

"It's just that I expected T. Calloway to pick me up

from the airport. I thought *we* were going to dinner... you know, so I could be better prepared..."

The sound of Tisa's laughter caught Stormy off guard. "Stormy, I *am* T. Calloway."

JUST LIKE STORMY THOUGHT THERE WOULD BE, there were suits in a row behind a table...seven pairs of eyes staring at her...

But all they wanted to know was if she had faith in the forthcoming magazine and what visions she had for her part in it. Name, rank, and social security number aside, Stormy relaxed and told them exactly what they needed to hear. She relaxed in her seat and told them exactly how she felt. She had already been to hell, twice over. If they did not like what she had to say, she would simply go back and start over. Or not go back, and still start over.

"You cannot hold a blog in your hands. You can't lay back in the bathtub with a website on your laptop without running the risk of shock, or rip out the pages of an internet recipe while you shop for the content of your husband's dinner. There is a future for print media," she said. "There is a future for *The Cutting Board*."

Fourteen minutes of deliberation was all it took for them to make a formal offer. It took Stormy seventeen minutes to renegotiate for a $150,000 annual salary and fifty-percent ownership rights to any radio or television broadcast of "Stormy's Cutting Board."

In any other field, it may have been unethical for Stormy to walk out of the newsroom door with the woman who had brought her there and presided over the board, but in the world of journalism, it seemed like this was perfectly normal. In fact, several board members who had been as captivated by her thighs as they had been by her presentation, had invited themselves to the celebration. But in the end, it was just Stormy and Tisa on a rollercoaster ride laid on a track of truth and trust.

"Do you love her?"

"Yes."

"Do you want her?"

"No."

"Do you envy her?"

"Not anymore."

Tisa's was the sweetest of kisses and when Stormy opened her mouth to her, it was as if she had that day in the Pastor's study to do all over again. It had been twenty-four years since she had lost her power. It was strange she had to go three thousand miles to find out that she had been the author and finisher of her fate all along.

"Go Stormy, go Stormy." She laughed and surrendered to love as Tisa did a stud dance in sea green cotton boxers and a yellow Lycra wife beater that did not match at all. "I could stay here forever, you know? But I have to go home."

"Do you?"

STORMY WAS FALLING IN LOVE BUT SHE WAS WAY behind Korea. Korea knew the very first night she got inside of Hartford. She didn't know how to explain it. Where she was from, you didn't explain. You cut your losses and moved on. But who could walk away from a woman as sweet as Stormy? How could she explain that she had grown bored, without her seeming primitive? Stormy had allowed more than the average wife when it came to sexual exploration, but Korea had learned in her lifetime that the way a thing begins is the way it will end. She had been consumed in her own conceit the night she had met Stormy. She had groped and kissed another man's wife. And although she had mentioned as much to Stormy when they joked about sexual deviance, she had never truly considered the weight of their words. The woman had practically made love to a perfect stranger in the bathroom of a business affair. Why then should it have surprised her that night at Club X, that she would have agreed to bareback with a man she'd never met?

And, she reminded herself, as she thought of Stormy again. *Why couldn't she just let her go?* Korea knew there was no room for her in her bedroom. There hadn't been a long time before Hartford had popped onto the scene. Was it love? Perhaps it was, but what does love really have to do with anything?

If it meant giving up home-cooked meals, Korea would have to hire a cook, as she had always threatened to do.

Korea didn't know why she hadn't been fucking men this way for years. It was the only way she wanted to fuck for the rest of her life.

"DIVORCE HER," SHE SAID.

"It is as good as done," Hartford said, dialing his home number. "Hey, baby girl?" he said to Raven. "Let me talk to your mother."

Raven hummed into the receiver as she walked down the hallway to her mother's room. "Mommy! The telephone is for you."

Raven sat on the floor by her mother's bed, trying to make herself invisible so she could listen. Her daddy could be gone for a week without calling. This must have been important.

There was something about being in the presence of Korea that made him feel invincible. Hartford did not wince when he told his wife of nine years, the mother of his eight-year-old daughter, "I don't love you anymore. I want a divorce."

If she had pleaded with him, Hartford was prepared to say, *'there's someone else,'* just as Korea had told him to.

But Shawna could not plead. She could only repeat the word, "Divorce?"

SHAWNA LOOKED DOWN AT THE PISS STICK AND SMILED. "Gotcha," she said. *This could not have come at a better time,* she thought. She didn't know where Hartford had been spending his time lately, but this baby was going to bring him back home and make him rethink getting a divorce. She had very strong intuition, bordering on a sixth sense, and her intuition was telling her that there was something foreign inside of her.

"This baby is a boy," she said. She knew how much Hartford wanted a son.

She called until he finally answered his cell phone. "Happy Father's Day," Shawna said.

"Excuse me?"

"Hartford. I'm pregnant. It's going to be a boy. I just know it."

CHAPTER 15

EFFECTIVE IMMEDIATELY

"Let's be honest. You are finished." Grace Riley was talking to Korea. "That old white woman, with a wrongful termination lawsuit that I hear you tried to bury, is the very least of your problems. You're romantically linked to a child endangerment case and the suspicious death of a woman infected with HIV. I'm so sure the ADA will find some kind of way to tie you into that. And now, you have sexual harassment charges? Very few nonprofits can afford the distraction, or financial consequences, of a lawsuit *even alledging* sexual harassment, and you think the City of Oakland, Alameda County Social Services, and the State of California want to be affiliated with you or Project W.H.Y.? Ever again? To be frank, my friend, you're a nonprofit nightmare."

"I know it looks bad, but I'm telling you, I wasn't harassing Melody. I don't care what she says," Korea said in her defense. "Tell me the truth, Grace."

"I am."

"No, tell me the real truth. Are you ditching out on

me because I'm fucking a man now? Is that it? Because it's not what you think. He's not the man in this thing. I am."

"You know what? What you do in your bedroom is your business. I really wouldn't give two flying fucks to know about it. But what is clear is that you haven't been handling your business. Maybe being *the man* has gotten you all caught up in some new kind of pussy. But the real truth is that you held the key to over half a million dollars in funding to decriminalize prostitution and save young women from street life and subsequent imprisonment and all along, you've been fucking and degrading a seventeen-year-old girl."

"What?"

"Seventeen," Grace said, pulling a cigarette from a wrinkled pack, and a lighter from her pocket.

"I thought you stopped smoking?"

"Bitch, are you listening? You and I are joined at the pocketbook like financial Siamese twins. If you go down, I go down, if I don't shake you loose. And, baby, you are going down." Grace lit up, took a drag of the little white stick, and exhaled smoke into the air. "It's bad, Korea. It's real bad. Still, it may be in your favor that she came to me instead of the police. You must have done something right."

"She's in love with me," Korea said, still stunned.

"In love or not, from what she tells me, you've been doing a whole lot more than fucking. I mean for Christ's sake, Korea, spitting on her? Choking, whipping her with newspaper, and making her bark like a dog? When did sex with women become so hard for you that you had to resort to such things to get off? I thought you were a woman; I thought you loved being one. But I see, you are a man, even if, as you say, you are fucking one."

"Those were her ideas, I swear."

"Maybe, but as you already know, if seventeen-year-old girls can't sell their own pussy, they certainly cannot negotiate how their pussy is used. So tell me, girlfriend, what is it that I'm supposed to do? I can give you recommendations for some good lawyers but, Korea, I'm afraid you're on your own with this. Do yourself a favor," she told her friend. "Shut it down. Start all over. Put somebody else in charge if you have to, but shut it all down now."

"Grace, this is crazy. I thought we were friends? I thought we had each other's backs. I'm telling you, that woman is not seventeen years old. There is no fucking way a seventeen-year-old can even know the stuff she knows."

"It's true; I talked to Sally in your own Human Resources department," Grace said sadly.

Korea did not even bother pleading her case any further. Thinking about the parade of young women who had been in Melody's place over the years, Korea realized that Grace was right. She had also underestimated the gaze of Big Brother. She had been sloppy in not doing more thorough background checks.

"I wash my hands of it," Grace said, standing up.

When Grace walked out of her office, Korea instantly began shutting it down.

"First things first," she said. She wrote a check out to Martha, *Ten Thousand Dollars and no 100's*, she wrote. Just as she was getting ready to sign it, the strangest feeling was coming over her. It started with a lump in her throat and then there was a burning in her eyes. Korea shook her head and attempted to swallow, but it was as if everything in her head was throbbing and her sinuses ached. She reached to her eyes to pinch the aching nerve between them; there was wetness there. She pulled her hand away from her face and looked at her fingers. *Are those tears?*

"Sixteen will get you thirty-two!" she heard herself scream at Keith through the bars. The day Korea found out he had infected her, was the first and last time she actually remembered crying. Her mother had told her that when she was a baby, she only cried when she was hungry. Gladys often told the story of how she would sometimes have to pinch Korea to make her cry from time to time on her doctor's orders. Korea didn't even cry when they took her mother away. But the thought of writing a check for $10,000 that Martha hadn't earned was bringing the tears, one after the other. She opened her desk drawer to look for a tissue. There lay Melody's panties, signed, sealed, and delivered with a kiss.

"If that bitch is seventeen, I'll gladly go to jail," she said to herself, remembering all the ID cards she had seen in Melody's bedroom.

"*Effective immediately*," the letter to all of her employees began...

Korea decided, from that day on, she would do all her own typing. She printed the letter and called Sally in Human Resources.

When she had the $10,000 check couriered to Martha's house, Martha called her and sang like a canary. She told her that she and Sally and Melody had been in cahoots to get paid. She said Melody had expected her to pay her off without ever having to go to court. She said the whole thing was Melody's idea.

hawna sat in the nurse's station getting blood drawn, thinking of how her son would change everything between her and Hartford. Now that she was giving him a son, he would love her more. He would respect her position in his life and quit threatening to leave her. He would put her and the baby in his will and dispose of that ridiculous prenuptial agreement he was so proud of. She hoped for all this, anyway, though all he actually promised was not to leave her right now and to stick it out until the baby came.

"Haven't things been getting better already?" she thought as she was escorted back to the waiting room.

"Right this way, Mrs. Crow," the nurse said.

Hadn't Hartford said that he was very happy about the baby? Shawna thought. *Had he said* happy *or* pleased? She couldn't remember. Man, she'd been so tired lately; her memory was starting to fail.

Hasn't he been coming home most nights? It's been at least a month since his last trip to L.A.

"Excuse me?" Shawna asked whoever was barging into her thoughts.

"I said, you need to cover your mouth when you cough," another patient said.

Now that she was pregnant, Shawna promised herself that she would change, too. She would slow down on the extracurricular fucking and dress up for him more. *I wonder if Bebe has a maternity line.* She would let Hartford get involved this time around. She would let him put cocoa butter on her belly, and talk to little Hartford while he's still in her stomach, instead of being embarrassed by the whole thing, as she had been with Raven.

"Mrs. Crow, the doctor will see you now," another nurse said.

Now that she was pregnant, she would try to find joy in motherhood, instead of looking at it as a sacrifice she had to make to be taken care of. She would change diapers this time. She would only use a nanny after her tummy tuck. She would let him fuck her until the moment she went into labor.

"Doctor, you know Mrs. Crow," the nurse said, opening the door to let Shawna in.

"Hi, Shawna. How are you feeling?"

"I'm tired, but otherwise good. This pregnancy was unexpected. I'm tired but very excited. *We're* very excited."

"Hmm, hmm. Well, it looks like you're about six weeks along."

"Yes, well, Hartford would've come but he's so busy these days. I'll let him know that we're six weeks along," Shawna beamed. *That bastard is embarrassing me already. Where in the hell is he?*

"Mrs. Crow? Shawna?"

"I'm sorry; did you ask me something?"

"That cough; how long have you had it?"

"Oh, I don't know. About two weeks, I guess."

"Alright, Shawna, I want you to listen very carefully to what I am about to tell you. I ran your blood work. You're definitely pregnant and you also tested positive for HIV..."

"HAVE YOU BEEN DRINKING?" HARTFORD ASKED when he walked into the house and found Shawna with a bottle in her hand. "Are you crazy?"

"Yeah, I'm crazy. I was crazy to marry you. I shouldn't have married a pretty-ass metro-sexual I met at a god-damned nail shop. You selfish asshole," Shawna said to her husband. "I've been to the doctor. Thank you so much; thank you for giving me HIV."

"Giving you what? You have HIV? Are you saying I'm gay? Are you calling me a fag, huh? You think I did some shit to you. Gave you some shit. You fucking cunt. I should beat your ass."

"Yeah, that's what I'm saying. I told them about your ass, too. They want you to come to the doctor's office on Monday and give them a list of..."

"Oh, no, we don't have to wait until Monday, you little skeezer. We're going to get this shit straight right here, right now, tonight," Hartford said, snatching Shawna up by her arm. He practically dragged her to his car.

"Dr. Maddox," Hartford said into his cell phone as he peeled away from the curb. "This is Hartford. Look here...can you get your hands on two of those twenty-minute HIV tests? No, right now, it's got to be right now. Come on, man; it is. Trust me; it's a matter of life and death. Thanks, man." He clicked the OFF button and threw the phone at Shawna, who had begun to cry.

"Me and this cheating BITCH are on our way!" Hartford screamed from his open car window. Hartford turned to his wife. The heat in his eyes could have bent steel. "You whore! You had better fucking pray I don't have HIV. You had better pray I don't have so much as a yeast infection. Ooogh!" Hartford said, choking his steering wheel. "You had better pray."

SHAWNA CRIED, SOBBED AND ROCKED IN HER CHAIR in the lobby of Dr. Maddox's office. Hartford didn't sit. He leaned calmly against the wall and looked smugly at her from across the room for the longest twenty minutes of her life.

"You look scared," Hartford said. "You should be scared. You weren't HIV positive when Raven was born. I'm only going to say this once. I have not fucked a man in my entire lifetime. Nor have I been fucked by one. Until this month, I have never stepped out on you. You hear me? I've been faithful to you. And now that I'm fucking her, I haven't been fucking you. I've only been with one other woman, my true wife, and she did not die of AIDS."

"Okay. Would you like to get the results together or separately?" Dr. Maddox asked, entering the room.

"Cut the formalities, Doc. Please. Just tell me if this bitch has gotten me sick."

Dr. Maddox looked at Shawna and shook his head. "I'm sorry," he said to the woman. Then he turned to Hartford. "Your text was negative, Hartford."

"Thank you, Jesus!" Hartford said, falling to his knees and clasping his hands together." He dropped his head for a moment, in deep thought or prayer; Shawna was not quite sure which. She was shaking now. Then, with his head still down, he turned it slowly to the right, looking at her out of the corner of his eye. "I'm going to need you to get your shit out of my house immediately. If you're not gone by the end of the week, I'll file charges of attempted murder against you. You cannot have any money. You cannot have any property. You cannot have my daughters. Just get your nasty, disease-ridden ass out of my fucking house."

"Hartford," Dr. Maddox said, snapping Hartford out of his rage. "Can you step into my office for a moment?"

"And if that baby is mine..." His tongue stabbed Shawna again. "Don't even think about pushing it out of your sick little pussy."

"Hartford!" Dr. Maddox yelled. "My God, man! Come in here. Let me talk to you."

Hartford followed his friend through the waiting room door into his office.

"Have a seat, Hartford." Hartford sat, as his friend spoke. "I know how you're feeling right now, having come so close to becoming exposed to the virus. It's a blessing that you weren't. But Shawna's very distraught and probably unstable right now. The reason the HIV test is administered the way that it is, with on-site counseling available and *not* in the middle of the night, is so people don't completely freak out and hurt themselves, or someone else when they get positive results. I'm telling you this, as your doctor and as your friend. Your body has been spared this time, but don't go throwing your soul away on hatred and vindictiveness. I mean, learning you have an incurable, deadly disease is traumatizing enough, but you rubbing salt in her wounds is…well, it's…the word *evil* comes to mind but I will just say ungodly."

"Come on, Jim; *ungodly*? Really?"

"How about diabolical?" Jim asked jokingly. "I'm just saying, your wife doesn't need to be alone and unsupported right now."

"Jim, have you ever read about all those people, especially men in Africa, who find out their woman is HIV-positive and they just start stomping a hole in a bitch?"

"Of course," Jim answered.

"Well, that's how I feel right now. I love you, man," Hartford said, giving the doctor a hug. "But I can't even talk about this right now. I can't even look at her face; I'm so disgusted. I'll make sure she's all right, if that's what I have to do, but right now she has to get the fuck out of my house."

When Hartford came back into the waiting room, Shawna was gone.

THE PASSENGER DROP-OFF WAS CROWDED WITH CARS as Tisa pulled up to US Airways departing flights at Ronald Reagan Washington National Airport. Stormy sobbed softly in the passenger seat next to her.

"Oh, Stormy," Tisa said, freeing her hand from the grip Stormy had on it, wiping her tears with her thumb. "Why are you crying?"

"I just...I don't want to go home."

"Okay," T. Calloway said without hesitation, pulling away from the curb.

"What are you doing?"

"I'm taking you to my place. That is what you want, isn't it?"

"Yes."

"Okay then. You think long, you think wrong. Women have intuition for a reason. Call your girl. Tell her you have to stay in D.C. a while longer. In the meantime, you can stay with me, and we can talk about it some more."

Stormy dialed Korea's cell phone, but did not get an

answer. "Korea, I missed my flight. I'll call you tomorrow."

"Stormy, why did you lie?"

"I just...I don't want any confrontation until I figure this out."

"No, that's unacceptable. Call her back."

"What for? She's not even answering the phone."

"Call her back. Tell her you have more business in D.C., and you will have to stay a while longer."

"Why? What difference does it make? She's going to be pissed off, no matter the reason."

"Because it's the truth, and telling the truth is for your own benefit. Do you want to spend tonight worried and riddled with guilt? I would much rather you were present when we're making love; how about you?" Stormy blushed. "Do us both a favor, then. Call her back."

Stormy hit the redial button.

Korea could hardly tell what Hartford was saying on the phone, he was so frantic. "Hold on, Hartford. Hold on a second, Stormy's on the other line." She clicked over. "Hello?"

"Hey, Korea, it's me. I have some other business here. I have to stay a while longer."

"Whatever." Korea clicked her cell phone back over to Hartford. "Hey, honey," Korea said, walking into the master bathroom. "You said you went to take an AIDS test? Did I hear you right?"

"That's right," Hartford said.

"Was it negative?" Korea braced herself for his response.

"Yes, of course," he said hurriedly. "But my wife... she's positive. I can't go home. I can't, I'll fucking kill her."

"Don't go home just yet. Whatever's going on, we can work it out together. Why don't you come over here so we can talk?" Korea hung up and then drained the sink of the water that her dick had been soaking in. "Well, buddy," she said to her little friend. "It'll have to be another time for you."

THERE WAS A LOUD CRASH AND A THUMP IN THE KITCHEN. Alex sat up in her bed. She had heard some fighting earlier and thought, for a moment, that maybe her father had had enough and was finally whipping Shawna's ass. But if that was the case, she was going to have to stop him. He had way too much to lose. Alex looked at the clock as she put on her robe and yawned. It was almost two in the morning.

Alex opened the door to her room and crossed the hall to Raven's door and opened it. She wasn't in her bed. She ran down the hall and leapt down the stairs. There was only a tipped wine bottle on the floor in the living room. She looked around and found nothing stirring. But there was a light shining from beneath the kitchen door. Through it she could hear whispering. Fear mounted her as she grabbed a wooden Ebo statue and proceeded closer to the light under the door, toward the whispering. Alex pushed the door open with one hand and brandished the African idol with the other as she stepped into the kitchen.

The knife drawer had been pulled out of its place among the cupboards. Alex could see that from the door. There were knives scattered about the floor and blood trailing between the Spanish tiles. The whispering was coming from the other side of the island.

"Get up," it said. "Get up." Alex recognized the voice of her sister as she walked closer, around the island, and peered over its marble top. Raven looked up at her sister, startled. "I didn't do it," she said. "You did!" The little girl was tugging, trying to pull the knife out of her mother's stomach.

"Shawna!" Alex screamed, dropping the figure, and falling to her knees at the dead woman's side. "No, no, no," Alex said. "Oh, my God!"

"God can't help you now," Raven said as she stuck her sister with the knife.

"HARTFORD, WHAT THE HELL IS GOING ON IN YOUR HOUSE?" Korea asked him as he stepped out of the elevator into her penthouse.

"I thought I was a man who would always know the answer to that question." Hartford looked defeated. He crumbled into Korea's arms and cried like a baby, explaining what he could through his wails and tears.

"It's alright. I'll be strong when you can't be strong,"

Korea comforted him. "I'll be strong for both of us."

His cell phone buzzed in his pocket. Korea reached in and pulled it out. She read the caller ID to him: "Hartford Crow."

"It's her," he said, snatching the phone from Korea's hand. "It's that fucking cunt!" He threw the phone against the wall and watched it fall apart. He didn't move a muscle until the morning light woke him, still in Korea's comforting arms.

IT DIDN'T TAKE ALEX LONG TO KNOCK THE KNIFE-wielding eight-year-old out cold with the statue her mother had called the African God of protection. The first person she called when she found her stepmother, lying there in a pool of blood and blades, was her father. When he didn't answer his phone, Alex got nervous, that her father may have killed Shawna. So she called her aunts, Dream Crow and Blue.

"Hold tight, Baby Crow," was all Blue had said and she knew they were on their way before they had even hung up the phone. Even with a dead woman on the kitchen floor and an injured child on the living room sofa, Alex never even considered calling the police. That was Raven's vindictive idea, and for a time, it would cost Alex her freedom.

"Hello?" the little girl whispered into the phone with desperation in her voice. "Is this 9-1-1? If you know some police, can you send them to get my sister? She hit me in the head and she killed my mother."

STORMY AND TISA HAD BEEN UP ALL NIGHT, talking and making love. Stormy had forgotten what it felt like to be gently touched and softly caressed. Tisa was a confident lover with no inhibitions. Tisa proudly opened her legs to let Stormy see her flower and she kept them open when Stormy climbed on top and gave her the rollercoaster ride of her life.

"So what do we do now?"

"Now we find you a place."

"Oh. Yes, of course," Stormy said, "My own place."

"What's wrong?"

"Nothing, it's just that…"

"Haven't you ever lived on your own?"

"No."

"Don't be afraid. When you're feeling lonely, I'll come visit you. Or you can come visit me. But it's important that you do this. You do understand that, don't you?"

"I understand. Six months ago, I might've been scared. Now the thought makes me a little nervous, but I'm good with it. I'm ready. What about Korea?"

"What about her?"

"Should we call and tell her?"

"No, not yet. Never let your left hand know what your right hand is doing. She will only try to stop you."

"Why would she do that? She doesn't want me any-more."

"That doesn't matter. You're like any of her other prized possessions. She sounds like a woman who doesn't like to lose. When the time comes to tell her, I'll take care of it. She'll probably back down if she thinks you have somebody already."

WHEN HARTFORD GOT HOME THE NEXT MORNING, Raven was in the custody of Child Protective Services and Alex had been arrested and taken to juvenile hall on charges of first-degree murder and aggravated assault. And there was a cop car waiting outside to take him in for questioning.

He used the telephone at the police station to call the one person he knew could fix this mess, before it was too late, but Dream Crow wasn't home.

"SO YOU SEE, JUDGE," DREAM CROW EXPLAINED TO HER old friend. "My brother wasn't home when his wife died. He hadn't left the children alone; they were at home with their mother. How was he supposed to know she would die?"

"I sure do miss you," the judge said. "Don't be such a stranger." He picked up the phone and called Child Protective Services.

"I miss you, too. There's just one more thing. The other little girl, Alex; they're holding her in juvie, saying she killed the woman. But I'm sure this couldn't be. I mean, they had their issues, like most teenage girls, but Alex wouldn't kill anyone. Is there anything you can do?"

"Well, if the girl didn't kill her and your brother wasn't home, what do you think happened?"

"She was unstable, real unhappy. My brother said he was leaving her. I think she killed herself."

"Still, I'm afraid I can't help you."

"Why not?"

"Dream Crow, I'm a family court judge. You're talking about murder, Dream Crow. That's way out of my hands."

"But, Your Honor," Dream Crow said, feeling herself slip too easily back into professional mode. "I don't want my niece to spend another night in that place. You know the kinds of things that happen up there. She's a good kid. She'll be ruined. I couldn't stand to see her end up…" She stopped to choke back her tears.

"You know, I never looked at you that way. Sure, I paid you, because that's what you required of me, but I always…I didn't know how to feel when you stopped taking my calls. It was like you dropped off the planet. I thought about you all the time. When I saw you on TV, singing like an angel, I was so proud, I cried. You should've seen the crazy way my wife looked at me, crying over some song on *Soul Train*. It was later, when I saw you and the old man on the cover of a magazine, that I realized I loved you." Dream Crow's eyes grew large in her head. *Is he really saying this?* "Of course, I couldn't do anything about it then. But she's gone now." The judge looked a picture of his wife on his desk somberly.

"I'm sorry for your loss," Dream Crow said, not sure what to make of the rest of his confession.

"I don't mean to make you uncomfortable, Dream Crow. It's just something that I wanted you to know. What you did for me back then was a beautiful thing. She had been sick for a long time and I was very lonely. You helped me through. I never thought of you as a whore, never once. You were more like an angel."

The tears were now flowing freely down her cheeks. As Dream Crow stood up and walked over to the judge and hugged his neck, she said, "I appreciate that so much. Thank you."

"No. Thank you," the judge said, wiping his eyes with the sleeve of his robe. "Here…" He wrote a name and number down on a piece of paper and handed it to her. "If your brother's wife killed herself, it shouldn't be hard for this guy to prove it."

Dream Crow smiled, took the little piece of paper, and kissed the judge on his cheek. "You know you're wrong about me?"

"How is that?"

"I was ready to give you a piece to help me out, just like I always have. So I guess I'm a whore after all."

"To get your niece out of jail? There are worse things to fuck for. That doesn't make you a whore. That makes you a mother. Come to think of it. Did you and the old man ever have children?"

"No."

"Hmm. I would've thought you would be raising a small army."

Dream Crow promised she would call him when all of this was over and walked out of his chambers into the hallway where Blue was waiting.

"Let's go get our baby girl," she said.

"DON'T WORRY," Hartford heard Korea say. "I was built for trials like this. I'll help you in any way that I can."

"Well," Hartford said. "I'm picking my baby girl up right now. I have to replace my cell phone and then get a hotel room. I'll call you when we're settled."

"Why are you getting a hotel room?"

"I don't think it would be good for Raven to be in the house her mother died in. I've already contacted my agent. I'm putting the house on the market."

"Stormy won't be back for a while. You two can stay here until you figure things out."

"Are you sure it wouldn't be an imposition? I mean, would it bother Stormy?"

"This is my house. Actually, this is my building. I don't have anything open right now but you can stay here as long as you need to. Stormy won't have anything to say about it."

Korea was right. Stormy didn't have anything to say about it. In fact, Stormy hadn't called her or returned her calls for almost two weeks. The first week had gone by without Korea really noticing, because she was so deep into Hartford's ass. But the carry-out was beginning to annoy her so she was missing her lady in waiting. She tried calling her cell phone again. But it went straight to voicemail.

"I BET YOU CAN'T GET HER TO SUCK YOUR TITTIE," a small girl said to a bigger one. They were standing over Alex's bed.

"Hey, wake up. You've been up in here for a minute now and you haven't chosen anybody yet. So I'm choosing you."

Alex kept her eyes closed and quietly whispered into the dark. "I'll choose you back, if you're gentle." She let the girl put her tittie in her mouth. She let the girl feel under the covers for her sticky virginity and play in it.

"I knew it," the smaller girl said. "I knew she was too quiet not to be a freak. Let me get some of that."

"Get back, bitch. You heard her, she's choosing me. Take your ass back to bed."

"What's your name?" the big girl whispered as she climbed into the bunk with her new girlfriend.

"Alex."

"My name's Keisha. Alex, you ever been with a girl before?"

"No."

"You ain't never had your pussy ate out?"

"No."

"You want to though, huh? Don't lie. I'm not trying to catch any more cases, so don't lie. I just want to make you feel good. You don't have to do anything. If you don't like it, I'll stop."

"You will?"

"Yep."

"Okay then. You can eat me out."

"Use the pillow to cover your mouth. You might feel like screaming. If you feel like you want to pee, roll over or something. Don't do it in my face. Okay?"

"Okay." Alex covered her face and let the girl part her legs with her hands and her vaginal lips with her tongue.

KOREA WAS GETTING READY TO LEAVE THE OFFICE and pick Raven up from school when her cell phone rang.

"I'm glad you picked up," Tisa said into the phone. "I know Stormy's been avoiding your calls."

"Who is this?"

"You don't know me. My name is Tisa...uh, T. Calloway."

"T. Calloway? Are you from that stupid-ass website? I thought you were a dude."

"The Cutting Board is a national publication, Ms. Smith." Korea did not respond. Tisa cleared her throat in the silence. "Listen, I don't want to be petty, and I don't want to take up too much of your time. This is a courtesy call."

"Courtesy call?" Korea asked. She could feel her skin getting hot and her nerves tingle up her spine. She loosened her top button. "What reason would you possibly have to call me on Stormy's behalf? If you plan on making up some excuse for her, as to why she is not back here, you can forget about it. And you can forget about her writing that food column, too. You tell Stormy to call me herself so we can get to the bottom of this. That's all you can do for me."

"Oh, I think I have the bottom of this covered," Tisa said.

"Excuse me?

"As I was saying, I'm busy, you're busy and Stormy... well, Stormy's always busy. I just didn't think we should leave you hanging out there, in the event your relationship actually meant more to you than she knows. I'm calling to tell you that she won't be coming back to you. She won't be coming back to California at all. She's mine now."

"She's what? So, who the fuck are you? You find lonely little housewives on the internet and seduce them with bullshit. You know what?" Korea stood to her feet and paced around her office. "I don't even care. Tell that bitch that. She can't eat pussy, she's messy. If it wasn't for her cooking I'd have put her out a long-ass time ago. Shiiiit," she said, forcing herself to laugh. "Stormy wasn't anything but my cook. Tell her I said that. Tell her she wasn't anything but my cook!" Korea picked up a paperweight and threw it at the door. She cleared her throat of the painful knot that was forming inside of it. She swallowed hard but cracked a little when she said, "She can't take anything I bought her..."

"No problem. Stormy is well-provided for."

"Fuck you. You know what? Let me talk to Stormy."

"As I explained to her, contact between you would be counterproductive. Save us all the drama. She says there isn't much there besides some clothes, and kitchenware. But, I would like to have UPS pick her computer up."

"Well, the bitch can't have that either."

"I figured as much; she told me how generous and supportive you are. That's why I had her store her files on my private server."

"Whatever the fuck that means...So you're going to take care of everything, reinvent her, buy all her shit all over again, manage her finances, and chauffeur her around?"

"Stormy? Oh no. I don't have to do any of that. Stormy can take care of herself. She has a new professional wardrobe and a car already. She'll be moving into her own place on the first."

"We must be talking about a different Stormy," Korea said in a confused voice.

"We must be. This one is earning six figures and only cooks when she feels like it. She's quite independent. And my goodness, can she cook," Tisa taunted, as she looked over Stormy's shoulder. "I'm watching her build a lobster lasagna right now." Tisa slapped Stormy lightly on her ass and kissed her cheek. Tisa walked away from Stormy and lowered her voice to a naughty whisper. "You know, you're wrong about her. When she sucks my dick, she's like a baby on a bottle; milking me."

"Fuck you, bitch. If you call me again, I'll reach all the way into Washington, D.C., tie a leash around your neck, and dog walk your ass."

"Yes, of course. Stormy told me how mature you are," she said, walking back into the kitchen. She pressed her pelvis against Stormy's ass, and kissed her neck. "Like I said, this was a courtesy call. You can have this number disconnected now. She has a new phone. Have a nice day." Tisa smiled at Stormy and dropped the cell phone into the kitchen trashcan.

"Wow, Tisa, you make me sound really great," Stormy said.

"Stormy, you are really great. I fell in love with your mind, months ago. Now that I love all of you, I never want to see anyone hurt you."

Tisa was a real smooth operator. She always kept her cool and was as confident as any man but she was clearly all woman. Her body was long, lean, and strong. Stormy loved to watch her walk. She kind of glided in and out of a room without devouring the energy that had been in it before, the way Korea had. She was nurturing Stormy into womanhood with devotion and respect and Stormy was healing nicely.

Tisa took the spatula out of Stormy's hand, spun her around and pinned her to the kitchen wall. She kissed her neck and nibbled on her earlobe. "What would you say if I asked you to stay with me?"

"I'd say, no."

"Why?"

"Because I'm working on me right now."

"Even if I kissed you like this?" Tisa slid down Stormy's body, lifted her dress with her teeth, and gently sucked her inner thigh.

"Yes," Stormy answered.

"And if I kissed you here, would you stay?" Tisa cocked her head to the side and kissed Stormy's fat lips as if they were the lips on her face.

Stormy gasped and felt her body temperature rising. "I would still get my own place, but you could definitely come to visit."

"That's my strong little lady. Lay down for me, baby."

"Here on the kitchen floor?"

"Yes. Lay right there on the floor." Tisa opened the refrigerator and reached inside.

Stormy lay on her back with her hands over her eyes. "What are you doing?"

"Did I ever tell you how much I love grape jelly?" Tisa said, smiling, with a jar of Smuckers in her hand. "It' so good on pussy they should call it Sucker's."

"You are so crazy."

"Crazy over you," Tisa said, kneeling between Stormy's legs. "Spread 'em."

Stormy spread her legs open and relaxed her mind. It seemed things were moving so fast for her lately, she could never relax. She let her legs fall open and told herself to let go. For a moment, Korea was waiting behind her closed eyes. The jelly was a cold slick as Tisa spread it over the layers of Stormy's Punany. She played in it for a few minutes with her fingers, moving her thumb in circular motions over her clit until Stormy began to grind against her fingers. Tisa could barely contain her own desire as her lady began to swell in her hand. She leaned into Stormy's body and blew through her pretty pursed lips, cooling the jelly again. The slightest quiver ran through Stormy, presenting Tisa's opportunity to devour her with instant results. Stormy did not expect the heat of Tisa's tongue to take her so completely, as she took all of her lips into her mouth and licked her inside out. Suddenly, she was open, completely open. And she knew, she had a brand-new handler, in whose hands she could entrust her future, until the game of love had run its course once again.

KOREA SAT, STEAMING IN HER CAR outside of the elementary school. She didn't know how long she had been sitting there, but the children were already going home when she finally moved a muscle.

"I can't believe she left?" she said to herself. "After all I did for her. That ungrateful little…" Korea searched for a word to describe the woman who had been the joy of her life for so many years. She thought of Stormy's smiling face, her girlish pout and of her wild curly hair. She thought of her fat lips and even fatter pussy lips and tried to remember the last time she had kissed either pair. "Damn, Stormy."

Just then she heard Raven's voice, and remembered she was there to pick her up. Except for Raven and another little girl, the school ground was empty. Raven had the girl hemmed up against the schoolyard fence. "If you don't give me your Now and Laters, I'll tell everybody you let Bobby put his finger in your you know what."

"But I didn't let him put his finger in my you know what," the girl said.

"Well, after I tell everybody, that won't matter. You might as well let him do it, because everybody will already believe you did." The little girl surrendered the pack of candy to Raven and ran away from her.

Korea honked the horn. "She'll be a beast of a businesswoman someday."

"Hi, Korea," Raven said, hopping into the car and buckling her seatbelt.

"Do you mind hanging out with me today? Your father

is handling some business today. He'll be over my place later."

"YAWL SHUT THE HELL UP," KEISHA WAS TELLING THE girls in the recreation room. "Shut the fuck up and listen to my baby sing." Alex got up off of Keisha's lap and began to sing, taking the juveniles to church with her rich alto rendition of the Reverend James Cleveland's sermonic song. *"I don't feel no ways tired, I've come too far from where I started from, Nobody told me, the road would be easy, I don't believe He brought me this far to leave me."*

When Blue and Dream Crow walked up with the staff counselor, there wasn't a dry eye in the room.

Keisha was hugging Alex, holding her tight. "Thank you, Alex; thank you."

Alex watched her family approaching from over Keisha's shoulder. "I think I have to go now. Aunt Blue! Dream Crow!" she screamed. "What are you doing here?"

"Girl, was that you in here belting like that? My Lord, Dream Crow, this girl can sing!" Blue said.

"Hey, why's everybody in here crying?" the counselor said with her hands on her hips.

"Come here, baby," Dream Crow said. "We came to take you home." They held each other in a family embrace.

"Alex!" Keisha screamed, "No! Don't take her!" Her eyes were red and full of tears. "No! Bring her back." She started to run after Alex when the counselor motioned for security to hold her back. "Alex, I'm getting out. I'm coming for you. I'm gonna manage you, baby. I'm gonna make you a star!" She was pinned to the floor. All she could see were Alex's feet as they walked out the door.

"Looks like you made a few friends in there," Dream Crow said.

"Yeah, one in particular," Blue said.

Dream Crow cut her eyes at her sister. "Alex, were you alright in there? I mean, nobody hurt you, did they?"

"No, Dream Crow. Nobody hurt me."

Blue said, "Well, how did you keep 'em off of you? You did keep 'em off of you, if you know what I mean?"

Alex's eyes were beginning to tear.

Dream Crow said, "Now, Sister Blue, you know that ain't none of our business. So long as she wasn't hurt, all is well."

"Well, I guess you could say music calms the savage beast."

"Come again?" Blue asked.

"I sang to them, Aunt Blue, every day for the last couple of days at rec time. They liked it, too."

"Oh yeah? Is that why that big sugar bear-looking dyke was howling over you leaving? It seems to me, a friend would be happy about you getting sprung up out the joint."

"Sister Blue, this place ain't the joint. Those are children in there. Every last one of them is somebody's child. And you should know, but for the grace of God go you and me."

With that Blue was silenced and thankful for knowing

that her sister was right. If she had not whored herself out for her and Hartford, there's no telling where any of them would have ended up, she thought and stayed quiet for a time.

"I don't understand," Alex was saying as she walked away from the juvenile grounds with her aunts. "Did Raven finally tell them the truth?"

"Ha!" Blue spat.

"How did they find out I was telling the truth then?"

"It was simple forensics. I hired my own investigator. It was the angle of the blade. They could tell by the way it entered Shawna's body that the wound was self-inflicted," Dream Crow said. "I'd figured as much."

"Oh. So she killed herself?"

"Didn't you know that?" Dream Crow asked.

"No. Not really. I thought maybe…"

"You thought maybe Raven did it." Blue finished her sentence. "I thought the same thing. Not that I wanted Shawna to die or anything, bless the Lord; I just thought it would be great if somebody would lock that little hooligan, Raven, up."

"I don't think they lock people up for putting laxatives in cookies, Aunt Blue."

"Well, they sure should. I still got hemorrhoids." Blue reached around and grabbed her own ass. "Damn."

"You'll have to go back to court to testify again, so we can enter the new evidence and they can close the case."

"Get on with it, Dream Crow. Go ahead and ask her," Blue said.

"I was getting to that."

"Ask me what?"

"Alex," Dream Crow said, "how would you like to come live with us out in Black Hawk?"

"I would love it."

"All right then. Let's go talk to your father."

"You know your daddy is shacking up with some woman already, don't you?" Blue asked Alex as they got into the car.

Dream Crow interrupted her messiness. "That's not even appropriate conversation for you to be having with a child, Sister Blue."

"Why not? That's what's wrong with kids these days. They're too damned ignorant. Grown folks don't want them to know anything, so they guess about it. Then, they do what comes natural for them to do. If we don't talk to them, how are they supposed to know anything? How are they supposed to protect themselves from anything?"

"Aunt Blue does have a point, Dream Crow," Alex said supportively, wanting to know more. "Who is he shacking up with?"

"I give up!" Dream Crow said to anyone in the car who was listening.

"I don't know exactly. Some woman he met before your stepmother died. Raven's there with them. It ain't too far from your daddy's house."

"Really? Raven was right then."

"Right about what?" the Crow sisters asked in unison.

"Raven said Daddy was with another woman. She told me that the night Shawna killed herself. She said, he asked for a divorce. She also said Shawna was pregnant."

"See, Dream Crow; it does no good to keep the truth from children. They're going to find it all out sooner or later," Blue said. "You're going to stay with your aunties, baby. You stay with us, and we'll help you with your singing career. You had a couple flat notes in that song you were singing."

"I just plain give up," Dream Crow said, looking at her sister as she hit the highway, headed for Hartford's new home.

"WHAT DO YOU MEAN YOU DON'T HAVE ANYTHING FOR me?" Melody asked Tom. He was sitting in his favorite chair, in the back room of his favorite youth program: The Blossoming Flower Shop on Grand Avenue.

"I meant just what I said, Melody. With all of that shit you started over at that dyke's place." He paused and sipped from a small crystal glass of scotch. "No, no. I can't have it. You're not worth it. I sent you on a simple mission, and you got it all fucked up."

"Admittedly," Melody said, removing her left dress strap from her shoulder. "It was messy, but I got you what you wanted, didn't I? I mean Korea's out of business, and you have the contracts." Melody let out a gentle purr as she removed her right dress strap from her shoulder, releasing her blue silk dress to fall on the floor at her feet. "Are you sure you don't have anything for me, Mr. Tom?"

Tom adjusted himself in his seat. "Well, uh, what did you have in mind?" He watched her hard brown nipples spilling through peach bra lace like melting Hershey's Kisses as she pinched them and smiled knowingly at his weakness. "First, I would like my job back. Then I'll take some of that stiff dick you got in your pants."

"You are rehired," Tom answered, unzipping his pants and releasing his golden brown shaft for Melody.

"Damn, you've got the prettiest dick I've ever seen." Melody was on all fours, ready to suck Tom's soul through his shaft when the flower shop doorbell jingled.

"Hello, is anyone here?" The voice of the council-woman was unmistakable.

ouncilwoman Grace Riley had been calling Korea repeatedly ever since she realized she had been wrong. She learned that Melody had been lying all along and that Korea had given her old assistant Martha $10,000. The realization that Korea had shut down her entire operation on her misinformed advice was tearing her up inside. She had awarded most of her contracts to Tom Brown, the man Korea has stolen Stormy away from, and she felt just awful about it. Grace had no idea what she would say to her old friend but she wanted to begin with an apology. Since Korea hadn't returned her phone calls, she decided to pay her a visit at home, flowers in her hand and the sincerest apology on her lips.

"Hello, is anyone here?" Grace yelled from the counter in the flower shop.

Melody was still giggling when she emerged from Tom Brown's office. Grace watched her hard nipples poking though her dress as she approached the counter.

"Hello, Councilwoman Riley," Melody said. "How can I help you?"

"I have an order for flowers." Melody fished around behind the counter looking for Grace's order. "You look familiar. Do I know you?"

"I don't think so," Melody said, smiling as she noticed Grace eyeballing her breasts.

"Do you have my order?" Melody looked around again. "Hold on."

"Mr. Brown," Melody called out, turning to the office door. "Grace Riley is here to pick up her order."

Tom Brown walked through the door, talking fast. "Melody, the order is on the table by the door as always."

"I'm sorry, Tom; you know it's been a while, uh, Mr. Brown."

"Melody? That's your name," Councilwoman Riley asked, as Melody whisked past her to collect the beautiful arrangement of Bird of Paradise and Stargazer Lilies.

"Wow, this is pretty," Melody said, picking the arrangement up and smelling it. "Toggle," she said absently. "My name is Melody Toggle."

Grace turned to Tom. "Is this the Melody I think it is?"

The look of guilt on Tom's face told her she and Korea had both been played. Grace didn't have to force a confession. It came spilling easily over his tongue. "She took something of mine. She had it coming."

GRACE EXCHANGED NICETIES WITH MRS. DAVENPORT in the lobby of Korea's building and greeted Charlie O at the elevator door. "It's a beautiful day for an elevator ride," he said. "Come on, lady; step inside."

Korea opened the door and greeted her old friend with a cheery hug and a smile. She accepted the flowers and said, "Follow me while I go put these in some water."

"Are my eyes deceiving me?" Grace Riley asked. "Or, do I detect a new switch in your stride?"

Korea laughed, smiled again, and said, "Girl, never underestimate the power of some good dick."

"This might be coming kind of late, now that I've already moved in and put my house on the market, but who's going to do the cooking?" Hartford asked Korea. "I've seen how you get when you don't have a home-cooked meal."

"I don't know. Maybe we can hire a chef."

"We'll figure it out."

"I can cook for you, Daddy," Raven said.

"That's sweet, baby. It's getting late now. Go get ready for bed."

"Okay, Daddy. Good night. Good night, Korea."

"Good night," Korea said. "She has really great manners. I'm looking forward to getting to know her."

"She's like a changed little girl, now that Shawna is gone."

"Didn't they get along?"

"It's complicated." Hartford could feel the tension in her shoulders as he rubbed them. His hands were strong and he effortlessly massaged deeply into the muscles, squeezing the pressure out.

"That's weird," Korea said.

"What's weird?" Hartford asked her, running his hands down her arms.

"Don't feel vulnerable with you. I feel supported."

"That's a good thing," Hartford said, not surprised by her finding. "Don't you know me by now? That's what I do. I support people, in music and in life. I'm a musician. I create the music babies are made to. I give life."

Korea lay back in Hartford's arms and watched the fire logs burn until they both fell asleep.

WHEN DREAM CROW STEPPED OFF THE ELEVATOR, she gave Korea a big hug, as if she had known her for years. "Korea Smith, I'm so pleased to meet you after all of these years. Who would've ever thought you would end up a part of my family after all."

"I'm pleased to meet you, too, Dream Crow. I've heard so much about you, and you, too, Blue, of course. Have we met before?"

"Oh, forgive me. Everyone calls me Dream Crow; have since I was a child. My married name is Bandarofski. I guess you could say that I've been your sponsor for years. It's a shame you shut your businesses down. I've been donating for years to your girls program." Dream

Crow put her arm over Korea's shoulder and said, "Now is not the place or time to talk about this in detail, but you and I have an old friend in common. Do you remember Keith?"

Dream Crow could have knocked Korea over with a feather. She stood there with her mouth gaped open, remembering the man that had left her with a piece of him she could never forget. "No worry," Dream Crow said, reaching for her hand. "He's long gone. We can have coffee some time. I will tell you all about it."

Blue and Dream Crow sat their brother down and promised him they would raise Alex in love. Hartford cried, but was completely agreeable.

"So," Korea chimed in. "You don't want to take Raven?"

"Oh no, no, honey, bless the Lord," Blue said. "If I were you, I'd think about getting her an exorcism. Here you go, baby," she said, handing her a small paper bag. "I brought you some something."

"Gee," Korea said, looking in the bag curiously. "Thanks."

"It's sage. You might want to start burning it now in Raven's room."

"Sage? I'm not sure it agrees with me."

"You don't say. Maybe you two will get along then," Blue said, looking at her suspiciously.

"Hi, everybody," Raven said, skipping cheerfully down the hallway. She stopped by her father's leg and reached for his hand. She eyeballed her big sister and gave her a crooked smile. "Hi, Alex," she said sweetly. She dropped

Hartford's hand, put earphones on, and scrolled through the playlist on Alex's iPod screen.

Alex stabbed her with her eyes. "Can we go now, Auntie?" she asked Dream Crow.

"Sure thing. Blue?" She nodded at her sister. "Are you ready to take off?"

Korea called for the elevator.

"Well, we need to get on out of here, Hartford. I'm sure Alex has a lot of things to get from your house."

"Let's go," Hartford said.

"Daddy, can I go?"

"No, baby, you stay here. You can help Korea with dinner."

"I would do that, if I were you," Blue said.

"Hmm," Raven pouted, adjusting the volume on the player. "*I shot the Sheriff…*" she sang as she walked back down the hall.

"Hey there, Charlie O," she said when the elevator doors opened.

"It's a fine day for a ride, ladies and gentleman, step right on inside," Charlie O said, smiling broadly. Hartford ushered his sisters on board. He turned to help Alex onto the elevator but she was charging down the hall after Raven. She caught her by her ponytail and pulled her to the floor.

"I told you not to touch what's mine!" Alex smacked her repeatedly in the head. "Take them off! Take them off!" She snatched the headphones and iPod from the little girl.

"Hey, you two, what's going on?" Korea asked, running down the hall to pull Alex off of the little girl.

"I'm just taking what's mine," Alex said, putting the headphones on. Raven shook the ass whipping off, as Korea helped her to her feet.

"I can respect that," Korea said.

Raven rubbed her head and looked at her sister in disbelief. "I can respect that, too. I guess jail made you hard."

Alex rolled her eyes and strutted victoriously back to the elevator.

KOREA STAYED HOME WITH RAVEN, who was clicking away on Stormy's computer. "What is it about this room that causes everyone to become a clicker?" she said to herself, reaching for the door. She stuck her head in the door.

"Hey, you," she said. "Is everything all right in here?"

"Hey," Raven said.

"Can I come in?"

"Sure, Mommy."

Korea wasn't sure how she felt about Raven calling her "Mommy."

"You can call me by my name," she said. "Korea or Ms. Korea will do for now."

"But I like to call you Mommy."

If I'm going to be anything around here, I'm going to be Daddy, Korea thought. She would talk to Hartford about it. "Hey," she said in her friendliest voice. "What are you doing?"

"I'm looking up recipes so I can make you some special cookies."

CHAPTER 18

COMFORT FOOD

tormy had quickly become the food critic to be aware of in Washington, D.C, when her first review slammed a popular yuppie favorite, better known for its sexy, scantily clad waiters than for its overpriced food. It was said that the place was bank-rolled by a congressman's wife, who had found favor in the young grad student at Georgetown University who owned it. "The waiters wore midriff tuxedo shirts, with red bowties and low-cut slacks, and the hottest thing in the kitchen was the chef himself," Stormy wrote in her review... "My Nuclear Family platter, complete with meatloaf, garlic mashed potatoes, and mixed vegetables, was packed full of flavor. In fact, I think I still have some Lipton onion soup mix in my molar. I suppose the sugar-mommas who patronize the quaint little water-front joint (conveniently located across the street from an all-too-popular boutique hotel) don't need their meat-loaf so hot it could melt denture glue, but every portion of the meal was cold. Oh, except my iced tea; it, my friends, was room temperature...Oh well, the next time

I want my vanilla bean crème brulee served with college boy butt cleavage, I will definitely know where to go."

The subsequent threats and demands for retractions coming from the senator's office put *The Cutting Board* on the map, giving them power to rival *The Post* and the *Times'* Lifestyle news sections.

"Stormy Talbert," she read the placard on the door and smiled. She fished for the key and unlocked the door, closing herself inside with her laptop and carryout container from Capitol Hill Deli and Grill.

There was nowhere to sit, not for her or anyone else, inside the tiny mom and pop restaurant that had captured the hearts and bellies of senators, congressmen, and diplomats from all over the world with what was reportedly the best French onion soup outside of Mez. So, like everyone else, she had ordered hers to go.

"Savor the Flavor! Five kinds of onions; one grown on every continent," she read on the bag. She slid the bowl out to find her soup packed in a fancy ceramic bowl. When she removed the foil, she was greeted by a beautiful kaleidoscope of champagne colors and husky fragrances of provolone, Swiss, and parmesan cheeses, oozing over the bowl's edge. She savored the flavors, both rich and simple; beef and chicken broth, toasted sourdough, roasted garlic, thyme, olive oil, and sugar. There were sea salt and fresh ground pepper, bay leaf and maybe even a hint of vermouth, all spilling over her spoon as she dipped again through the cheesy brim and watched it fill with the famous day-old crystallized vegetables and mouth-watering, dry sherry-infused soup.

"The line was long and the wait, practically unbearable, in my new Joan & David shoes, but as they say, anything this good is worth waiting for. And for this heart-warming experience, I would gladly stand in the soup line," Stormy typed. She saved her article and emailed it to the copy editor's desk, turned her laptop off, and packed it. She grabbed her coat and headed for the door. "Oh, my God," she said out loud. Her new assistant had framed her invitation to join the Food Critics Guild and hung it next to the door. There was a little sticky note on it that read: *"Congrats! Come home."*

She missed Tisa's call in the elevator, but she knew her lover would call her before she could reach the garage and start her car. "Hello?"

"Hey, baby, I'm so proud of you."

"Thanks, Tisa."

"Are you on your way?"

"Yes."

"Good, I have a surprise for you."

"What is it?"

"If I told you, it wouldn't be a surprise."

"Hmm…you have a point. I will be there in twenty minutes."

"I'll be waiting."

Stormy drove through the maze of lines and circles that made up the streets of downtown D.C. She wasn't a very confident driver, so she was used to getting stuck in a circle or two nearly every day. But that day, she was full of confidence. She had everything she had ever wanted and so much more. She was a highly paid columnist and an official member of the Food Critics Guild. She was respected and she was loved by a woman who was powerful enough to have anyone in the world of journalism. So when a man tried to force her to stay within the boundaries of Dupont Circle, she honked until he let her turn in front of him. She smiled and waved at the man as she passed and reflected on her new life, spread before her like a perfectly set table. Her newfound confidence and emotional resilience were scintillating appetizers that made her mouth water for more of this good life. Tisa's love and loyalty were the sweetest dessert. But Stormy's career was the main course that had won her the respect of her readers and peers that nourished her soul. Her self-respect emitted a bountiful bouquet that washed all doubt away and Stormy felt just like comfort food.

ABOUT THE AUTHOR

Best known as founder of The Punany Poets, Jessica Holter, also known as "Ghetto Girl Blue," is a mother, an author, a gifted orator, a talented visual artist and an activist for AIDS awareness and sexual abuse recovery. She created The Punany Poets in 1995 after the untimely death of Eric "Eazy-E" Wright of AIDS. Her theater group, The Punany Poets, has appeared on HBO's *Real Sex*, Black Entertainment Television, Playboy TV, London's Channel 5 and Cinemax. Her sexy stories are in rotation on Playboy Radio (XM) and she has self-published six books under The Punany Poets Entertainment, LLC. Best-selling Author/Publisher Zane compiled her most riveting poetic works into a hardback anthology, *Verbal Penetration*, in 2007. *The Punany Experience* is Holter's first novel from Strebor Books. Holter continues to tour the country in live stage plays and cabaret performances. She actively promotes AIDS awareness and female empowerment though her growing line of public service advertisements, print media, audio/radio, video and film and novelties. Visit her at www.punanypoets.com.